Annie Fields

James T. Fields biographical notes and personal sketches

Annie Fields

James T. Fields biographical notes and personal sketches

ISBN/EAN: 9783743351813

Manufactured in Europe, USA, Canada, Australia, Japa

Cover: Foto ©Raphael Reischuk / pixelio.de

Manufactured and distributed by brebook publishing software (www.brebook.com)

Annie Fields

James T. Fields biographical notes and personal sketches

JAMES T. FIELDS

BIOGRAPHICAL NOTES AND PERSONAL
SKETCHES

WITH

UNPUBLISHED FRAGMENTS AND TRIBUTES
FROM MEN AND WOMEN OF LETTERS

BOSTON
HOUGHTON, MIFFLIN AND COMPANY
The Riverside Press, Cambridge
1882

The Riverside Press, Cambridge:
Stereotyped and Printed by H. O. Houghton & Co.

James T. Fields

" *Il n'y a pour les âmes d'autre solitude que celle de l'oubli.*"

IN MEMORY.

As a guest who may not stay
Long and sad farewells to say
Glides with smiling face away,

Of the sweetness and the zest
Of thy happy life possessed
Thou hast left us at thy best.

Warm of heart and clear of brain,
Of thy sun-bright spirit's wane
Thou hast spared us all the pain.

Now that thou hast gone away,
What is left of one to say
Who was open as the day?

What is there to gloss or shun?
Save with kindly voices none
Speak thy name beneath the sun.

Safe thou art on every side,
Friendship nothing finds to hide,
Love's demand is satisfied.

Over manly strength and worth,
At thy desk of toil, or hearth,
Played the lambent light of mirth, —

Mirth that lit but never burned;
All thy blame to pity turned;
Hatred thou hadst never learned.

Every harsh and vexing thing
At thy home-fire lost its sting;
Where thou wast was always spring.

And thy perfect trust in good,
Faith in man and womanhood,
Chance and change and time withstood.

Small respect for cant and whine,
Bigot's zeal and hate malign,
Had that sunny soul of thine.

But to thee was duty's claim
Sacred, and thy lips became
Reverent with one holy Name.

Therefore, on thy unknown way
Go in God's peace! We who stay
But a little while delay.

Keep for us, O friend, where'er
Thou art waiting, all that here
Made thy earthly presence dear.

Something of thy pleasant past
On a ground of wonder cast,
In the stiller waters glassed!

Keep the human heart of thee:
Let the mortal only be
Clothed in immortality.

And when fall our feet as fell
Thine upon the asphodel,
Let thy old smile greet us well,

Proving in a world of bliss
What we fondly dream in this, —
Love is one with holiness!

                    JOHN GREENLEAF WHITTIER.

NOTE.

It will be observed that great care has been taken in these pages to omit, so far as possible, all personal mention of living friends. Some of those only who have passed beyond this narrow scope and vision have been recalled as making part of a life not to be altogether forgotten.

A few poems and extracts from letters, where friends may speak for themselves, have been incorporated as properly forming a part of this memorial.

BIOGRAPHICAL NOTES

AND

PERSONAL SKETCHES.

———+———

PORTSMOUTH, New Hampshire's only seaport, is one of the few places in America touched with the hue of decay. During the Revolution, when our humble navy consisted only of seven ships, New Hampshire furnished one from the Portsmouth navy yard. But the city reached "the highest point of all" her "greatness" during the latest five years of the last century, and a quaint, fleeting glimpse of the old home world that so called "greatness" was. Calm after storm, the calm of closing day, was already brooding over the town when the boy who is the subject of this memoir was born, in 1816. His father was a ship-master, "much respected," writes one of his town's-people, "by all who knew him." His early death at sea left his widow with the care of his two little sons, and the ship-yards and wharves, attractive to every boy, became places of danger and distress in her eyes. The rapid Piscataqua,

1

where the older and more adventurous boys loved to launch their boats and be carried down to the great sea, was forbidden to them. There was, however, no disobedience to the maternal authority. James used to say, as it is quoted of Barry Cornwall, " My mother was simply the kindest and tenderest mother in the world."

The loss one Sunday afternoon of summer, in a sudden squall, of a sailing boat containing a party of his school fellows and one of their teachers, — a company James to his boyish sorrow had been forbidden to join, — was held up to him long afterward as a righteous judgment on Sabbath-breaking as well as an end to be looked for when boys entered sailing boats. He never forgot this incident, referring often in later years to the grief which overspread the whole school at the loss of their beloved teacher and comrades, but with a keen memory, also, of the narrowness and folly which attempted to instil the idea of a God made angry and revengeful by an afternoon of simple pleasure upon the summer sea.

He was brought up in the straitest sect of the Unitarians of those days, being carried twice and frequently three times a day to Dr. Parker's church, the front house-door being duly locked as the little family party sallied forth. While he trudged along holding his fond mother's hand, thinking, doubtless, of the box of unread books which he had just unwillingly quitted, he was unconsciously forming in his own mind a new sense of what religion really signified and the beauty of the world. That box of books! He never forgot what they were to him! A friend and neighbor of his mother having lately lost her own only son, offered to let James enjoy his books. They were to be borrowed a few at a time, read, and returned before others should be taken. It was not long before he knew every one the box contained, and to his latest years, could name them over. "I wonder if that good woman knew all she did for me," he said latterly; "if I could find her people I should be so happy to do something for them now."

One of the privileges and pleasures of his early life was connected with Dr. Parker's church. There was a flourishing Sunday-school, chiefly, I believe, under the minister's own care, but James's teacher was a man of singular integrity and beauty of character. "I think there never was a better man than Mr. F.," he used to say, " and his teaching was as simple and true as the man himself. We could not help understanding it or loving him. He was a model Sunday-school teacher." There is a small book of prayers still in my possession prepared by Dr. Parker for this school. He treasured this little volume to the end, and it took the place of the prayer-book with us, one of the last Sundays he passed on earth.

Although the boy was denied the pleasures of boating and of horses, — which were considered equally dangerous and terrible by his careful parent, — it must not be supposed that he was a stranger to boyish sports and exercises. From an early age he became a great walker and was fond of open-air games. There never was a boy who was a greater favorite with his companions. His out-of-door life with them, in those quiet shaded streets, or in their excursions to Rye Beach and shorter wood-land rambles, or journeys to Dover and Greenland, were always delightful reminiscences. Often by the half hour he would amuse others as well as himself recalling the companions of those days by the names they each assumed, and recounting their boyish fun. Who can ever forget, having once heard, the tales of " Gundy Got " and " Shindy Clemmens " and others, whose nicknames I cannot now recall ; or the story of his first pocket-knife named " Sharper," and the way in which the reputation of Sharper spread among the boys ; or the Saturday afternoons in the famous garrets of those days when they re-galed each other on sweetened water until one boy, having made his beverage a week beforehand in order to be on time, was exposed by the quick sense of James and brought to confession? Who ever failed to be amused at his own amusement over these boyish follies? His exuberance and love of nature made every step of the long road from the south end of Portsmouth to Rye Beach like turning a fresh page of an unread book, and to the end of his life the great book of nature was his chief curiosity, his unchanged early love. However tired other boys might become, he was always fresh, with a first-rate appetite for luncheon, when he arrived at the end of his walk. The memory of those boyish pleasures made the old places dear to him forever, and he was always ready for " a day or two in Portsmouth."

In one of the little addresses given at some academy in his later years, we find him saying, " Remember, boys, it is not so much the books you study as the books you read which will be of permanent value to you." In saying this he was only speaking out of his own experience. From the box of books to which I have referred, it was an easy step to the Portsmouth library (the Athenæum), still preserved in the same pleasant old building of the last century, looking out upon the public street. The honors of the High School seem to have been easily won, leaving time enough beside for those hours in the broad window seat of the old library room, which he loved to point out to me in our visits to Portsmouth. The window was shaded by a fine tree tempering the summer sunshine, making his chosen retreat a most delightful resort both in summer and in winter. Before the age of fourteen, when he came to Boston, there were few books in the library which he had not mastered. Everything possible to his years, and much more, he seems to have read and remembered. He used to say with amusement, that he chose to go into a book-shop when he came to Boston, because he thought he could sit behind the counter and read all day; but the first thing he was told was that boys were not allowed to read in business hours.

His companions and play time were not meanwhile forgotten. Upon one of the numerous occasions of late years for calling together the "Sons of Portsmouth," he said: "It is good for us to be a troop of happy boys once more. I am glad to see the companions of my school-days; boys who have knocked the chip off my hat, boys who have dared me out three times, boys who have met me in those fierce encounters between the Northern and Southern tribes of our native town, and who are my excellent friends now that these bloodless but terrible Saturday afternoons are all over."

When the boy of fourteen quitted his native town " to go into business," he left a happy memory behind him. All the boys who could go, or who were in any wise ready for college or business, left when he did ; and he never forgot that morning when the little company clambered up the coach-side full of hope and excitement for an untried future. There was some boyish grief for his mother and those who must be left behind. On the whole, however, it was a very happy and exciting journey, the longest he had ever taken, and he arrived in Boston full of new life for the days to come.

I have before me now, carefully preserved through these many years, the letter of Mr. Richard Sullivan, telling James that he had found a place for him according to his request, with Messrs. Carter and Hendee. " Excellent young men and much respected in Boston. If you like the trade, and are pleased with the place, you can come as soon as your mother pleases." It was in accordance with this note that when the school term was ended James came to Boston. His new life was full of interest to him, in spite of his not being allowed to read all day as he had fancied ; but his employers were extremely kind to him, soon discovering that he could be much better employed than in the usual routine imposed upon boys. After a very few days he was relieved from the work of taking care of the shop and given clerk's work instead, and he shortly became one of the trusted members of the establishment.

Speaking of his employers in later years, Mr. Fields said: "Mr. Hendee was an indulgent master and pleased to make the boys in his shop happy. According to the fashion of those times he had a box at the theatre, and always invited one or more of the clerks to go every night. In this way I saw the elder Booth, Fanny Kemble as Juliet, her father, and in short all the good actors who came to America at that time."

A certain wholesome pride of character early manifested itself. He quickly learned all details of business; wholesale and retail prices, orders needing to be filled, honest and dishonest buyers and sellers, persons prompt in payment and otherwise, and with especial quickness at once observed by his masters, he was able to discover what books were to be popular. He acquired also a power, considered "very queer" by the other clerks, of seeing a person enter the shop and predicting what book was wanted before the wish was expressed. For some time he kept this to himself, but after a while, on its being discovered, it was one of the interests for the day among the clerks to see how many times James would be right, and he seldom made a miss. He thought no more of reading behind the counter, that idea was only remembered as a boy's idle fancy, but every night he would carry home an armful of books, and he became acquainted with a goodly portion of their contents before morning. In after years he used to deplore the foolish habit, as he called it, of doing without sleep, for his love of nature and open-air life caused him to be up with the dawn, that he might have an early walk and taste the fresh air before the world was astir. The fullness of life which never knows weariness except as the downward sweep of the pendulum, the brightness of the sun of human existence, the untamed spirit of action and desire were never more fully seen than in his nature. From the first he was sufficient not only to take care of himself but others, and as is universally the case with such natures there were needs enough presented early and always continued, to absorb a large portion of whatever might be his. "The heart at leisure from itself to soothe and sympathize" was native to him. The best thing he gave, or had to give, was "that good which is effused by a kind nature, and is not lost or wasted in vacancy. The surrounding natures must catch a portion of it, as of a portion of the sun or air, and diffuse it in their turn."

In the few pages of autobiography left by Barry Cornwall, I find the following passage upon the value and the choice of reading. I quote it here because it is another spirit bearing testimony to what was a religion with Mr. Fields, a code of law reproduced by him for others, in some form, every day of his life : —

" In the village where I dwelt [wrote Mr. Proctor], there was a circulating library. Its contents were of a very humble description. It contained the novels and romances of fifty years ago, a score of old histories, and a few volumes of biography now forgotten. The books had been bought at sales for the value of waste paper. Nevertheless it was out of this dusty collection of learning that I was enabled to select a few books which spurred me on the great road of thought. When we encounter a new idea it surprises us, and we begin to doubt and examine it, and this is thought. For it is not simply the admission of another man's ideas, for these sometimes present themselves so that we neither dissent nor sympathize. They do not spur the mind on its road at all. I had already read Cæsar and Virgil, and Ovid, and some parts of Theocritus, and passages of Homer ; but these passed unprofitable over my mind, like shadows over the unreflecting earth below. They were read as words only, and left no trace or image. But now a more effective agent was at work, which moved my heart at the same time with my other faculties. Let no one despise the benefits which thus open the young and tender heart. They are the gates of knowledge. . . . . If I had never become intimate with Le Sage, and Fielding, and Richardson, with Sterne, and Inchbald, and Radcliffe, I should, perhaps, have stopped at my seventeeth year disheartened on my way. But they were my encouragers: they forced me to travel onwards to the Intellectual Mountains. I have now forgotten all my mathematics and arithmetic, all my Greek, and almost all my Latin ; but I cleave to those who were true nurses of my boyhood still."

It is interesting to read this passage in connection with the following extracts from an informal address made by Mr. Fields to the young men of Phillips Academy, Exeter, in 1874. He says : —

" FELLOW STUDENTS, — I count myself still a scholar, a seeker after knowledge and the true meaning of things. And it is always a great pleasure to me when I stand face to face with a hundred or more busy young gentlemen thirty or forty years younger than I am. You would scarcely believe it to look at me now, but I was really once young myself and studied Latin. I actually once had a smooth cheek and dug away at my Greek verbs, and spaded about among my mathematical roots like yourselves. And so, as I have suffered in these things myself, I know how to sympathize with you. You can't tell me what it is to wake up in the morning with a thundering great mathematical problem lying in wait for you ! I know all about it. . . . Just see how simple the whole matter of acquiring information is. Given *Brains* (and we always claim the privilege of knocking a man down, if he disputes with us the fact of this possession), and all we can require, and *must acquire*, are these three — *Attention, Perseverance*, and *Memory*. These can all be had for the asking; they can all be strengthened if they happen to be weak in any special case. You notice I do not reckon in *Morals*, for I cannot conceive of a *real* student, a young man of brains or common sense, who loves learning, and means to be a first-rater, by and by, I cannot conceive of *his* having any time or inclination for those idiotic immoralities which turn a man into a brute. I take it, that sort of a thing is not in our line, and so I do not intend to insult you by mixing up baser matters with the things needful, which we are all striving for, namely, the *Great Truths* of life. Go in for fun and genuine enjoyment. It is a capital rule to *play* a little every day of our lives."

This was quite as much as was wise or possible to say to students still under their master's supervision, but in his lecture on " Fiction " he reiterates his faith in the value of literature of the imagination in forming the young mind.

James Russell Lowell has lately given expression to this same truth, in his speech at the Literary Fund Dinner in London. "Science," Mr. Lowell says, " can never extinguish imagination, nor that thirst which human nature feels for something more piercing than facts are apt to be. I think that as long as the human race lasts wonder and delight in natural things, which, perhaps, are not useful, and which are certainly not scientific,

will be born into the world with every child." In
a sphere where the gospel of work is rigidly en-
forced the rare individual natures who give ex-
pansion as well as expression to something deeper
and more enduring within us cannot be too highly
prized. One of this beloved company has said,
" If life itself were not a pleasure the utility even
of its necessaries might very well be questioned."

In rehearsing the story of a life the fact of pri-
mal importance is the individual. Be careful to
preserve the corners, Goethe has somewhere said,
lest if we are too well rounded off there will be
no personal recognition in the hereafter. Therefore it is a happiness even to recall the limitations
of certain natures. Defining what they are not,
however, cannot define what they are. That is
quite a different labor. To define what they are
not would only be to lose ourselves in God's il-
limitable plan.

" A man may earn the gratitude of the world by
speaking, writing, or acting admirably [writes Coventry
Patmore], but its most delighted and enduring thanks
are given to individuality of character, in other words,
to a living addition to the visible scope and variety of
humanity. This individuality, whether in action or in
art, is always more or less, and often wholly, unconscious. Consciousness is the destruction of individuality, . . . but all true character is individual, and incapa-

ble of being acquired by any amount of effort, or quite abolished by any amount of neglect. It is so rare and delicate a quality that to be able to recognize it at first hand in a poem or other work of art is in itself a sort of originality, the gift, or rather the grace of the few whose verdict is sure to prevail after a time, commonly a long time."

In this age of much scientific study and noble advance, the character of which we write was marked by quiet progress in its own direction. The paths of science were reverently left to other feet as quite outside his own province. By the modest and almost unconscious acceptance of himself he was laid open to much misapprehension from the learned and dogmatic, but the recognition universally and instinctively accorded to him wherever simple human intercourse was possible, made his life rich. He was incapable of envy, and had no ambitions beyond doing his best in his own direction. He was continually surprised, and rejoiced afresh by the appreciation which came to him.

One of Mr. Fields's earliest interests, outside his business, was connected with the Mercantile Library Association. Of this portion of his life, Mr. Whipple has lately written in the "Atlantic Monthly." These few extracts from his tender and able tribute shall stand here to speak for these years, more perfectly than any words of mine could do : —

" My acquaintance with Fields began at the Boston Mercantile Library Association when we were boys of eighteen or nineteen. It happened that both of us were inflamed by a passionate love of literature and by a cordial admiration of men of letters; that we had read — of course superficially — most of the leading poets and prose writers of Great Britain, and had a tolerably correct idea of their chronological succession ; that both of us could write verse in various measures, and each then thought that the ten-syllabled couplet of Dryden and Pope was the perfection of poetic form ; and that Fields had made his reputation a few days before our acquaintance began as the first anniversary poet of the association. Before a large audience he had read an original poem which commanded general applause.

" It was my fortune, or misfortune, to follow Fields in his brilliantly successful anniversary poem. Of what I wrote I can hardly remember a line. The whole thing has gone out of my memory as thoroughly as it has gone out of the memory of the public. But what I do remember is this, that Fields was anxious that I should succeed. Being under the age when a free American can vote, I naturally thought my couplets were quite bright. Fields did all he could to confirm me in my amiable illusion. He suggested new ' points ;' worked with me as though he desired that my performance should eclipse his own ; and was the foremost among the lads who, after the agony of delivery was over, were pleased to congratulate me on what was called my 'success.' This disinterestedness made me at once a warm friend of Fields.

"One of the most notable facts in the lives of clerks with literary tastes and moderate salaries is the mysterious way in which they contrive to collect books. Among the members of the Mercantile Library Association, Thomas R. Gould (now known as one of the most eminent of American sculptors), Fields, and myself had what we called 'libraries' before we were twenty-one. Gould was a clerk in a dry-goods jobbing house, Fields in a book-store, I in a broker's office. Fields's collection much exceeded Gould's and mine, for he had in his room two or three hundred volumes, — the nucleus of a library which eventually became one of the choicest private collections of books, manuscripts, and autographs in the city. The puzzle of the thing was that we could not decide how we had come into the possession of such treasures. We had begun to collect before we were in our teens, and as we had neither stolen nor begged we concluded that our 'libraries' represented our sacrifices. In the evening, after the day's hard work was over, Gould and I drifted by instinct to Fields's boarding-house; and what glorious hilarity we always found in his room! He was never dull, never morose, never desponding. Full of cheer himself, he radiated cheer into us. On one occasion Gould and I introduced the question of our salaries, and somewhat gloomily resented the fact that there was no prospect of their being increased. 'Look here, Tom and Ned,' Fields broke out, 'I have none of your fears in this matter. I was originally destined for Jupiter, but the earth caught hold of me, and hauled me in. Don't you see, by thus impertinently interfering, the earth is bound to give me a good living?' This joyousness of mood lasted through his life.

" The conversation of Fields had, even in his boyhood, the two charms of friendliness and inventiveness. The audacities of his humor spared neither solemn respectabilities nor accredited reputations ; yet in his intercourse with his friends his wildest freaks of satire never inflicted a wound. His sensitive regard for the feelings of those with whom he mingled was a marvel of that tact which is the offspring of good nature as well as of good sense. When he raised a laugh at the expense of one of his companions, the laugh was always heartily enjoyed and participated in by the object of his mirth; for, indulging to the top of his bent in every variety of witty mischief, he had not in his disposition the least alloy of witty malice. When seemingly delivered over to the most unrestrained ecstasies of his jubilant moods, when his arrows flew with lightning-like rapidity, hitting this person and that on the exact weak point where their minds or characters were open to good-natured ridicule, there never was the least atom of poison on the shining edge of his shafts.

" Those who knew Fields in his youth as well as in his manhood must have noted that he was two widely different persons, according as he talked with intimate friends or chance acquaintances. He never was his real self except in the company of the former, for with them he had to put no rein on his impulsive feeling or his quick intelligence ; but the latter utterly failed to comprehend

2

him as he was in himself. To them, indeed, he appeared as an eminently polite person, irreproachably dressed, irreproachably decorous, guarded in his conversation, pleasing in his manners, relying for his modest position in literature on what he had privately printed for distribution among his friends, and never presuming to be anything more than a publisher, who not only sympathized with literary genius, but had a singularly swift power to discern it. To us who were in his confidence he was ever the maddest of mad wits, of inexhaustible inventiveness and unconventional audacity. . . .

" I cannot help lingering on these early days of our friendship, for his forth-rushing ebulliency of nature was never more delightful than at that period, though his capacity of self-command was even then as remarkable as his spontaneity.

" As years rolled on, and Fields became a partner in the house which he had served as a clerk, the proofs multiplied that he was, among American publishers, one of the most sagacious judges of the intrinsic and money value of works of literature. . . .

" As I happened to witness the gradual growth of what became one of the leading publishing houses of the country, and as I know that its germinating root was in the brain of Fields, I may be able to give some testimony as to its rise and progress. Fields from the start had deliberately formed in his mind an ideal of a publisher who might profit by men of letters, and at the same time make men of letters profit by him. He thoroughly understood both the business and literary side of his occupation. Some of the first publications of the house be-

longed to a light order of literature, but they still had
in them that indefinable something which distinguishes
the work of literary artists from the work of literary
artisans.

"One thing always puzzled me in reference to Fields,
and that was how he contrived to get time to attend to
his own affairs. His place of business always seemed
thronged with visitors. Some dropped in to have a chat
with him, and they dropped in every day; others had
letters of introduction, and were to be received with particular attention; others were merciless bores, who severely tested his patience and good-nature. On some
forenoons he could hardly have had half an hour to himself. Then he was continually doing kindly acts which
required the expenditure of a good deal of time. In
spite of all these distractions, he was a singularly orderly
and methodical business man. He made up for the hours
he lost, or was robbed of, by accustoming himself to
think swiftly and decide quickly on business matters.
. . . . I have done small justice to my own conception
of the brilliancy of his wit, the alertness of his intelligence, the variety of his information, and the kindness
of his heart. I shall have to take some other opportunity to speak of his numerous writings, and of his career
as a lecturer on literature."

Neither public interests nor private friendships
are sufficient to round the full life of the natural
man. The instinct of home is as deep in our natures as the instinct of common joy. During the
period of which Mr. Whipple has spoken, Mr.

Fields became engaged to a beautiful girl, Mary Willard, eldest daughter of Mary (Adams) and Simon Willard. She seemed in every way suited to make him happy, but disease had laid its hand upon her, and a few months after the engagement she faded out of life. This was his first sorrow. He felt incapacitated for the old routine of life for the time, and as soon as possible he sailed for Europe. Sea-sickness, lasting forty days, was a novel experience, and one not to be repeated. There *were* steamers even in those days, and he returned in one after a visit of a few months, but his fortune in the steamer was hardly better than in the sailing vessel. His own diary shall serve to give us particulars of this first rapid tour in Europe. During the voyage he writes : —

" Here my observation ceases for many days. That dreadful destroyer of all personal comfort at sea got hold upon me and kept me chained to my berth. At intervals I was able to enjoy the fine sights about me: the rising and setting sun, the shifting clouds, the rolling swarms of fish, from the huge black-fish to the little nautilus. Life at sea is so new and strange to my experience I have something to attract my attention every hour of the day, and only want bodily strength to note down what I witness of interest. My nights are passed mostly in uneasy snatches of sleep. C—— reads to me every night till ten or eleven, and I manage after that to toil through the hours."

The days and nights were chiefly a repetition of the above, save when he was able to pursue his studies of the French language and French and English history. One day we find him reading Lockhart's Scott. "I should like it better if I had not read it so often," he writes.

This hurried diary gives an interesting picture of how much may be crowded into a single day, and digested, too, by a young and enthusiastic traveler. Days grow to be as long as weeks. Such travelers may truly say, —

"I moments live who lived but years."

"*July* 9, 1847. This morning we got into Havre with the ship at about eight o'clock. I jumped ashore as soon as possible with the Captain and M——, and was enchanted at every step of the way. Everything was so new, and land so glorious once again. After breakfast I went about with a young French gentleman who was kindly introduced to me in the counting-house of MM. Lemaître and Cie. We went first, at my request, to the house in which St. Pierre, author of 'Paul and Virginia,' was born, now occupied by a refiner of sugar.[1] Then to the end of the superb 'pierhead' and to the Round Tower of Francis the First. The day is a delightful one, and I never saw human faces so happy before in the streets. Dined at two

---

[1] Mr. Fields has recorded the suggestions of this visit in his paper upon "The Author of Paul and Virginia," included in his volume of Sketches called *Underbrush.*

P. M., and left for Rouen in the three P. M. train." [Then follows a list of towers, castles, cathedrals, towns, and villages, en route.]

"My companions were a young Scotchman and a young Englishman, intelligent and most communicative, one inviting me to visit Edinburgh, and the other London. . . . After dining [We may observe it was for the second time that day, but he had divided the cherry and made two of it] I sallied out and walked among the crowds, the women in high Norman caps, and made my way to the great Cathedral famous over Europe. It was just vesper time, and the effect of the nuns singing behind the high altar was an utterance of music so thrilling it went to my heart. The light came dimly down the aisles, and I lingered till the priests walked by me to their cloisters. . . . The Seine runs directly by my windows; and as I write this a bugle from a descending steamboat steals along the water like an echo. I am tired, but could not help recording, before I slept, my first day in Europe. . . .

"*July* 10. My second day in Europe. Rose at five and went to the great Cathedral to attend matins." [Here follows a description of churches, monuments, and places seen before half past nine, when he returns for coffee to the hotel, but sallying forth again directly he visits and enjoys the market, Palais de Justice, Museum, where he mentions particularly the autographs of Richard Cœur de Lion and William the Conqueror. He says of two old houses which he visits:] "They look like carved objects that have escaped some great museum. . . . I have run into the flower-market twenty times to-day and gaped with delight at the curious old damsels who offer their bouquets in unknown tongues. Notwithstanding I have got lost in a dozen streets, I manage to come out right at last, everybody is so complaisant and so ready to go any distance with you to set you going in the true direction again. . . . The old concert gardens near the St. Ouen Church are well worth the half hour occupied in looking at them.

"Left Rouen at four P. M. for Paris, by the railroad, which runs through a highly interesting country all the way." [He gives a detailed account of every village, and of glimpses of the Seine, its bridges, of châteaux, avenues of trees, scenes of historical interest, etc., until he sees Paris "towering mistily into the skies."]

"My heart beat rapidly as I made out in the evening light, indistinctly, familiar objects from the memory of pictures I have seen."

And so ended the second day in Europe.

The third day being Sunday, the best day of all, so it was crowded the fullest. Again we read, "Rose at five, dressed, and sallied forth," — and after a long list of things seen and done, he writes, "To bed at one." Speaking of his visit to the Hotel des Invalides, he says, "I saw stumps of men to-day, the major part of whose bodies had been left scattered on battle-fields before I was born." "Home to bed at twelve," and "rose at half past four," or, the latest hour recorded, "rose at seven,"— such were his habits as a traveler, the same as when at home.

Mr. Goodrich (Peter Parley), our consul, was at this time living in Paris with his family, and our traveler seems to have found a warm welcome at his house. Mr. George Sumner was also in Paris, and Mr. Henry Baird of Philadelphia. All three gentlemen were his intimates, and he owed much of his pleasure in Paris to their companionship. From the Rhine he writes of himself as still indefatigable: "Went to bed at ten, got up and saw the Drachenfels by moonlight; saw the sun rise; walked out at five around the town. . . . In the cars we had opportunity of observing how a kind deed or a gentle word atones for an ugly face."

His first day in London was, of course, full of delight to him.

"Dined at a chop-house. Loitered in book-shops. Went to Bath Court (Dr. Johnson's lodgings), Covent Garden, The Cock and Magpie of Jack Sheppard memory, and to Wolsey's house, now a barber's shop. . . . Took a cab and drove to the booksellers', Moxon's, Bohn's, Pickering's, and Murray's, whose rooms are interesting as connected with English literature. Mr. Murray's nephew showed us about the apartment, where are original portraits of Byron, Scott, Campbell, Moore, Irving, and other eminent men."

It was during this first visit to London that Mr. Fields enjoyed that exceptional evening at the Italian Opera (Her Majesty's Theatre), when

Jenny Lind, Lablache, Gardoni, Coletti, Corelli, and others made their appearance. Who of his friends cannot remember his humorous description of that night, the intense excitement, the wonderful fulfilment of excited expectation? "After the opera we had 'Le Jugement de Paris.' Taglioni and Cerito were the principal dancers. We went home at half-past twelve, entirely satisfied that the fame of these singers and dancers had not been overstated or overrated. Coming along home we were accosted by a little child in the street, who swept the sidewalks, begging for pennies, — a contrast to the splendid scene we had just left by no means pleasant." We find notes at this period also of breakfasts, dinners, and visits to Mr. John Kenyon, Mr. and Mrs. Howitt, Mr. and Mrs. Procter (Barry Cornwall), and Mr. and Mrs. S. C. Hall, all of whom became his life-long friends.

"Sunday, went to hear W. J. Fox preach. Fox gave out a hymn, read a passage from the Bible, from Wordsworth, Southey's translation of Michael Angelo, Milton, and Herder. No text, but a consideration of the literature of the day: Leigh Hunt, Wordsworth, the 'Economist' newspaper, etc. Told anecdote of the Society for the Suppression of Mendicity. 'What shall be done with the poets?' Fine singing at Finsbury Chapel, and an original preacher. . . . . Mr. Kenyon recalled at Mr.

Procter's dinner-table Rogers's description of dining with Sheridan, Talleyrand, and C. G. Fox. 'Barry' himself told me more privately of his young days at school with Byron and Sir Robert Peel. He also spoke of his love of 'Hyperion,' by H. W. L. 'You don't drink, Fields,' he said to me. 'Ah! he is languishing for his Susquehanna!' . . .

"Left London for Brompton and 'The Rosary,' the beautiful cottage of Mr. and Mrs. S. C. Hall. Mrs. Hall's library is a most tastefully decorated room. A fine parrot, whom Mrs. H. calls her secretary, added by his presence to the beauty of the apartment."

He describes an interesting company of persons assembled at Mrs. Hall's, and returned to London delighted with his visit.

"Walked through the college grounds at Eton, and on towards Stoke Pogis." [Recalling, doubtless, as he went, those exquisite lines of Gray, "Ye distant spires, ye antique towers," which were favorites of his; indeed, the last words he heard on earth were from Mr. Matthew Arnold's beautiful sketch of Gray's life, published in Ward's "English Poets."] "Just as twilight came on we rambled into Gray's churchyard, and read the tablet nigh his tomb. The hour was happily chosen, and the whole scene most touchingly beautiful." [Copied from the tombstone in Gray's churchyard:] "In the same pious confidence, beside her buried sister, here sleep the remains of Dorothy Gray, widow, the careful tender mother of many children, one of whom alone had the misfortune to survive her."

A few days later he writes : —

"In company with Leslie, the painter, visited Mr. Rogers's house, in St. James Place. He was not in; saw his Rubens, Sir Joshua Reynolds, Rembrandt, and all this beautiful collection by the most tasteful poet of his time. . . .

"Tea with William and Mary Howitt at Clapton, who gave me a hearty reception. Freilegrath came in and stayed during our visit, talking of Longfellow and Bryant with enthusiastic admiration. . . .

"To-day Moxon showed me the remnant of Elia's library, and gave me a copy of the ' Rape of the Lock' that once belonged to Charles Lamb, and contained some manuscript pages in his handwriting. . . .

"*August* 26. Had a delightful interview with the author of 'Our Village.' . . .

"Nine A. M. Rose at five, and rambled round the old city of Bristol; went to Radcliff church, and reconnoitered the old place thoroughly, thinking of Chatterton and his wretched life and death."

Of course his visit to Stratford is most enthusiastically described, but there are no special points to mention here. Mr. Fields's friends will never fail to recall his amusing story of one of his stage companions thither, who asked why he was so eager to stop at Stratford. "Because Shakespeare happened to live here," was the reply. "Shakespeare," said his interlocutor, "*he'd* never been thought anything of if he had n't written them plays!" Unhappily these little trifles do not bear transcription. If occasionally they slip, as it were, from the point of the pen, because the mind so indissolubly connects them with certain places, persons, or things, an apology should go with them, since the voice and manner which gave them grace are vanished.

"A kind note from Colonel Wildman inviting us to Newstead Abbey. Saw an old lady at the Hut who had seen Byron and his mother alight at the 'old place' which formerly occupied the ground, where the present inn stands. Spent many hours at the Abbey, where we saw the chapel, tomb over the dog, the drinking cup (skull), tree with Byron's name beside his sister's. Also from an eminence in the garden saw Annesley Hall, (Mary Chaworth's residence), old mill at the lake side, boat, Byron's canoe in the hall; rode over to Hucknall Church where Byron lies buried, — sexton just locking the doors, — walked into the Byron pew; saw the spot where Byron lies; tablet erected by his sister. . . . Arrived at Edinburgh at half-past five in the morning, the castle looming proudly up in the sunlight. After rattling over the pavements many a weary mile, the hotels being all full, we were set down at 31 St. Andrew's Square, and were received by the landlady at the top of the stairs in her night-cap, nothing abashed at our presence. Poor old Mrs. H——, can I ever forget her welcome, and her offer of all sorts of spirituous liquors! . . . Went to Blackwood's. Saw Wilson's portrait in his back room; strolled about this glorious old city. . . . Went into old churches, and I made bold to ascend a Dissenter's pulpit and think of John Knox. . . .

"Rode down to Gallashiels on top of the coach beside a young Scotch lady who knew every inch of the ground; had seen Scott when a child, and knew Lockhart. She pointed out all the noted hills and castles, and I was sorry when she bade us good-by at the door of the little inn by the roadside in Gallashiels. At G. we took what is called a dog-cart, a queer vehicle enough but quite comfortable, and drove down to Abbotsford; we walked along in sight of Scott's proud growth of young trees planted by himself with so much pleasure, and pretty soon entered the gateway to his dwelling. There it stood on the green and beautiful slope, so quiet and still that it seemed the tomb of greatness departed. Not a sound disturbed the solitude. . . . We walked down the avenue to the hall door and rang the bell very softly. The housekeeper bade us enter the apartment first shown, where armor hung about the walls and everything breathed of war and border minstrelsy.

"I sat in Scott's library chair, walked about among his books, examined his pictures, looked upon his hat and cane and the last coat he ever wore. After spending all the time we could spare in the house we went into the grounds and sat down by the Tweed side. A chamber window was open and we imagined that room the one in which Scott died. Lockhart describes the scene and no one can forget it. . . . As we sat in the evening in the little parlor at the 'King's Arms,' Melrose, we heard the voice of a woman singing one of Burns's songs in another room. We rang the bell and the music ceased.

It was the landlady's daughter who had been singing, and who came to spread the table for our simple supper. We read till midnight, and then as the moon had risen sallied out into the quiet village. There stood the old Abbey waiting for us. We rambled about in the moonlight and climbed into the broken windows. . . . It was a great night, that at Melrose. To bed but not to sleep.

"Up at five, a dull, misty morning, and set off in a drosky for Dryburgh Abbey, where Scott lies buried. As we went on the sun came out and the whole scene was full of beauty. We passed the Eildon Hills, Chiefswood, Ravenswood, and Wallace's Monument. Crossed the Tweed in a small boat and leaped ashore just on the rim of a waving forest filled with birds. Walked on in silence through rows of superb trees till we reached a low cottage, where reside the family who show Dryburgh and its grounds. The Tweed was rippling by us as we stood around the grave of Scott, and a robin from a neighboring tree kept up his morning melody undisturbed. We picked some pebbles out of the river to carry with us, and left a spot no change can ever wipe from my memory."

It was upon this visit that Mr. Fields met John Wilson (Christopher North) and William Wordsworth, but he has recorded his memory of these visits both in prose and verse more satisfactorily than in these meagre jottings from his diary.

To return briefly to the journal : —

"My last day in London. The old apple-woman at the corner of Arundel Street wishes me all sorts of luck wherever I may go ! I have eaten her pears till she seems like a friend I am leaving behind. . . . ·

"*September* 5. Sunday. On board the steamer Britannia. Wind fair. Head pretty steady. . . . Sat near the bows ; read Bible and prayer-book. Began Irving's ' Astoria.' . . .

"*September* 8. Walked with Judge K. and a Scotch gentleman who is to travel a year in America ; thinks New York is in New England and New Orleans near Boston.

"*September* 9. Bed most of the day. P—— very funny, but I can't laugh at his jokes. Much obliged to him, however, for trying to amuse me.

"*September* 15. At five o'clock this evening, while lying in my berth talking with B——, the steamer ran ashore ——

"*September* 16. Leaking badly. . . . can't help laughing at —— behind his back. His courage has dwindled to a pin's point. He has just left his stateroom with a face like a tombstone.

"*September* 17. Leaking badly — nearing Halifax. . . . Jumped ashore and walked all over the city. . . .

"*Sunday morning.* Sailing up Boston Harbor. I have walked the deck two long nights thinking of home and friends."

Once more in the old places Mr. Fields took up his renewed life with increased vigor. The following note to Miss Mitford in 1849 gives a hint of his literary occupations : —

Boston, U. S. A., *November* 10, 1849.

" Dear Miss Mitford, — Many weeks have elapsed since I received your welcome letter, and I have delayed answering it till now that I might send you a book I have been editing.   It is called ‘ The Boston Book,’ because it contains the contributions of our metropolitan writers.   Among our Boston men you will find the names of Webster, Prescott, Longfellow, and others not unknown across the waters.   I did not include Channing because I have not printed the writings of any deceased authors. The book is intended as a souvenir to be handed to a friend as a memento of our city, and I am happy to say a large edition is already sold.

" Mr. George Ticknor's ‘ History of Spanish Literature ’ is going through the press rapidly.   It will be ready in a few weeks for publication.

" I made your compliments as expressed in your last letter, and he in return, with his family, begs his kindest regards.   I have read some portions of his book, those devoted to the ballad literature of Spain, and am greatly charmed with the perusal.

" In the course of next month I intend to prepare, if I get the leisure, a brief article on some of the less known and more recent English poets for one of our Boston periodicals, called the ‘ Examiner,’ and hope to please B—— by saying in print how well I like him.   I am busy just now superintending the republication of the complete poems of Robert Browning, the first American reprint.   It will be issued by our house in a few weeks. I asked my friend Mr. Whipple to send you a copy of his ‘ Lectures,’ which, I am sure, you will like.

"Mr. Webster has lately made one of his great speeches touching Hungarian affairs. I think I have never seen the lion more roused.

"Mr. Prescott is still busy with his 'History of Philip II. of Spain.' He is not determined as to the extent of his labor, but it will undoubtedly be one of his longest efforts, and I think one of his most successful ones.

"With all my best wishes for your health and happiness, in which I am heartily joined by my friends,

"I remain, dear Miss Mitford, always

"Yours most truly,   JAMES T. FIELDS.

"P. S. Has there ever been made a good engraved portrait of yourself? If so pray send me one. I have that which appeared in Chorley's work some years ago, but I should like a better one if possible."

In 1850 Mr. Fields married the younger sister of his first betrothed, Eliza Willard. For a few brief months they were supremely happy, but before a second summer ended she also vanished away. His suffering was very great. Being in the full vigor of manhood he could not help feeling that his life, some life to him in this world, still remained, and he must face it alone. He was blinded and unequal to his duties, therefore he was advised again to leave America and pass a year in Europe.

The happy season of his marriage was also fruitful of much labor in his career as a publisher. In October, 1850, he writes to Miss Mitford: —

"Many months have elapsed since I have had the pleasure of writing to my kind friends in England. I have been absent from home, and more than ever busy. The older I grow, thicker and faster comes upon me from every quarter, work, hard and unremitting work. The matter of a publishing house never moves out of the way, but is continually crowding itself before one's eyes, so that I now find at night huge piles of unfinished labor all ready to stare upon me in the morning."

Again he writes : —

BOSTON, *January* 7, 1851.

"MY DEAR MISS MITFORD, — A few days ago I read from one of our American newspapers a fresh paper from your delightful pen descriptive of English scenery in and about your own residence. It was copied from the 'Ladies' Companion.' How charmed I was with it, and how it roused me again to wishing myself once more in the dear old lanes of England. My passion for rural life in your country amounts to a disease. Sometimes when I get musing about my rambles in England in 1847, I become very impatient that I see no chance of my visit being repeated the next summer. . . . Pray accept my thanks for Carlisle's speech. It is well done, and is another evidence of his honest good sense. I send you a brace of volumes by his friend Charles Sumner, a man whose splendid talents (albeit his politics are unpopular) will send him to the Senate the next spring we hope. I also send you Holmes's other volume of poems and his late pamphlet. I am sure you will like Holmes. He is a prodigious favorite in Boston, and one of our most eminent physicians. Hillard's

address, which I enclose in the same parcel, is very
well thought of here and all over New England. Hillard is one of our most eloquent speakers, and idolized
greatly among the young men. We intended to republish Mrs. Browning's new edition, but another house in
New York claims the right, so we give it up.

" You would be amazed to see what a call we have for
Bohn's new edition of ' Our Village,' about Christmas.
I always order from him a good stock, but we generally
run out long before the New Year. By the steamer just
in (which brings me your kind letter), I see we have a
fresh lot, redolent of the woods and fields of Old England.

" I forget if I have sent you a few new pieces of mine
printed since the little volume. I will try, however, to
pick them up from the newspapers and enclose to you in
some future letter. Hawthorne is writing a new romance, to be called ' The House of the Seven Gables.'
When it is printed, I shall send it to you." . . .

We find the correspondence of this period in-
cludes, almost without exception, all the men and
women of any literary note in America. His correspondence with some of them was only the beginning of friendships which were uninterrupted
to the end, and bringing the fruitage he most
valued to his life. Among the letters, beginning
at this time, from those who have gone from this
earthly scene, I find those of Hawthorne, Willis,
Mrs. Anna Cora Mowatt, the actress, of whom

Edgar Poe wrote : " Her sympathy with the profound passions is evidently intense. . . . This enthusiasm, this well of deep feeling, should be made to prove for her an inexhaustible source of fame. . . . Her step is the perfection of grace. Often have I watched her for hours with the closest scrutiny, yet never for an instant did I observe her in an attitude of the least awkwardness or even constraint, while many of her seemingly impulsive gestures spoke in loud terms of the woman of genius, of the poet imbued with the profoundest sentiment of the beautiful in motion. . . . A more radiantly lovely smile it is quite impossible to conceive." Mrs. Mowatt was much beloved by her friends, and always counted Mr. Fields among them.

Fitz Greene Halleck's letters are also before me, and brief notes of Margaret Fuller and Mrs. Kirkland ; letters of Miss Catherine Sedgwick and Epes Sargent, Lewis Gaylord Clark, J. G. C. Brainard (whose beautiful sonnet upon Niagara was one of Mr. Fields's favorite poems), Bayard Taylor, Charles Sumner, and Henry B. Hirst.

The mention of Brainard's name recalls a half-forgotten anecdote Mr. Fields related of him, as told by Mr. S. G. Goodrich. Brainard was a young lawyer, and had an office very near Mr. Goodrich's. They were too poor to keep a boy to

make their fires in the winter, so they were in
the habit of going down together and making
them with their own hands.   One morning Brainard had his stove open ready to put in the fuel,
when the sonnet upon Niagara came to him.
He called G. in and repeated the lines.   " Write
it down, write it down," said G., " it is superb."

Mrs. Seba Smith, also, and the Davidsons, are
found in this somewhat heterogeneous collection ;
and Dr. Channing, George P. Morris, Rufus Gris-
wold, George S. Hillard, Thomas Crawford, the
sculptor, T. B. Read, and many others.

The following lines were sent to Mr. Fields by
George S. Hillard, on the occasion of the publication of the latter's " Six Months in Italy " in
1853 : —

> " Dear Fields, it is a pleasant thing to find
> My name upon a page with yours conjoined.
> For us that launch upon a sea of ink
> Our foolscap argosies, to swim or sink,
> No better flag than yours to sail beneath,
> E'er felt the sunbeam's kiss, the breeze's breath.
> The ogre publisher whom poets paint,
> That sucks the blood of authors till they faint,
> The stern pasha of Paternoster Row,
> Whose scrawl portends ' the everlasting no,'
> Is a mere myth to us, who see in you
> A heart still faithful to the morning dew.
> Had I a draught of Hippocrene sustained,
> 'T is to your health the goblet should be drained.
> Large sales your ventures crown, and may your **books**
> Reflect the cordial promise of your looks."

The correspondence with Mr. Hillard is one of the earliest date, and the friendship was sustained until the end. In 1856, upon the introduction of "the blue and gold" books, wherein the poets were so many of them conveniently enshrined by Mr. Fields, the following lines were again addressed to him by Mr. Hillard: —

TO J. T. F.

"When your new Tennyson I hold, dear friend,
Where blue and gold, like sky and sunbeam, blend, —
A fairy tome — of not too large a grasp
For queen Titania's dainty hand to clasp, —
I feel fresh truth in the old saying wise,
That greatest worth in smallest parcel lies.
Will not the diamond, that fiery spark,
Buy a whole quarry-full of granite stark?
Does not the flaunting holly-hock give place
To that pale flower, with downward-drooping face,
Which summer fashions of the moonbeams' sheen
And sets in tents of purest emerald green?
Well suits your book with this sweet month of June,
When earth and sky are in their perfect tune.
For, when I read its golden words, I think
I hear the brown thrush and the bob-o-link; —
I hear the summer brook, the summer breeze,
I hear the whisper of the swaying trees.
Between the lines red roses seem to grow,
And lilies white around the margin blow.
Cloud-shadows swift across the meadow pass
And fruit-trees drop their blossoms on the grass.
Thanks to the poet, who to dusty hearts
The balm and bloom of summer fields imparts;
Who gives the toil-worn mind a passage free
To the brown mountain and the sparkling sea;

Who lifts the thoughts from earth, and pours a ray
Of fairy-land around life's common way.
And thanks to you who put this precious wine,
Red from the poet's heart, in flasks so fine,
The hand may clasp them, and the pocket hold; —
A casket small, but filled with perfect gold.

G. S. II.

"*June 6, 1856.*"

Willis writes with his accustomed grace in 1848, " Your press is the announcing-room of the country's Court of Poetry, and King People looks there for expected comers." Again, " When are you coming this way? Slide down upon us with the autumnal rainbow and see how lovely it is here."

In response to an invitation extended him through Mr. Fields, to come to Boston to deliver a poem, Willis writes : —

"*Saturday.*

" My dear Fields, — I beg a thousand pardons for my neglect to reply to your letter. The truth is, I took the time to consider whether there *could be* such a thing as an effective *spoken* poem. I am satisfied, now, that my style depends so much on those light shades which would be lost on more ears than two at a time, that I should make an utter failure. I would risk even this, if it was not in Boston, for (to confess the " morsel under my tongue ") I have few plants growing in my hope-garden like that of being one day acknowledged among the Boston boys with whom I was snubbed and brought up, as a good fellow and worth taking back into their hearts. A failure would damage the growth of this.

So, dear Fields, make my thanks and excuses acceptable to the committee and believe me

" Yours much indebted and most truly,

" N. P. WILLIS.

" J. T. FIELDS, ESQ.

" Remember me to Whipple.

" What a *ne plus ultra* of a translation that is of 'Consuelo' by Shaw. And what a delicious book it is. I have just finished it and am going to write a word or two about it for Morris.

" Many thanks for your kindness to dear good Fanny Forester."

In spite of his incessant occupation as a publisher, Mr. Fields was continually writing and printing verses and *jeux d'esprit* in the current journals or magazines, or for occasions. Any continuous literary work was of course out of the question, but such as he could do was done cheerfully for others or to stop some gap. Few, almost none, of these early effusions has he wished to preserve, but it is interesting to note the activity of his powers.

As early as September, 1838, we find him invited to deliver a poem before the Mercantile Library Society, and later the committee ask the favor of printing his " Poetical Address." Doubtless before this as well as later, his pen was busy, indeed it was never idle.

In the autumn of 1851, Mr. Fields left America

for a prolonged visit in Europe. He wrote cheerfully to Miss Mitford as usual, before his departure,
informing her of his plans, which were to go directly to the Continent (after a possible call at her
cottage door), where he intended to remain until
the following spring, when he hoped to visit England. He never referred in speech, and scarcely
by letter, to his own grief, from the time he left his
bedroom after the first terrible shock to the day
of his death, never directly even to those nearest
to him, except to whisper once his gratitude that
he was to possess what he never again expected to
enjoy. The tender letters written him from his
friends at the time were carefully preserved, but
all was silence.

In the same letter to Miss Mitford already referred to, he says : —

"You ask me particularly about Hawthorne. He *is*
young, I am delighted to say. His hair is yet untinged
by Time's sure silver. . . . A few days ago the author
of ' The Scarlet Letter ' came to Boston after an absence
of many months. Every eye glistened as it welcomed an
author whose genius seems to have filled his native land
quite suddenly with his fame. . . . He blushes like a
girl when he is praised . . . . I shall send you shortly a
new juvenile book from his pen, as fine reading, by the
way, for grown people as I happen to remember from the
press for many a day. . . . Cooper, the great novelist, is
gone. He died a few weeks since at his residence in the

State of New York. His fame belongs to his country, while his name is world-renowned."

The spring of 1852 was passed in England, as he had proposed, and he writes again to Miss Mitford, first from Rome, later from Paris, and finally from Regent Street.

In Rome he says: —

"I can see the almond trees in full bloom from my window and hear the birds about the orange trees, but I shall be glad once more to hear the English tongue even in a bird's mouth, and look upon the hedges which skirt the lanes down which we rode that fine autumnal day which seems so long ago. . . . I had a charming visit while in Paris, to the Brownings, and only regretted I could not see more of them. I was glad to find Mrs. Browning in better health than I anticipated and hope she will live to write many more great poems."

Again in Paris he writes: —

"Partly on my own account and something on yours (knowing your enthusiasm for the Bonapartes) I went to the President's ball. It was a splendid affair. . . . I was looking intently at Jerome Bonaparte, who stood talking with General M., when the President himself, with Lady Cowley on his arm, came into the great hall and took his seat directly in front of the spot where I was standing. He looked pale, and although he bowed with a smile to those who stood near, I thought I discovered a deeper meaning in his look than he meant to be exhibited then and there. I cannot but think he is a

man for the time and will show himself competent to
carry out all his designs. His face I think better than
his portraits. It is folly to call him ill-looking. . . . I
have seen a great genius since my last note, Rachel ;
you may judge how delighted I was a few nights since
to read her name underlined at the Theatre Français.
The play was *Diane*, a new drama of the time of Louis
XIII. When the curtain drew up she was discovered
coming down the stairs of a rude cottage with the step
of a queen. She advanced with a mien so noble and yet
so natural — so simple and so regal at the same time,
that I hardly knew which to admire more, the quiet or
the majestic in her deportment. Throughout the whole
drama she was magnificent. At one time she stood such
a living monument of woe, that Niobe herself is not so
drowned in sorrow as she appeared. I was charmed
with this superb creature, and shall not soon forget her
splendid manner when she replied to a young gallant in
the first act as she was going off the stage. He followed
her crying out, ' *Ne saurai-je pas qui je salue ?* ' She
turned round very quietly and said in a voice, that made
music of the reply, these simple words ' *Une femme.*' It
was worth a voyage across the billowy Atlantic to hear
that voice and see that manner. You remember Fuseli's
remark, when some one in his hearing said the existence
of the soul was a doubtful problem. Rachel might truly
affirm, that, however badly off other people might be in
that way, *she had a soul.* I hope some day you may have
the opportunity of seeing this great creature on the stage.
She is worthy of all the praise that has been lavished
upon her. I understand she has had the good taste to

preserve among the ornaments of her splendid salon, the poor little guitar which used to accompany her voice when a child she went about singing at the doors of the cafés on the Boulevards.

" I am delighted at what you tell me about your portrait and hope I may get an engraved copy to carry home with me. I have now hanging up in my little library room in Boston your likeness engraved for Henry Chorley's ' Authors of England,' and there is a nice little niche for the engraving now on the tapis, wherein I hope to place it. In a few weeks I hope to find you in Swallowfield and as much improved in health as my heart could wish.

" Very sincerely yours always,

" J. T. Fields."

" 72 Regent Street, London, *May* 21, 1852.

" My dear Miss Mitford, — As soon as I sweep away this load of pressing business I shall run down to Swallowfield, and I must find you well again. Then we will *talk* over the contents of your kind letter received in Paris a few days ago, and which I did not answer as I knew I should so soon meet you again. Your requests about a portrait of Louis Napoleon and the Memoir of the President were curiously enough complied with before the receipt of your letter. I had already packed away in my trunk a little bust of the Prince and one of Béranger for you, together with the Memoir, a recent one, and a copy of Galignani's edition of your ' Reminiscences.' This last is not yet published, but I got from the bindery a copy in advance, thinking you would like to know how you look across the channel.

When I go down to Swallowfield I will bring these with me. I cannot tell you how delighted I am in the perusal of your book, which I read in the cars between Paris and Boulogne. How happy you must be in the thought of what a world of pleasure you have given to your readers. I must not forget to tell you that I found letters in London from Holmes, Hawthorne, and Longfellow, all of whom are delighted with your praise. And I must not forget to say how grateful I am for the too kind manner in which my own name is mentioned. I see in the American papers your chapter on *Webster* is copied weekly everywhere. He cannot but be delighted with your charming account of his visit.

" Hawthorne has just finished another romance. Whipple, who has read the manuscript, says it is admirably done; that it is full of thought and beauty, and pathos and humor. The story turns on the new ideas of the day. One of the characters is a ' Woman's Rights Woman,' says Whipple, and although one is all along doubting her system, she is of such surpassing loveliness, in Hawthorne's description, that the reader falls in love with her person. The sharp, penetrating, pitiless scrutiny of morbid hearts which Hawthorne is so celebrated for, appears in this new novel in some transcendent examples.

" I am glad to see that Holmes is to be immediately reprinted in London. Since you copied his ' Punch-bowl' into your pages, that lyric has gone everywhere, I am told. Holmes writes me that he wishes to be most heartily remembered to you, and begs me to say how much he feels your kind mention of him. Hawthorne says, 'tell Miss Mitford I mean to write her a letter one of these days and thank her myself.' "

Again he writes: —

"June 24.

"When I tell you I have eaten twenty-nine dinners out of the house where I lodge, during the past month, you will know how to pity me. A return to hard biscuit and beef on board ship will be a relief. But ah, these warm English hearts! . . . De Quincey's daughter Margaret writes me from Lasswade (near Edinburgh) with reference to my 'Editorship' as she calls my humble labors, and I think before I leave England I shall go down and see the author and his family. . . . Ah, how much I enjoy London! Not the dinners and the opera solely; my tastes are low in some departments and what many others would call ungenteel I dote upon. For instance, I like those small specimens of humanity in the shape of ragged boys who sweep the crossings, and have established such an intimacy with them that in certain streets they scent my coming afar off, and run to receive my trifling gratuity with a grin of satisfaction that is perfectly delightful. It is my delight on returning from an evening party, on foot late at night and sometimes early in the morning, for Londoners keep untoward hours, to encounter a poor devil barefoot and hungry, and surprise him with a Niagara of hot coffee and a round of meat-stuffs ordered for him at a cheap establishment near Covent Garden, or in the Strand. One of these boys I picked up a few nights ago, sitting on a pavement smoking the end of a cigar which some passer-by had thrown into the street. He looked as he crouched along-

side the wall like a bundle of rags smouldering away in
the cold night air. I wish you could have seen those
sausages descend into his poor empty stomach, and hear
the gurgling of two pots of beer as they went down to
join company with the solids! This is my *fun*, better
sometimes than sitting through a play or an opera.

"I do not know how you will like Hawthorne's new
book, but it seems to me (I have read a few sheets only)
quite delightful in its way and full of fine pictures of
New England scenery.

"I must not forget to tell you what a charming morning I had in Mr. Lucas's studio. . . . The portrait was
not in his house; it is still at the engravers.

"Pardon this long note and believe me,

"Dear Miss Mitford, ever yours,

"J. T. FIELDS."

"I have not seen Mrs. Browning yet. 'Sordello'
himself I met a few days ago at Mr. Kenyon's, where I
had the honor of being sandwiched between Carlyle and
Landor at table. . . . While you were writing your note
to me I was walking with De Quincey home to his cottage from Roslin Castle, where we had been spending the
afternoon together. A more delightful day I do not remember to have passed in this beautiful country. . . .
He is a most courtly gentleman."

In the autumn of 1852 Mr. Fields again returned to America, where he was beginning to be
sadly missed at "The Old Corner." The publishing business which he had enlarged and yet con-
centrated so closely in Boston, began to need his
hand at the ship's helm.

" Hazlitt's writings," he continues to Miss Mitford after his return, " have been all reprinted in America or I should at once set about it. De Quincey is still the rage and I have got two new volumes which I shall send you the very first opportunity. . . . That elegy on the death of Mr. Webster was written by my friend, T. W. Parsons, a fine poet who has done but little, yet everything well. Have you seen Longfellow's lines on the Duke? They are much admired here. Dear Dr. Holmes, who has just asked for you and desires his love, has been delighting all Boston with a most sparkling lecture on Poetry and Science. He will not publish or I would send it to you. I told Hawthorne of his Russian eminence. He says ' Give my love to my dear friend Miss Mitford and tell her I thank her heartily for all her kindness.' Mrs. S——, Heaven forgive me, I have not called upon yet. Since my return home my friends have flocked about me so pressingly that I do not sleep or eat as I once did. However, next week I shall go to Cambridge and sit down with Mrs. S—— for a long chat. She is a charming person. As you refer to the ladies of England who have so modestly told us what a set of wretches we are in America, I must tell you of a paragraph which I introduced into a lecture a few weeks ago before the Boston Mercantile Library Association. ' Our country is sure to advance even its present position if the Duchess of Sutherland and her illustrious coadjutors can only be persuaded to remove their satin slippers from the neck of the Republic.' The allusion seemed to give the audience — I had 3,000 listeners — great fun.

" Our President is only a General by appointment

from his native State in a volunteer regiment, consequently he is only a General *pro tem.* and may give up his honors in that way any week he chooses. 'How do you do, *Captain*,' said one Western man to another. 'Call me *General*, if you please, sir,' replied the man spoken to, —'I have killed a rattlesnake and am plain *Captain* no longer !'

"How provoking it is that you do not own the copyright of 'Our Village.' By this steamer we have ordered *one thousand* copies of ' Bohn.' "

"Yours, dear Miss Mitford,

JAMES T. FIELDS."

"BOSTON, U. S. A., *March* 8, 1853.

"MY DEAR MISS MITFORD : — I am beginning to feel sadly uneasy and fidgetty about these days. The truth is my English fever is most strong upon me. I want to turn my face toward the English land again and I see no signs as yet that I shall be able to do so. Not a day goes by but I think of the far-off country across the ocean. I open a book in my library room of an evening and try to read, but as I go on, straightway the printed page slips from my mental vision and I am in ' distant climes and lands remote.' Now I am looking from the roadside on a cricket ground. There is a small pony chaise quietly resting on the opposite side of the way. A very dear friend of mine is talking cozily with other dear friends who cluster about her side. A gentleman on horseback is looking across the fields. Somebody says it is the author of 'Alton Locke.' I walk up to the aforesaid gentleman, but am disappointed. It is some

4

other fine-looking man who has come out to enjoy the day. There is a picturesque old mansion in sight. The air is clear and bracing and off we go to explore the grounds. Sam talks to us by the way of by-gone times when merry scenes were going on within the fine old house. Now all looks dull and dreary. There are dilapidated houses where the dogs used to live on 'the fat of the land.' Now the whole scene is changed and the tall ancestral trees seem to sigh amid the desolation. Now I am riding through the Duke's grounds and the pony is full of spirit and dashes through the gates like mad. Cattle are grazing all around, and I can smell the hay among the meadows. Now I am sitting in your pleasant room looking out across the road. K. has sent away several carriages, and we all listen while you read to us dear friend Bennoch's charming May poem, ' And welcome in the glorious May.' I can hear it as distinctly as when we sat together that pleasant afternoon (it seems but yesterday) and heard your beautiful and never-to-be-forgotten reading of those verses. Now we are at your hospitable dinner table and I am trying to carve, an art I never shall learn. Then ' the carriage is ready ' and we say ' good-by,' and drive toward the station, talking of the happy hours we have spent with our dear friend, the lady of ' Our Village.'

" Oh, those days ! When shall we all meet again un-der those glorious old trees and under your cottage roof ?

" It seems as if I could not possibly get through the summer without taking the voyage once more. My friends hang on to the skirts of my coat and say, ' You shan't go again ! ' But I will. I want to see Swallowfield and Miss Mitford and that famous illustrated copy of the ' Recollections.' I want to shake off the Yankee dust for a season and revel in a good substantial English fog. I want to see English faces and hear English voices once more. In short, I want to be in England and embrace the whole Island! I like England and I can't help it, and I don't want to help it! Why could I not have been born with a stout traveling fortune, ample and sufficient for me to see the shores of Great Britain as often and as long as I would like to? What a plague is this busy atmosphere of books all about us." . . .

"Ever, my dear Miss Mitford, affectionately yours,

JAMES T. FIELDS."

In June, 1854, Mr. Fields again sailed for Europe, but he became very ill and was carried ashore at Halifax. In writing to Miss Mitford of his disappointment, he enclosed some farewell lines addressed to him by T. W. Parsons the day he went on board the steamer. In October of that year, however, he writes again in a different vein, asking her " if she has room in her heart for one more American? Her name is Annie Adams, and I have known her from childhood, and have held her on my knee many and many a time. Her father (and this must recommend her to your favor) is one of our leading physicians, and a great admirer of Miss Mitford. . . . On the 7th or 10th of next month we go to church."

The Divine Disposer who "shapes our ends" had thus far denied something which seemed indispensable to his existence. He felt the power and sacred rest which a home can give as deeply as it is possible to understand it, but hitherto he had been turned, as it seemed, violently from such hope or rest to stand in the white light of the world. His gay temper and conversation allowed no one else to feel the void and unrest; but when at last the doors of home opened to him he entered reverently, and with a tenderness which grew only with the years. What an exceptional experience, also, for a young girl, a younger member of a large family, with less reason for special consideration than any other person of the household, to be swept suddenly out upon a tide more swift and strong and all-enfolding than her imagination had foretold ; a power imaging the divine life, the divine shelter, the divine peace. The winds of heaven might not visit her too roughly, and every shadow must pass first through the alembic of his smile before it fell upon her. There was no more thought of Europe for the present ; by and by he wished his wife to go, and they would travel together. He desired nothing further for himself, working with fresh interest and vivacity over his plans for new books, and for the extension of influence and usefulness of the firm of Ticknor and Fields.

Mr. George William Curtis has lately portrayed with beautiful skill and feeling the publisher and friend as he knew him in these and previous years:

" The annals of publishing and the traditions of publishers in this country will always mention the little Corner Bookstore in Boston as you turn out of Washington Street into School Street, and those who recall it in other days will always remember the curtained desk at which poet and philosopher and historian and divine, and the doubting, timid young author, were sure to see the bright face and to hear the hearty welcome of James T. Fields. What a crowded, busy shop it was, with the shelves full of books, and piles of books upon the counters and tables, and loiterers tasting them with their eyes, and turning the glossy new pages — loiterers at whom you looked curiously, suspecting them to be makers of books as well as readers. You knew that you might be seeing there in the flesh and in common clothes the famous men and women whose genius and skill made the old world a new world for every one upon whom their spell lay. Suddenly, from behind the green curtain, came a ripple of laughter, then a burst, a chorus; gay voices of two or three or more, but always of one — the one who sat at the desk and whose place was behind the curtain, the literary partner of the house, the friend of the celebrated circle which has made the Boston of the middle of this century as justly renowned as the Edinburgh of the close of the last century, the Edinburgh that saw Burns, but did not know him. That curtained corner in the Corner Bookstore is remembered

by those who knew it in its great days, as Beaumont recalled the revels at the immortal tavern : —

> " What things have we seen
> Done at the Mermaid ! heard words that have been
> So nimble and so full of subtile flame,
> As if that every one from whence they came
> Had meant to put his whole wit in a jest!'

What merry peals ! What fun and chaff and story !
Not only the poet brought his poem there still glowing
from his heart, but the lecturer came from the train
with his freshest touches of local humor. It was the exchange of wit, the Rialto of current good things, the hub
of the hub.

"And it was the work of one man. Fields was the
genius loci. Fields, with his gentle spirit, his generous
and ready sympathy, his love of letters and of literary
men, his fine taste, his delightful humor, his business
tact and skill, drew, as a magnet draws its own, every
kind of man, the shy and the elusive as well as the gay
men of the world and the self-possessed favorites of the
people. It was his pride to have so many of the American worthies upon his list of authors, to place there if
he could the English poets and ' belles-lettres ' writers,
and then to call them all personal friends. Next year it
will be forty years since the house at the Corner Bookstore issued the two pretty volumes of Tennyson's poems
which introduced Tennyson to America. Barry Cornwall followed in the same dress. They caught all the
singing-birds at that corner, and hung them up in the
pretty cages so that everybody might hear the song.
Transcendentalism and ' The Dial' were active also at

the same time. The idyl of Brook Farm was proceeding in the West Roxbury uplands and meadows on the
shores of the placid Charles. The abolitionists were
kindling the national conscience at Chardon Street
Chapel and Marlborough Chapel. Theodore Parker was
appalling the staid pulpits and docile pews. There was
a universal moral and intellectual fermentation, but at
the Corner Bookstore the distinctive voice was that of
'pure literature;' and hospitable toward all, and with
an open heart of admiration for the fervent reformers,
Fields had also the most humorous appreciation of 'the
apostles of the newness,' but minded with zeal what he
felt to be especially his own business.

"It was a very remarkable group of men — indeed, it
was the first group of really great American authors —
which familiarly frequented the corner as the guests of
Fields. There had been Bryant and Irving and Cooper,
and Halleck and Paulding and Willis in New York, but
there had been nothing like the New England circle. It
was that circle which compelled the world to acknowl-
edge that there was an American literature. Of most
of these authors the house at the corner came to be the
publishers, and to the end they maintained the warmest
relations with Fields, who was not their publisher only,
but their appreciative and sympathetic friend."

In spite of his pleasant preoccupations behind
" the green curtain," a whole new life began with
his marriage. No threads of this unseen weaving
were ever dropped or forgotten. The day seldom
wore from end to end during all the years of his

business life without some brief note or token sent homeward from his part of the city. "As this is a day to pick and choose and be dainty in the selection of a book for the fireside hours, I send you a couple of volumes more than you have in our bright room." Or, "It is such a fine walking day I shall call for you." Or again, "Here are three letters, they are only intended for your perusal. They are not well done, I fear; but it is difficult to manage the pen over such a subject. A woman could have said what I wanted to say much better than I have done, but I doubt if any one could FEEL more in this sad business —"

Within this note I find enclosed the two letters to which he refers. They were indeed intended only for the persons to whom they were addressed, but they may be of use or comfort now to some one else whose eye may chance to fall upon this page when the writer and those for whom they were intended have gone beyond and above the difficult problems presented to them.

"BOSTON, *October* 6, 1854.

"My DEAR ——. Your letter has given me more real heart-grief than I express when I tell you it has cost me a sleepless night. But I know not what to say in reply to your communication. You ask my advice in a matter so delicate and unusual that I feel almost like asking you to release me from tendering a word of counsel. But our friendship of so many years, and the tender affection expressed in your letter, will not suffer me to be silent.

"You say you have lost 'the love of your husband, and that he no longer makes you his confidant or even his friend.' Do not, I pray you, my dear ——, hastily conclude on this point. A man's love is not quenched so suddenly. Do not mistake my meaning. I have always been of the opinion that the affection of a man is equal, nay, may I say it, — stronger oftentimes than that of a woman. If F. does not evince the same fondness for your presence as formerly, and treat you with the same tender regard as of old, may he not be won back to your heart, and join his as fervidly to yours by a deeply expressed solicitude on your part to gain back the love of other days. It too often happens in married life that husband or wife do not come more than half way in reconciliation. It is hard, very hard to doubt and weep alone the loss of affection. Let me tell you what I would do if my case were yours, as you describe it. I would hang about my husband with a gentle kindness, and although I would not hide my grief for the loss I had felt, I would still be as cheerful and kind as I could be. Love begets love. Try to make *home* necessary to a man's happiness and you will almost always succeed. Your husband is a man of intellectual tastes and habits. Feel an interest in his pursuits and spring to his side with a smile and a kiss of welcome, for a sensitive shy scholar must appreciate this, and I am sure another influence will be exerted in his bosom. I would not abate one jot of womanly tenderness in your daily life toward

F., but I would rather increase in it. Depend upon it no man constituted as he is will repulse the feeling of a true wife. With regard to your suspicion that he has conceived a 'liking and perhaps a love' for another, don't believe it. I know whom you mean and I know all her attractions for a student like F., but I also know the human heart. She is too vain and overbearing in her intellectual gifts to win his regard even. A poetical temperament like his clings to a warm nature and a simple, beautiful character rather than to a showy intellect and cold heart. You have every quality in the way of attraction that a man gifted as F. is demands in a woman. God bless you. I pray that all may yet be clear in your way of duty and love.

" Yours affectionately,

J. T. F."

" Boston, *October* 8, 1854.

" MY DEAR FRANK, — I am glad to hear from your welcome letter that you and yours are well again, that the cloud of sickness has been withdrawn from your dwelling. In your prosperous country you cannot but succeed in your profession. ' Be industrious and you will be happy ' is a motto so strongly recommended in Gray's letters that I have never forgotten its meaning. You speak of ' jolly times ' among the natives of your city, and days and nights of pleasant intercourse with your friends in the country. I am glad to hear, if you are happy, of your new friendships.

" Dear Frank, did it ever occur to you how dependent a *wife* is on her husband's constancy at home ? Did it never strike you how strangely a word or a look falls on a woman's heart if wrongly applied? We men, knocking about the world and jostled by one another, are apt to forget how much a *word* signifies or how much a tone implies. I let fall this sentence simply because your letter led me to suppose your pleasures were mostly away from your own dwelling. Come now, my dear fellow, let us be honest with each other. —— is unhappy that you do not seem to her the same as in former days, the affectionate lover of times past. You must have seen unquiet thoughts were gathering in her heart. Be a man, my dear Frank, and heal the temporary wound that has been inadvertently opened in her young bosom. The female character demands something more than the *forms* of life. I hold that husband and wife should be *lovers* all their days. Why not? You speak of your ' humdrum life at home.' This ought not so to be, my dear fellow. In your beautiful library, beside that glorious well-filled book table, the evening lamps lighted, your sweet wife sewing opposite to your chair, listening to your rich voice as you read to her from Tennyson or one of your own ballads, — there is no hum-drum in all this, depend upon it, for it will *last* when your out-of-door friends fail and disappointment comes in to break up your intimacies. Don't call me foolish and think me officious. I love you too well not to drop a word of suggestion even in your excellent heart.

" All your friends here are well. Longfellow finds plenty to do, and Lowell is probably laying up treasures for the Lowell Institute, where he lectures this year.

" Ever yours, my dear Frank,

" J. T. F."

Five busy, peaceful years at home succeeded his marriage. These years included a period of large literary activity among our American authors, and Mr. Thackeray's second visit to our shores. Closer friendships were formed, partly by means of a social club, then first established, and visits to New York created ties between Mr. Bryant and his family, Mr. and Mrs. Godwin, and Washington Irving. In Boston, Mr. Emerson was delivering his wonderful lectures, surely never to be forgotten, — this master and helper, with the voice and manner of a lover and a seer ; and Starr King was preaching at Hollis Street Church, and illumining the air with his bright presence.

After collecting books enough, " to read on the voyage," — to answer for three voyages, as his wife thought, — the midsummer of 1859 was passed in Europe, chiefly in England. In an old diary I find : —

" LONDON, *June* 27. Mr. Hawthorne and Julian (an interesting boy) came to breakfast. Hawthorne wishes us to take a villa near Florence, where they lived ; he said the bells of the city sounded exquisitely there, — besides the place was haunted ! Talked nervously about his new romance, the muscles of his face twitching, and with lowered voice ; he thought some time he might print his journal also. . . .

" Mr. and Mrs. Bennoch kindly obtained places for us at lunch at the Lord Mayor's. The occasion was made in order to present Durham's bust of the Queen to Madame Goldschmidt. Her sweet face was calm, yet there were unmistakable signs of deep emotion. A gentleman, a relative of Florence Nightingale, spoke of the happiness Madame Goldschmidt had given Miss Nightingale by her interest in the cause. (Madame Goldschmidt had arranged and sung at a concert, the proceeds of which were very large, and devoted to the care of the soldiers at the Crimea.) Mr. Grote, the historian, also spoke. . . .

"*Friday, the* 27*th.* Mr. Tennyson is in London, at the Temple. . . . Went to see Robson in 'The Porter's Knot.' He is a man of original power. . . . The second time we saw Robson, he played ' Uncle Zachary ' and ' Mr. Benjamin Bobbin.' Nothing could be more touching than the former characterization. When Uncle Zachary comes up to London in his best clothes, with that most excellent Tabitha (Mrs. Leigh Murray), to visit 'the little 'un,' the mixture of pathos and comicality seems almost too much to endure; also in the drunken scene, when it becomes so unfortunately easy for him to see people and things as they really are, and he recognizes Wiggins the barber under his stately disguise ! It is inimitable, indescribable, unrivaled ! . . . Mr. Dickens came in the morning, . . . Arrived at Mr. Thackeray's, . . . passed the evening with Mr. and Mrs. Martin. . . . It was nearly eleven o'clock before we reached Mrs. B.'s house, where we were to meet Elizabeth Sheppard, the author of ' Charles Auchester.' " . . .

This interview was the first and the last we ever enjoyed with this interesting woman, — she died shortly after. Not, however, until we had received notes and manuscripts from her hand, chiefly short stories, which were printed in the "Atlantic Monthly," and some stories for children. Beside these, the friend who was constantly by her side during the last six years of her life frequently wrote, giving us particulars of Miss Sheppard's condition. This friendship seems to have been one of those absorbing relations between two women which are occasionally to be seen. In one of her first letters this friend writes: "I must feel for those who appreciate one whom I venerate as I do my only friend. . . . She has been my companion since I was ten years old." In speaking of the article which appeared in the "Atlantic Monthly," after Miss Sheppard's death, she writes : —

"Will you allow me to say that the notice of the 'Author of Charles Auchester,' considered merely as a composition, is perfection, — as a criticism, it is most subtle and powerful, and could only come from the pen of an accomplished writer, showing, as it does, that minute appreciation of difficulties surmounted and beauties achieved, which only the initiated can display; but more than all, it touches so tenderly and reverently the memory of herself and her writings, that it renders any comment unnecessary. . . . There is only one trifling mistake, which I am sure you will forgive me for rectifying. I allude to the surmise that Miss Sheppard was not a great reader. It is, indeed, a perfectly harmless error, as it proves how perfect her taste must have been, and shows she had that charm as an author which is alike the test of good writing and good breeding, — an absence of all mannerism. But she was indeed and truly a bookworm : she read everything, or rather devoured everything, from the most abstruse works, such as Gall's and Reichenbach's (taking in all metaphysical writings) theology, occult books, history and travels, physiology, poetry, children's story books, etc., and she read in French, German, and Latin with equal ease ; nothing escaped her. Yet again you are right in saying she could not be called a student, for (setting aside all partial views which I might be supposed to entertain) she made all information her own as if by magic, and her memory was wonderful. As a child of eight years old she learned 'Childe Harold' through, in twice reading it, during play hours ; Shelley's ' Prometheus Unbound' as quickly ; and everything, by the same kind of intuition, she mastered in the spirit while others were hammering away at the letter. Goethe and Schiller she translated from with ease at fifteen, and amused her teacher by writing long German critiques and imaginary magazine articles as an exercise.

" I mention these particulars knowing you must like to hear everything about her that I can tell. Also I approach the latter part of her dear life with a cowardly sickness at the heart, which is only like ' life in death.' Now I will endeavor to answer every point of your letter without delay.

" She often talked of you and ——. Her sufferings made all reading and writing impossible for some time before her death. I inclose a little sketch in her own handwriting, which you may like to keep. . . . For the poems, I have quantities. . . .

" No stranger ever touched her or looked at her, or knew anything about her. Thank God! We were by ourselves till the last few hours of her life, when a dear Hebrew cousin of mine, who knew her intimately and loved her as a brother, came into the room. . . . To have had her to talk to, to consult on every intellectual subject, leaves me in that sense alone, now she is gone. . . . You made a good guess at Cecilia." . . .

Several manuscript poems are found among these letters and papers. One is headed " Extracts from Memorials of the Flight of Mendelssohn," but they seem to be productions chiefly of her early youth, and such as would not advance the maturer reputation of " Charles Auchester." Personally she was not handsome, but with a fine brow and presence, sensitive, and refined.

The diary continues : —

" *June 30th.* Drove to Hammersmith, where we found Leigh Hunt and his two daughters awaiting us. It was a very tiny cottage, with white curtains and flowers in the window, but his beautiful manner made it a rich abode. The dear old man talked delightfully about his flowers, calling them 'gentle household pets.' He told us also about Shelley, declaring it was impossible for his loving nature to hate any one, yet once he said 'Hunt, we write *love* songs, why should n't we write *hate* songs.' He said he meant to, sometime, poor fellow, added our host. Shelley disliked the second Mrs. Godwin, particularly, believing her to be untrue. He used to say, when he was obliged to dine with her, he 'would lean back in his chair and languish into hate.' 'No one could describe Shelley,' continued Leigh Lunt, 'he was always to me as if he were just arrived from the planet Mercury, bearing a winged wand tipped with flame.' . . .

"P. J. Bailey, the author of 'Festus,' came to lunch. Fine brow and head. He is a student by nature, and confessed to his hatred of crowds. He told us he passed two charming evenings with Hawthorne, who did not know him nor discover him to be a writer. . . .

"Went to Cheltenham to see Captain Robertson, the father of Frederick Robertson of Brighton. Saw the various portraits of Robertson, also the few notes and papers remaining in the hands of his parents. Captain Robertson has made extracts from his son's sermons, which will be published by Ticknor and Fields for the benefit of the children. Mrs. R. a most lovely woman, such as I hoped to find the mother of Robertson. She gave me her son's history. . . . They have lost four daughters also. . . .

"Later Captain Robertson wrote: 'What you say of your being continually bereft of your copies of the sermons is gratifying indeed. . . . I fear the publication of the letters on theological and other subjects may be delayed. I hear they are of great interest. Indeed, the dear departed told me they might some day be published. . . . The last of the Napiers is gone. You recollect seeing the portrait of my friend, that glorious soldier, Sir Charles Napier, in our sitting-room. . . . In the early part of February, as I had taken my seat in the College Chapel, a little before three P. M., I had a mental vision that Sir William was at that moment dying. Next morning I said, 'Mark my words, Sir William Napier died yesterday afternoon while I was in chapel. . . . Tuesday morning brought a letter saying that Sir William died on the Sunday afternoon without a sigh. Two other instances in my life have occurred of this spiritual communication with me of departing friends, so that I can have no doubt of the intercourse of spirits in this nether world ; and I think we may see from Holy Writ that even departed spirits have held communion with those not yet glorified. . . . Sir William said he had a second self following him continually, and essaying to be joined to him. I have no doubt that 'the second self' of which Sir William spoke, was the one, to use the words of the sermons, attendant on a life of spirituality : ' A living Redeemer stands beside him, goes with him, talks with him, as a man with his friend.' . . . I have had some most interesting and extraordinary letters sent me, to be added to the forthcoming volume of my son's letters. What editions have the Sermons reached in Boston ? Do my dear friends indulge me occasionally with a few lines. . . . I am seventy-three years old, and am anxiously looking forward to the publication of my son's correspondence.

"I received lately a letter from a Mr. ——, a stranger

to me, whose name is a household word at Brighton, saying, ' Bigotry and prejudice prevented me ever hearing your son preach. I have now read his works (and by way of amend), have had a marble bust executed (from a cast taken after death), and have had it put up in the Pavilion', — thus corroborating what the ' Saturday Review ' said a year or two ago, ' Many a man either in secret or in public has been constrained to do penance at the graves of Arnold or Robertson of Brighton.' In fact, the voice from the grave is doing more than even the voice from his pulpit. . . . I am glad to find the approbation you speak of regarding the Corinthians. . . . I have the Boston editions of all the other works, and I hope to have them in every tongue in which they shall appear. I have a German copy of the first volume published at Manheim, an English edition by Tauchnitz of Leipsic ; and I hope soon to have the sermons in French, as they are coming out in Paris ; also two of them, ' The Glory of the Divine Son,' and ' The Glory of the Virgin Mother,' which are translated into Italian for distribution as tracts over Italy. . . .

The diary continues : —

" Arrived at Cleve Tower — the residence of Sydney Dobell. Mr. Dobell came down the hill to greet us, accompanied by his fine deerhound, a gift from the family of Flora Macdonald. We clambered up the little lane, fascinated by his talk, and soon wholly at our ease. An interesting and delightful home. Mr. and Mrs. Dobell are of the same age. Engaged at fifteen and married at twenty, they are, — which is not always true of such

early marriages, — deeply attached. Alas ! they are neither of them in good health. . . . We slept at the cottage
in the garden, with a lovely panorama stretching far and
silently below. . . . We can never forget the wonderfully
varied flow of Dobell's conversation.' . . . 'Came to dine
in Magdalen College, Oxford, in one of the queer old
rooms (the place was built in 1485), with a cider cup
in the middle of the table quite as old as the College,
of silver overlaid with gold. Heard C. R.'s interesting
talk. . . . He finished reading to us that night, his last
new story, ' A Good Fight.'

" He has a cheerful, affectionate smile, and seems truly
beloved by all about him. . . .

" Zurich, *September* 1. — This evening the news of
Leigh Hunt's death reached us. It came most unexpectedly, following closely upon his last letter."

Unhappily the letter in question I do not find :
only two or three notes full of personalities, which
are not possible to reproduce here.

From early youth Mr. Fields suffered from pros-
trating headaches, lasting from twenty-four to
forty-eight hours, when he would lie pale and
cold, and conscious only of intense agony. Nothing could be found to arrest them — hot and cold
baths and inhalations of ether being only useful
palliatives. The climate of Switzerland was more
conducive to them apparently than that of England, but no change seemed to prevent their occasional recurrence. Only those persons, — and alas !

they are too many, — who suffer in this way know all that the word "headache" signifies! How many good days and good things lost! For those who watch by the bedside, also, their part is not to be forgotten. The interrupted plans to be explained, the disappointed persons to be satisfied, the letters to be answered, and above all the utter stillness to be preserved at all hazards; the word "headache" is full of significance to them and often full of awe, bringing them face to face with the sudden semblance of death. No habitude can make the coming less terrible.

From the diary : —

"PARIS, *December* 18, 1859. — A sadly eventful week. The news of Washington Irving's death and of De Quincey's reached us on two successive days, and on the third ——— [1] . . . Met Mr. Thackeray on the Boulevard, — like his old self and delighted to be in Paris. 'Father Prout' (Mr. Mahoney) held him by the arm. At night, dining at the 'Trois Frères,' whom should we see but Thackeray again. He came and sat with us, chatting during the evening in his inimitable way. He said Father Prout was 'good but dirty!' As we parted, he shouted 'Good-by, neighbor,' from down the Arcades in his own gay fashion." . . .

"FLORENCE, *February.* Drove to call upon Walter

---

[1] The space which is not filled signifies the death of John Brown, and the unspeakable sorrow and fear for the future of our country, which took possession of every American.

Savage Landor.   He remembered his friend of ten years
ago perfectly, and his reception was most cordial. ' Ah ! '
said he, ' I am eighty-six now, and forget everything.   I
can't remember the name of my new book published the
other day by Nichol in London. Deuce take it ! ' Talking of Louis Napoleon and of Mrs. Browning's faith in
him, he said, ' If that woman should put her faith in a
man as good as Jesus, and he should become as wicked
as Pontius Pilate, she would not change it.   No ! not
wicked as Pilate, because he was n't so bad, perhaps ; he
fulfilled the laws of his country only, but any wretch
we might name.'   He has around him but a handful of
pictures from his large collection.   They are mostly at
his villa, now occupied by his son. . . . He showed us
what he believed to be original portraits of Petrarch's
Laura and her husband, and a fine head by Salvator
Rosa.   He said the whole collection was the finest private
gallery of old paintings in the world except that of the
King of Bavaria, and would we go out to see them without giving his name ? The name might make the pictures inaccessible.

" He spoke of George Washington as the greatest hero
in the noble galaxy. ' He had a large hand,' he said,
' which is an excellent sign.   Assassins have small hands.
Napoleon, the most wholesale of assassins, had a very
small hand.' . . .

" Dined with Mr. Landor ; were waited upon with
wonderful tact by Wilson, an old friend and servant of
Mrs. Browning. A missing spoon would have been quite
sufficient to cause the thunderbolts of wrath to descend,
which seem to stand ever ready at the smallest bidding

of this old man. Fortunately the regiment of spoons
and forks was unbroken, and all went smoothly. Wilson
had reserved a little surprise for him in a dish of *cignale*
which he said was certainly the best thing in the world.
The deep rich purple of the Montepulciano wine recalled to his mind a song of Redi, which he repeated
most musically. Then he told us how Italian wines
had degenerated, and of once meeting a man in his
travels whom he asked to dine with him at a way station. 'Sir,' said he, 'I fear if you knew my trade
you would not ask me.' 'Pray what may that be?'
said Landor. 'A wine-taster, sir.' 'Oh! then come
in by all means. I follow that trade myself sometimes.
And so,' continued Landor, 'I learned something in
our after-dinner talk, which is, that powdered orris-root
put into good claret will make fine Burgundy. Two
teaspoonfuls dissolved in brandy will work the wondrous charm. . . . I have seen some famous people in
my time, and not the least among them was Kosciusko.
A young girl who had heard him say he would like
to see me brought me to his door. She knocked and
said, "General Kosciusko, I have brought a friend to
see you." "I am sorry, my dear," he answered, "but
I can see no one." "I knew you wished to meet Mr.
Landor" — "What Landor" — and in one instant he
started from his couch and came forward to embrace
me. He had been severely wounded on the head, and
his pale face, bound about with broad black bands,
gave him a look of deathly whiteness. He was reading, as he lay, a volume of my poems, and called my
attention to the coincidence. . . . . Garibaldi is the

greatest man of modern times,' he went on to say; 'he it is who has saved Italy, he has done all that is done, he is the regenerator and savior of this distracted land. I hope to see him in Florence before long; he writes me to that effect.'

"While he was talking thus his grandchild came in, bringing him some trifling gift. At once he was like a child with her. He seemed perfectly happy to hold her on his knee and watch her playful ways.

"I asked if he ever met Byron in Italy. No, he said, because some speech of his was repeated once to Byron which put him in a great rage; B. wished to challenge him, but on receiving the information that Mr. Landor was quite ready, and a much better shot than himself, nothing ever came of the proposed rencontre. . . . Before parting, Mr. Landor took from his walls a painting which he believed to be an original Guido and presented it to me. . . . Yesterday Mr. Landor took the pains to walk round to make me a visit. He had not walked so far for an age, he said. His little dog 'Giallo' came with him. 'Ah, dear,' he said to him, 'I wish they would make a collar for the Pope, these people, and give me a piece of it to put round your neck.' "

I find only two notes of Mr. Landor; they were written after this period, chiefly about the publication of his books. There were many others. I remember them especially, because he became very angry with Mr. Fields for withholding what he calls "His Defense," from the public. This was an unfortunate paper, written in his extreme age, giving the details of a quarrel he had with a lodging-house keeper. It was sad enough to have such a paper in existence, but it was an act of the truest kindness to keep it from the public. Often Mr. Fields would say, laughingly, " How I wish poor Landor could be translated before he has time to write me again about his Defense." Unfortunately he lived long enough to be very angry with this friend as with so many others. Before matters came to this conclusion, however, the two notes at least, to which I have referred, were received; the rest, like so much else of interest in epistolary form, seem to have been plucked away by those devourers of the literary land — autograph hunters. One of these brief letters runs as follows : —

" MY DEAR SIR, — I am reminded of the hazard you offered to take in the publishing of my Latin poems. They would occupy about seventeen pages. I had just sent them to my friend Mr. Hare. Intelligence has this day reached me that he is somewhere on his travels. My parcel is not likely to follow him. Now, if you think it convenient to publish them, the peril would be less by the addition of a hundred pages more, partly poetry and partly prose, including my Defense, which is far more important to my fame than any other addition. Our friend Mr. Browning will show you a specimen of the poetry, which, I hear, does me no discredit. In my hands is much more of it, certainly not worse in the more important part. Some portions have been published of the prose. I would rather that you should possess these different pieces than any other publishers. I desire no advantage from them. If you think them worth your attention, I will transcribe them legibly.[1] . . .

> " Very truly yours,
> " WALTER SAVAGE LANDOR.

"*Feb.* 2.   *Via* NUNCIATINA 2671, FLORENCE.

" My ' Honores ' are not come."

This was the period of Mr. Fields's first intimate acquaintance with Charlotte Cushman, a woman of great energy and ability. Many of the pleasantest days in Rome that winter were passed under her roof and at her table. Here was to be seen, from day to day, everybody of interest either among the residents in Rome or the chance visitors to that city. Her dramatic talent and her courage made her a power in the social circle. Miss Cushman was a keen observer and appreciator of that disinterested power of doing for others, which was one of the distinguishing characteristics of her friend's disposition. It is amusing to see how full her letters are of suggestions for forwarding her own plans or those of others in whom she was interested.

---

[1] The idea of the publication of this book was given up by Mr. Fields because of Mr. Landor's insistance on the subject of *The Defense.*

"A thousand thanks about the something for me to read next season. 'Show, show, show!' It would have rejoiced your sympathetic soul to have seen 2,000 people under the influence of the 'Young Gray Head.' . . . You would have seen the reward of your search, and in pointing it out to me as a reading."

"I want very much to introduce to you the bearer of this, . . . and you will make something of him, . . . for you seem to have the power to make of people what you will. I think you are the great original philosopher's stone." . . .

Again she writes: —

"I want you to come to see me and give me some vitality. . . . I want to be taken up bodily and made to do whatever is right, and good, and pleasant. . . . We unite in declaring you are the most wonderful fellow for finding out just what will suit the friends you love and honor with your gifts. I sit down with double-barreled determination to write and say I am keeping well, seeming to contradict the 'malignancy' of disease which my surgeon feared for me. . . . Tell me one thing. Do the lines in the 'Adonais' of Shelley, beginning at stanza 31, 'Midst others of less note,' etc., refer to Byron? or to whom? Please tell me. . . . I know you are very busy, and I would not trouble you, but we cannot get —— to any *action* save through your *personal* pressure. . . . I will beg *you* to assume this responsibility. . . . E. S. has made such a lovely little figure of the Angel of Youth, . . . and a colossal head of the original (secesher, I call it) Rebel, 'The Archangel Ruined' as she calls it, alias Lucifer, which is full of power, and ought to be ordered by somebody at home. . . . How wonderful are the 'Biglow Papers;' there is more said in those papers than has been said by any writer and speaker yet."

The diary continues: —

" Came to Jermyn Street.　When Walter Scott was in London he always lived in this street, usually at the Cherry Hotel, just opposite."

" Met Mr. Edward Jesse at the British Museum at one o'clock.　Through him we were able to see and understand many things of which we should otherwise have been ignorant.　He introduced us to Professor Owen, who kindly escorted us over the department in which he is chiefly interested.　Mr. Jesse is over eighty years old, but hale and hearty."

A few extracts from the correspondence with this aged naturalist may not be out of place here. Mr. Jesse's books have given him a niche with lovers of out-of-door life and students of natural objects.

" East Sheen, Mortlake, Surrey, 1854.

" My dear Mr. Fields : I am become an old fellow and do not much like to look into futurity, as having any certainty of a prolonged existence, but if I am alive next year you have not any one in England who will be more glad to see you than myself. . . . I send you my last note from Mr. Mitford, received to-day.　He alludes to a large mass of papers of Shenstone the poet, now in my possession.　I am afraid that the unfair attack made

upon him by Dr. Johnson in his 'Lives of the Poets' has
done him an irreparable injury, though Shenstone was a
charming poet as well as letter-writer, and I have many
of his unpublished letters.

"I will send you my 'Country Life' as you desire.
Murray calls it a third edition, that he might introduce
the prints of former editions, but in fact nearly the whole
of the matter is new."

"Brighton, 1862.

"Old age creeps upon me very fast. I am rapidly
advancing to my eighty-fourth year. . . . It is time to
thank Mr. Flint for his beautiful and most interesting
work. It beats any of our modern works in binding,
printing, and paper. The subjects are most carefully
colored, and it is altogether a work that does its author
the greatest credit, and gave the recipient the greatest
pleasure. . . . We are very comfortably settled at this
place, though I miss our pretty cottage and its garden,
but I feel that I am doing some good among the fishing
population of Brighton, to whom I continue to give lectures, chiefly on Natural History, and which, when published, I shall hope to send you. . . .

"Professor Owen has been giving a very interesting
lecture here to a large audience. In the course of it he
did me the great honor to say that he was indebted to
my earlier works for his first love of Natural History.
This was a pleasing compliment from the first Naturalist
in Europe. . . . Mr. Agassiz' illustrated catalogue is a
curious and valuable book. Do you claim him as an
American?"

Again we find in the diary: —

"Our kind friend Mr. Flower, of Stratford, accompanied us to the door of Joseph Severn the artist, and friend of Keats. We found Severn a man of kindly nature with true devotion to his art. 'How strange it is,' he said, 'that we never tire of our labor! I have enjoyed working upon this picture more, I think, than upon any other in my life, and last summer I used to get up at six o'clock to steal the flowers from the Park to paint from.' [1] . . . He has just finished a picture of Keats's tomb by moonlight. It is filled with all the tender feeling for the spot which haunts his heart.[2] He showed us a letter, the last Keats ever wrote, in which he says his pain at parting from Miss Brawne would cause death to hasten upon him, but he never wrote a line, nor did Severn ever hear him speak a word, to intimate that newspaper criticism had caused him mortal grief. Severn told us several incidents showing the exquisite kindliness of Keats's nature, and while he told them the unbidden tears would overflow his eyes. 'One day,' he said, 'when Keats was dining with one of the Royal Academicians whose picture had been refused, while Severn's was admitted, the conversation turned upon this subject, and some one declared in a loud voice that Severn was an old man whose pictures had been sent and refused every year until this one was finally accepted

[1] Mr. Severn was at this time over seventy years old.

[2] I find this description of the picture in Mr. Severn's handwriting : "The scene is moonlight at the Pyramid of Caius Cestius. and a Roman Pastore is resting and sleeping against the poet's tomb, whilst a moonlight ray illuminates his face, and thus faintly realizes the story of Endymion. On the tomb is the inscription, ' Here lies one whose name is writ in water.' "

out of charity. Keats rose upon hearing this, declared Severn to be a young man who had never before sent a picture to the Academy, and a friend of his. "I can no longer sit," he said, "to hear his name calumniated in this manner without one person to join me in defense of the truth." Saying this he seized his hat and abruptly retreated from the room.' "

There are a few letters from Mr. Severn before me, and although we may recognize the truth expressed in an article printed just after Mr. Severn's death, "that he does not appear under his own name in any biographical dictionary," yet when all biographical dictionaries have floated into oblivion, Shelley's words will crown him with an aureole. In the preface to the "Adonais," the poet has written, after speaking of Severn's devotion to Keats, —

"Had I known these circumstances before the completion of my poem, I should have been tempted to add my feeble tribute of applause to the more solid recompense which the virtuous man finds in the recollection of his own motives. Mr. Severn can dispense with a reward from 'such stuff as dreams are made of.' His conduct is a golden augury of the success of his future career. May the unextinguished spirit of his illustrious friend animate the creations of his pencil, and plead against oblivion for his name."

I quote from Mr. Severn's letters : —

" You will be interested by the romantic incident in my ' Keats paper,' of my charming meeting with the poet's sister in Rome, and that we have become like brother and sister. She lives here with her Spanish family ; her name is Llanos ; she was married to a distinguished Spanish patriot and author, and has two sons and two daughters, one of whom is married to Brockman, the Spanish director of the Roman railways.

" She has been so kind as to get me from Madrid some fifty letters of her illustrious brother the poet, but as they were addressed to her when she was a little girl, they are not so interesting as his published letters. . . .

" I am officious (*sic*) representative for all the liberated Italian nations, and in my one year's consulate I have been able to liberate, indirectly, some fifty-five suffering political prisoners. The state of things at this moment would form a romance."

Again : —

" I am glad you saw my posthumous portrait of Keats. It was an effort to erase his dead figure from my memory, and represent my last pleasant sight of him."

Finally, on New Year's Day, 1879, from Rome, Scala Dante (when eighty-five years old), he writes : —

" To begin with Keats, I am anxious to know your opinion of the thirty-nine letters to Fanny Brawne, which I confess to you gave me *great pain*. . . . Lord Houghton's Life I admire very much, except that he has most obstinately given the poet *blue eyes*, whereas over and over again, I told him that the poet's eyes were *hazel brown*, all his family having blue or gray eyes, and I have always considered that it was a trait of nature to characterize the poet. . . . I am still at work, occupied on my Marriage of Cana, or the miracle of the wine. . . . I cannot finish without alluding to the wonderful translation of Dante by Longfellow, which I am now reading, and which I consider the first translation made by any poet.

"Good-by, my dear friend.

"Your ever faithful

"JOSEPH SEVERN."

It would be a work of supererogation, after Mr. Fields's own reminiscences of Barry Cornwall, to recall further particulars regarding him, or memories of his hospitable home. Mr. Coventry Patmore writes in his memorial volume to Mr. Procter: "Among his friends in later life no one seems to have won from him so much genial confidence and self-communication as Mr. Fields, to whose charming papers the reader may be referred for more information about the poet's ways and opinions than is to be found elsewhere."

This acknowledged power to win "genial confidence and self-communication" must excuse, if excuse be needed, the publication in these pages of so many fragments from the correspondence of various persons. It is curious how differently the same nature unfolds to different correspondents.

6

We may learn to know a friend by what he unconsciously draws from others almost as well as by his own conscious expression.

The diary continues: "Drove to Lasswade to see the daughters of De Quincey." It is impossible to reproduce or to quote from the private letters of these ladies, but it is most interesting to see their affection for their father and the care they took of him. They were of valuable assistance to Mr. Fields while he was editing De Quincey's works, giving him the dates when certain papers were written, and hunting up many details which would have been difficult if not impossible to discover otherwise, with the ocean rolling between him and the libraries where he must have searched. Very tender, grateful, and sparkling letters these ladies wrote, as to a trusted friend, full of home-like and individual touches.

"Alexander Smith called. Conversation interesting and sympathetic. He laughed about his unwilling confinement at the Isle of Skye in a storm of seven weeks' duration, which was the origin of his delightful paper called ' The Sky Bothie.' He talked especially of Carlyle and Dobell, giving a strong picture of the harsh and rough side of Carlyle. A. S. is a man of health and energy, who gives promise of a long literary career."

What could any record of Edinburgh be worth which should omit a tribute to Dr. John Brown, our friend of many years. The world is still made better worth living in by his presence, and though illness may prevent him from bearing an expressed share in this memorial, we are none the less confident of his unexpressed feeling and sympathy. " Rab" was not to be seen when we were there, save in the spirit, but " Dick," the household friend, was very well indeed.

In July, 1860, we returned to America, Mrs. Harriet Beecher Stowe and her family, and Mr. Hawthorne and his wife and children, accompanying us. It was an excellent passage, though all our little party were happy to touch the shores of home, I believe, except Hawthorne, who used to declare he would like to sail on thus forever, and never come to land. A large number of letters received at Liverpool were premonitory to the busy publisher, and he was soon again established in his home in Charles Street, Boston, with every moment occupied.

It was during this absence, though of course not without correspondence and consultation, that " The Atlantic Monthly " was purchased by Ticknor & Fields. Established in the year 1857, by Phillips, Sampson & Co., under the editorship of James Russell Lowell, it was already recognized as a power, when the failure of the firm who first gave it existence threw it into other keeping.

In 1861 Mr. Lowell resigned the position into Mr. Fields's hands, who continued to fill the place until 1871, when Mr. W. D. Howells became the editor. In 1881 he was succeeded by Mr. T. B. Aldrich.

From the diary: —

"*July* 26, 1863. — Yesterday morning came an article from H. G. upon Gerald Griffin, author of 'The Collegians;' at noon came two little lyrics from ——, pure in feeling, but not adapted for publication. At night a paper was returned from the printing office, a mass of corrections, nearly a week having been exhausted by the proof-reader vainly endeavoring to correct a bad style. Much must be omitted. This morning comes a poem from ——. Something had been done by the editor to bring it into rhythmical shape. The author writes that the deficiencies were 'intentional,' — nevertheless accepts the amendment!

" 'The Atlantic Monthly' is a striking feature just now in American life. Purely literary as it is, it has a subscription list, daily increasing, of 32,000. The labors of the editor and publishers are not light. . . . Looking over a historical article — fear poison — the author is a fierce democrat. —— has just sent a pleasing woman with a volume of poems. The first one is about 'The Frost,' but the fabric the frost builds melts in the sun before we can see what it is all about; so with each one; of course they must be refused. Professor —— sends a pleasant and quaint article; the only objection is he threatens to send more! Excellent paper upon De Quincey, written with great ability.

De Quincey stands in danger of being wronged by undue or unjust praise.

Have been in Concord this week, making a short visit at the Hawthornes. He has just finished his volume of English Sketches, about to be dedicated to Franklin Pierce. It is a beautiful incident in Hawthorne's life, the determination, at all hazards, to dedicate this book to his friend. . . .

"Visit from Charles Sumner. He is to speak next week in New York upon 'Our Foreign Relations.' Meantime he has prepared an address upon 'Our Domestic Affairs,' with which it was his intention to open the next session of Congress, but events move forward so rapidly he thinks it better to print his discourse at once in 'The Atlantic Monthly.' After this matter was satisfactorily arranged, Mr. Sumner proceeded to speak confidentially of Mr. Prescott and of their old friendship. On the day of his return to Boston after he was struck down in the Senate Chamber, a procession escorted him past Mr. Prescott's residence to his own house. 'I had no sooner entered the door,' continued Mr. Sumner, 'than Mr. Prescott's servant rang with a note containing these words: "Welcome home, my dear Sumner; I hope you saw me wave you a greeting from my piazza. What is the earliest moment you can appoint that I may call upon you.' When he came on the following day at the time suggested, he said, " How I wish I had known of the reception earlier, that I might have draped my house with flags and had a canvas printed in enormous letters, 'Welcome home!' with yesterday's date, and underneath May 22, the date you received your injuries; under these should have appeared the words: —

> ' Then I and you and all of us fell down,
> Whilst bloody treason flourished over us.' "

He was full of feeling during the interview.' Mr. Sumner was not only pleased with this sign of friendship, but he felt there had been some misrepresentation of Mr. Prescott's political position, and the idea had gone abroad that he was inimical to himself. Therefore he was glad to make this little incident known.

"Speaking of style in writing, Mr. Sumner said he had re-read Mr. Hawthorne's paper called ' Civic Banquets,' just printed, three times, for the style. ' I suppose De Quincey and Landor are the masters of style among moderns,' he continued. . . .

Signed a paper yesterday, just put into circulation, for raising 50,000 colored troops from New England. . . . Letter from ——, saying his article in the A. M. was shamefully mutilated. ——, standing by, says it is the editor's *duty* to cut off people's heads.' It does not make this duty more agreeable, however. . . . Franklin Pierce, formerly President of these United States, joined us unexpectedly as we were walking in the woods. He is at least a most courteous gentleman and interesting man, kindly and thoughtful. . . .

" *September*, 1863. — This autumn a most attractive list of books will be published by T. & F. Browning, Tennyson, Richter, Hawthorne, Ticknor, and not least, though last, a new volume just finished, called ' The Wayside Inn.' . . .

" *October* 14. — Inauguration of the Union Club. Mr.

Everett made a fine address. . . . Have laid plans for placing several works of art upon the walls. Two are already in position. . . .

" A rough old man from the Cape, half fisherman, half farmer, came in to see Mr. Fields. Said he, ' Mr. Agashy has been down to see the Cape, and we went exploring it together. We discovered some wonderful things down there, some things that air to come out in the next number of your paper (meaning the A. M.). But I wrote to Mr. Agashy and told him there was one partikler thing I was afraid he hadn't got in his article, something very important, and he wrote back and said, when he got through with his article I might write the rest and finish up the matter.' ' What was the new discovery which he had omitted?' ' Why, 't was just this, and I think I'd better write about it. Yer see, they 've been a-planting cranberries down on that are Cape and plantin' and plantin'. Now yer see 't' aint no more use than if they was planted down here in Washington Street; they *won't* grow. You see, the soil down there is all either shelving or 'luvial, and t'wont do for cranberries. Now I should like to finish Mr. Agashy's article, for he is a real good, queer man.' "

" TUESDAY, *November* 3. — Dinner given to the organ builders of our beautiful organ in the Boston Music Hall. Governor Andrew surpassed himself in interesting conversation. O. W. H. read a lyric, and J. T. F. a little drinking song."

January, 1864. Mr. Fields received frequent visits at this period from Professor Ticknor, whose life of William H. Prescott had been lately issued:

" Ticknor is delighted to have completed the work, and to see it in so fitting a dress. He has much that is interesting to relate about the incidents of his life, and as the years increase finds a greater pleasure than ever in recalling his memories of distinguished men whose careers have been parallel to his own.

" He has never ceased to be generous with his most precious possession, namely, his library. Not infrequently two hundred and fifty volumes at a time have been absent from his shelves, for he seldom refuses an applicant. It has been the same also with the loan of money in small sums. No one has been refused. He tells some interesting anecdotes of 'narrow escapes,' and of irresolution, upon his own part, when total strangers have asked to borrow his books. One night has been enough to restore his generosity.

" Called on Professor Ticknor. He said he should be happy to allow his picture of Sir Walter Scott, by Leslie, to be photographed if Mr. Fields desired it. It is, of course, a great privilege, and will be done immediately.

" Sir Walter was pleased with Mr. Ticknor when he visited him as a young man, and yielded to his wish to sit for a portrait. Therefore, in 1815, Leslie painted this one. Mrs. Lockhart preferred it to all the other likenesses of her father, and was unwilling to have it leave the country. Leslie at length concluded to make a copy in miniature, and this copy is still in England in one of the fine collections there."

March 5, 1864, came the news of Starr King's death. " It is hard to think of him as elsewhere.

He seems necessary still to our cause, which he has served nobly."

He was an early friend of Mr. Fields, and from among his letters I have been able to gather a few passages which may give some idea of his rollicking fun : —

"PIGEON COVE, SUNDAY, *July* 9, 1854.

" Heartiest thanks for your bundle and *Walton*. It's a luscious copy. I shall begin it this glorious Sunday afternoon which you have slighted. That will go into the choicest spot of my best book-case.

"I had a rich interview with old K—— last evening, at Sunset Rock. He said: 'I knowed suthin' would happen that week the nigger was lugged out 'er Boston, cos the 'old Farmers' said, Look out for Causaltis and Rascalities this week.'

" Somehow lawyers came into our talk, and especially ——. He grew eloquent on our legal friend. 'The d—d cuss pled agin me once. I watched him, — Gowod! He can *cant his countinince* so ez to draw the tears out of the eyes of the jury in two minits.' Some Biblical criticisms were equally shrewd, reverent, and rich. . . .

"Sir ! with great regard,

" Your friend and servant,

T. S. KING."

" BOSTON, *March* 30, 1860.

" MY DEAR JAMES : — I leave Boston to-morrow, and New York April 5th. Can it be ? No King in Boston after this ! No portly frame, and handsome mouth and nose which drives the artists crazy, belonging to the Presbyter of Hollis Street, to enter the dear old sanctum on the corner, and pester the poet-bibliopole! Is it possible?

" And then I go where there is no such compound as yourself. Fields there may be in California. Chinamen are there, and perhaps *tea fields*, but no James T. alas! ' He was very kind to me, sir!' . . .

" J. and I laughed over your note till we cried." . . .

" San Francisco, *October* 29, 1862.

". . . We are chipping the shell here, and are coming out northern eagles, not southern buzzards as the intention was. We have gone through a hard and very important fight, in fact have achieved the most remarkable revolution which the war has witnessed. The State must be northernized thoroughly, by schools, Atlantic Monthlies, lectures, New England preachers, Library Associations, — in short, Ticknor and Fieldsism of all kinds. I have worked the last eighteen months within an inch of my life, in speaking, preaching, orationizing, traveling, organizing, etc., and have arranged to deliver there six lectures, in addition to other labors, in order to set the taste of our irrepressible and noble community in the right path, and clinch the political nail that we have driven through the State. . . . Do help me and you shall be rewarded in this life, and shall have a copyright for the lyrics of Gabriel. . . .

" Your obliged friend,

" T. S. K."

. . . "Last night I spoke to a grand audience on Holmes. You should have seen and felt the reception of his tremendous lyric, 'Choose You Whom,' etc. I could hardly get out the line, 'And the copperhead coil round the blade of his scythe,' before the crash came, which shows that the lightning struck. . . . Lowell has sent me a perfectly charming poem showing his two faces, the humorous and the transcendental, and conveying the most delicate compliment to California bounty that the finest fibre in his brain could devise. . . . I shall clear about $2,000 for our organ. Oh, how I want to see you all, and to take our little Hesperus to an Eastern sky! Don't die, don't turn secesh, don't let the country break in two. . . . How I want to see you. How glorious Emerson's 'Titmouse' is! What vitality in the Biglow Papers! What excellence in the 'Atlantic' generally! Here we have been nearly two years, and have n't seen you for three; and we still *live*, eat three meals per diem, and are supposed to be tolerably content with existence! . . . I can't imagine what I should do if we should see Boston and you all once more. I fear the tether wouldn't hold. . . .

" Yours, always,

"T. S. King."

This year was marked not only by the incidents of war, but by the death of Nathaniel Hawthorne. His passing was like losing a portion of our own household, so closely interwoven had become the interest and affection of the two families. The

season of that parting was in the beautiful month
of May, as Longfellow has so exquisitely recorded.
Mrs. Hawthorne was not only uplifted herself
through the infinite beauty of spring, and the silence which surrounded her, in her wayside home
at Concord, but she shared a large measure of her
feeling with her friends when she sent them the
following letter. I print it because it contains a
breath of true life, and may breathe again upon
some soul whose joy is departed.

"MONDAY NIGHT.

"BELOVED; When I see that I deserved nothing, and
that my Father gave me the richest destiny for so many
years of time to which eternity is to be added, I am
struck dumb with an ecstasy of gratitude, and let go
my mortal hold with an awful submission, and without a
murmur. I stand hushed into an ineffable peace which
I cannot measure nor understand. It therefore must be
that peace which 'passeth all understanding.' I feel
that his joy is such as 'the heart of man cannot conceive,' and shall I not then rejoice, who loved him so far
beyond myself? If *I* did not at once share his beati-
tude, should I be one with him now in essential essence?
Ah, thanks be to God who gives me this proof — beyond
all possible doubt — that we are not and never can be
divided!

"If my faith bear this test, is it not 'beyond the utmost scope and vision of calamity!' Need I ever fear
again any possible dispensation if I can stand serene when
that presence is reft from me which I believed I must

instantly die to lose? Where, O God, is that support-ing, inspiring, protecting, entrancing presence which sur-rounded me with safety and supreme content?

" ' It is with you, my child, saith the Lord, and *seemeth* only to be gone.'

" ' Yes, my Father, I know I have not lost it, because I still live.' 'I will be glad.' 'Thy will be done.' From a child I have truly believed that God was all good and all wise, and felt assured that no event could shake my belief. To-day I *know it.*

" This is the whole. No more can be asked of God. There can be no death nor loss for me for evermore. I stand so far within the veil that the light from God's countenance can never be hidden from me for one mo-ment of the eternal day, now nor then. God gave me the rose of time; the blossom of the ages to call my own for twenty-five years of human life.

" God has satisfied wholly my insatiable heart with a perfect love that transcends my dreams. He has decreed this earthly life a mere court of ' the house not made with hands, eternal in the heavens.' Oh, yes, dear heavenly Father! 'I will be glad," that my darling has suddenly escaped from the rude jars and hurts of this outer court, and when I was not aware that an angel gently drew him within the palace-door that turned on noiseless golden hinges, drew him in, because he was weary.

" God gave to his beloved sleep. And then an awak-ing which will require no more restoring slumber.

" As the dew-drop holds the day, so my heart holds the presence of the glorified freed spirit. He was so beauti-

ful here, that he will not need much change to become
a 'shining one!' How easily I shall know him when my
children have done with me, and perhaps the angel will
draw me gently also within the palace-door, if I do not
faint, but truly live, ' Thy will be done.'

"At that festival of life that we all celebrated last
Monday, did not those myriad little white lily-bells ring
in for him the eternal year of peace, as they clustered
and hung around the majestic temple, in which he once
lived with God? They rang out, too, that lordly incense
that can come only from a lily, large or small. What
lovely ivory sculpture round the edge. I saw it all,
even at that breathless moment, when I knew that all
that was visible was about to be shut out from me for
my future mortal life. I saw all the beauty, and the
tropical gorgeousness of odor that enriched the air from
your peerless wreath steeped me in Paradise. We were
the new Adam and new Eve again, and walked in the
garden in the cool of the day, and there was not yet
death, only the voice of the Lord. But indeed it seems
to me that now again there is no death. His life has
swallowed it up.

"Do not fear for me, 'dark hours.' I think there is
nothing dark for me henceforth. I have to do only
with the present, and the present is light and rest. Has
not the everlasting

> ' Morning spread
> Over me her rich surprise?'

"I have no more to ask, but that I may be able to
comfort all who mourn as I am comforted. If I could
bear all sorrow I would be glad, because God has turned

for me the silver lining; and for me the darkest cloud has broken into ten thousand singing birds — as I saw in my dream that I told you. So in another dream long ago, God showed me a gold thread passing through each mesh of a black pall that seemed to shut out the sun. I comprehend all now, before I did not doubt. Now God says in soft thunders, — 'Even so!

"Your faithful friend,

"SOPHIA HAWTHORNE."

Again the diary : —

"*April* 3, 1865. Forever memorable! Our armies entered Richmond, — General Weitzel, with the colored troops ahead. The bells of the little town of Manchester, where we passed the afternoon, were ringing, and the sea and sky were in unison with the joyous sounds. Returning home we found Mrs. Hawthorne lying on the couch, where she might see the lovely sunset and moon rise over the Charles River bay.

". . . 'Carleton' delivered to John G. Whittier behind 'the green curtain' the key of the Richmond Slave Prison. He saw fifty slaves emancipated from this den a few days since." . . .

April 29*th*. "Saturday Club Dinner. Mr. Brownell, author of 'The Bay Fight,' was present, as Dr. Holmes's guest."

The Saturday Club was established in the year 1857, and has been maintained with unabated interest to the present date, meeting on the last Saturday of every month, at two or three o'clock in the afternoon, in order to accommodate **Mr.** Emerson, Judge Hoar, and other out-of-town members. It is entirely social, and therefore of necessity rather small, the whole number of members from the beginning until now amounting to but forty-five persons. Whatever may be said of the lack of social spirit in New England, this club will forever stand as a living contradiction to such assertion. I believe there is not a parallel in the world of such a company. Not more proud of each other's fame or achievement than they are attached to one another by sincere confidence and affection, they are enabled to speak freely when together, upon the subjects affecting them most nearly. When we consider the individual character of its members and its duration, it will remain as an exponent of our time. Jealousies, so often rife among men of kindred labors, have never darkened these friendships or altered the freedom of communication. Each member is privileged to bring one invited guest, and thus opportunity is made for any distinguished visitor who may be in our vicinity for coming face to face with the individuals who have made New England famous. Henry Howard Brownell, a man of high poetic gifts, was thus first introduced among his peers. His talent had already been recognized by **Mr. T. B.** Aldrich, who has written a beautiful sonnet **to** his memory, which should be reproduced in any mention of the poet.

HENRY HOWARD BROWNELL.

" They never crowned him, never knew his worth,
     But let him go unlaurelled to the grave:
     Hereafter there are guerdons for the brave,
     Roses for martyrs who wear thorns on earth,
 Balms for bruised hearts that languish in the dearth
     Of human love. So let the lilies wave
     Above him, nameless. Little did he crave
     Men's praises. Modestly, with kindly mirth,
 Not sad nor bitter, he accepted fate —
     Drank deep of life, knew books, and hearts of men,
        Cities and camps, and war's immortal woe,
 Yet bore through all (such virtue in him sate
     His spirit is not whiter now than then !)
        A simple, loyal nature, pure as snow."

The unrivaled tribute by "the Professor" in the 'Atlantic Monthly' also, must not be passed unmentioned. It was a generous and fitting recognition.

Who can forget having been present at that first reading of "The Bay Fight" in the Charles Street library one evening, when Dr. Holmes thrilled the little company with his impassioned presentation of the poem; from that moment we all felt that we knew Brownell, and whatever the future should bring us from him would be of value in our eyes.

7

The diary says: —

" Brownell's home is in Connecticut by the sea, where he lives with his widowed mother. He visits at a few houses only in Hartford, he says, but he finds a fisherman by the water-side who is blind, one J. H. (an excellent machinist also, and man of affairs), whom he likes much and whose companionship he often seeks. Brownell has a ' Life of Farragut ' under way, which he thinks would outvie Southey's ' Life of Nelson,' if he had eyes to finish it."

In connection with Brownell and his proposed Life of Farragut, I find the following extract from the diary : —

" *August*, 1865. Dr. Townsend called, at whose house Admiral Farragut stayed while he was in Boston. The Doctor came, bearing a courteous message from Mrs. Farragut, and her thanks for a copy of Ticknor's Life of Prescott. He said he begun his professional life as surgeon in the United States Navy, and he was upon the same ship with Farragut, who was then a midshipman fourteen years old. He was a clever, affectionate lad, whose observation nothing escaped, and a warm friendship grew up between them. The old surgeon remembers distinctly often holding the boy upon his knee. The intimacy between them has never ceased. Farragut is a marvel of muscular and physical power. He is sixty years old now, but on his tour to Rye Beach a few days since, he repeatedly walked up a five barred gate and stood upon the upper bar without touching anything.

His life has been a varied one, and, of course, of profound interest to Americans at present.

"When the government sent to beg his acceptance of some prominent position with a high salary, or the ministry at some foreign court, he declined, saying he wished to die as he had lived, in the navy. It was then asked what station he would prefer and what style of house, as they wished him to be appointed and settled where he liked best, but he replied, give your positions and houses to the men who need them, for they are many. I am well off, and shall prefer to live simply and take care of myself."

Mr. Brownell became personally attached to his publisher, and many jocose little notes passed between them. In one of them he says : —

"I don't know whether you like dedications. What do you think of this one? If you approve it return it to me, and I will send it to the Admiral, and see if he is willing that it should appear. Tell me just what you think about it. . . . I am taking you behind the scenes so much, in our rehearsal of this piece, that I'm afraid you will think 't is like Mr. Weller's watch — 'opens an shows the vorks'." Again he writes, "I see that you are doing me a kindness in a very delicate way. Accept my sincere thanks. I am not above receiving a favor from a man like you."

"EAST HARTFORD, *February* 28, 1866.

"MY DEAR FIELDS, — By some divine magnetic instinct, I had already, two days ago, anticipated one of your objections, and written to you to change the line to '*its breath;*' so you might let me have my way about the other.

> " Ac half the prayer wi' Phœbus grace did find,
>   The tither half he whistled down the wind."

" Don't be afraid of ' now for it,' it was the first line written, and is the very nucleus and key-note of the piece, and is really the only good thing in it. ' Be it known to you, Señor Gil Blas,' said the Bishop, ' that I never composed a better homily than the one you except to.'

" However, I would alter it if I could, since you wish it, but really don't see how.

" It is, indeed, the merest trifle after all, and if it wont go as it is, send it back. I shan't regret it, except that it does not please you, whom I truly wish to please. . . .

" H. H. B."

December, 1868. " Brownell has just returned from a voyage to Europe in the frigate Franklin with Admiral Farragut. He is now forty-eight years old. He has accomplished only six months traveling during his absence of a year and a half, the rest of the time being passed in monotonous sea-life. His vivid description of ship-board talk, long yarns, arguments where nobody is persuaded; tales of the sentry who tramped every night above his head until he found himself frequently compelled to sit up and meet the dawn; of the wonderful fall of a man through the rigging, one hundred and forty feet, who recovered his perfect health, — all these things told in his own striking manner, became exceedingly interesting. Also his sense of utter shallowness under

such circumstances, though he seems to have been the
life of the ship from his humanity and love of literature
and fun. He was full of appreciation of ' Mark Twain.'
Presently he spoke of the delight he experienced in finding himself on Shelley's ground. Spezzia, Pisa, the
Lido (where he picked up shells as Shelley did with
Byron), at his grave, and the baths of Caracalla. He
spoke of the injustice done to Byron; of his marvelous
descriptions ; how they reveled in his words as they stood
looking at Hymettus which ' flamed like a white pillar
on the sky.' He was deeply moved at the sight of our
copy of ' Diogenes Laertius ;' the one owned by Shelley
and Leigh Hunt. Brownell reads Greek fluently ; indeed, he has translated something of Homer, scholars say
remarkably, into hexameters. But this work was done
fifteen years ago, and will never be continued, he says.
. . . There is a pervading honesty in Brownell, by which
you recognize his religion. A full man. He has a small,
finely cut head."

The diary proceeds : —

"Went to see Mrs. and Miss Thoreau. They produced thirty-two volumes of Henry's journal and a few
letters. Their idea is to print the letters. . . . Their
house was like a conservatory, it was so filled with
plants in a beautiful condition. Henry liked to have
the doors thrown open that he might look at them
during his illness. . . . Miss Thoreau did not feel in
any haste to find the editor for her brother's journal.
She did not see the man, she said, but she thought he
would come."

Mr. Fields had no intimate acquaintance with Henry Thoreau. "I like to see him come in," he would say, "he always smells of the pine woods." The published volume of Thoreau's letters is selected with great care, and I do not find anything new or more important in those before me. We one day went to Lexington, and drove down to Bedford Springs, five and a half miles. We found a little lake there quiet and full of sunshine in the autumnal afternoon. The keeper of the house came to us while standing by the lake side and offered to row us about. The man had known Thoreau, and we found ourselves on Thoreau's ground. There were the houses for the musk-rats which he describes, and the red berries of the alder and the purple asters he loved so well. The brilliant trees and moving clouds lay reflected in the lake as he had seen them. Occasionally a hawk would glide over on still wings, but no human sounds were heard until the children came from school. We were delighted to watch some ducks in the pond. They were not wild, but they jumped into the pond as soon as they could move, and had fed and cared for themselves ever since. How calm and peaceful the scene was!

It was in the spring of 1863 that Forceythe Willson first became known as a poet. The two poems, "The Color Sergeant" and "In State," chiefly gave him his reputation. One of our eminent men, who first extended the right hand to that young poet, said, "He is as shy as Hawthorne, and has not learned that the eagle's wings should sometimes be kept down as we people who live in the world discover."

Willson had the singular power of reading character by the touch of manuscript. There was something almost weird at times in his presence and conversation. He took great pleasure in Mr. Fields's cheerful friendly character, and seemed to draw near to him as to a protecting and befriending presence.

I give one of his characteristic letters : —

"CAMBRIDGE, *August* 22, 1865.

"DEAR SIR, — Monday morning I promised myself this should be Lazy Week — no engagements — no work — nothing *positive ;* — that I should drift and float, and not lift a hand, forget myself and, as much as possible, everybody else (on the Mutual Insurance principle). Next week — if you don't interpose — I'll be on hand for a tramp with you; but out upon chaises and civilities, for I want to ride a whale bareback.

"Yours truly,

"F. WILLSON.

"N. B. I shall bring no poems."

In one of his notes he says : —

" Dear Mr. Fields, — Please draw your pencil along
the margin of the intrusive stanzas, and return me the
po——ttery.   Your Friend,

" Willson."

And again he signs himself " Yours ever

" F. W.

" Maker of earthen vessels."

"Cambridge, *August* 26, 1865.

" My dear Mr. Fields, — When the wind is south-
erly I know a hawk from a handsaw ; and unless it abso-
lutely rain on Thursday morning I shall come without
regard to the weathercock.

" Just this moment finished reading Lowell's ode. ' VI.'
is a good strophe, — the only thing of decent proportions
I 've seen on the subject in verse.

" There has really been no ode written in English (that
I know of) since Dryden ; but some of the shorter lines
in ' X ' are almost up to the old strain.

" As for poems — tut — tut ! —

" (the gods have quit making 'em !)

" Yours truly,

" F. Willson."

Mr. Fields was a warm friend of Charles
Sprague, who one day told him an incident relating to the composition of his fine Shakespeare
Ode, which should not be forgotten. Mr. Fields
had mentioned one passage which he thought especially good, the one descriptive of the murder.

"Ah!" said Mr. Sprague, "how well I remember the day I wrote that. I was keeping a grocer's shop on Tremont Row at the time. It was a cold, stormy winter's day and I was alone in the shop sitting over a sheet-iron stove. I had just reached this passage and was hoping nobody would come in, when a man opened the door and asked for a quart of train-oil. Well, sir, I filled his vessel for him and handed it back, and then, my hands reeking with train-oil, I finished that passage."

The diary continues: —

"One of the printing offices in revolt, which complicates 'Atlantic' responsibilities, and as for disappointed authors! they seem to hedge us in and shake their threatening beards."

"Went to get a few oysters for lunch. The oysterman lay down his guitar, upon which he had been improvising, and began to pry open the bivalves, singing as he pried, 'I call thy spirit back to earth!'"

"Note from ——, thanking the editor for his frankness in telling him his poem was bad, but *disagreeing with his opinion!*"

During these years I find references to the constant increase of business responsibilities. A weekly journal was started called the "Every Saturday," which gave the firm a quarterly, monthly, weekly, and juvenile magazine. The result was, that ultimate decisions on a large variety of matters were referred to Mr. Fields. In the diary he says: —

" An overwhelming week. Affairs crowd until it becomes impossible to accomplish what should be done.
The sight of a manuscript is like a sword-fish now-a-days,
— it cuts me in two."

Again, —

" A most fatiguing day. Numberless persons with
books which must be refused; among others ——, who
was full of grief, therefore it was harder to say ' No.'
Beside his book is a good one; . . . but Ticknor &
Fields have too many books already to make it best to
accept anything new at present."

The first letter I find from Mr. Bryant is dated
shortly before this period and the friendly correspondence remained unbroken until his death.
He writes in 1864 : —

" DEAR MR. FIELDS, — I send you a poem for the
' Atlantic.' Ask me for no more verses. A septuage-
narian has past the time when it is becoming for him to
occupy himself with

" The rhymes and rattles of the man and boy."

Pope was twenty years younger than I am, when he said
to Bolingbroke , —

' Why wilt thou break the Sabbath of my days? '
and, .
' Public too long, ah, let me hide my age.'

Uhland, who died in his seventy-sixth year, did not in the
last twenty years, or twenty-five, was it ? add a hundred
lines to his published verses. Nobody in the years after
seventy can produce anything in poetry except the thick

and muddy last runnings of the cask from which all the clear and sprightly liquor has been already drawn."

Again in 1867, he writes from Roslyn, Long Island : —

" DEAR MR. FIELDS, — It would give me great pleasure to be a guest at your dinner next week and to testify my admiration of the writings of Mr. Longfellow, in particular of his translation of Dante, but for the occupations in which I am now engaged and I must say, also, the habit of seclusion, incident to my time of life, and gaining strength as I grow older. Allow me to plead these as my excuse for not coming to the dinner to which you have so kindly invited me. Meantime I take this opportunity to express in words what my presence could not express more emphatically. Mr. Longfellow has translated Dante as a great poet should be translated. After this version, no other will be attempted until the present form of the English language shall have become obsolete, for whether we regard fidelity to the sense, aptness in the form of expression, or the skilful transfusion of the poetic spirit of the original into the phrases of another language, we can look for nothing more perfect. It is fitting that Mr. Longfellow's friends should congratulate him, as I heartily do, on the successful completion of his great task.

" I am, dear sir, very truly yours
" W. C. BRYANT.
"JAMES T. FIELDS, ESQ."

This letter refers to the dinner planned by Mr. Fields and given by " the firm " in honor of the completion of Mr. Longfellow's translation of Dante. The Dante Festival, as it was called, because it was given on the six hundredth anniversary of Dante's birth, was a beautiful and successful occasion. Mr. Bryant's absence was regretted, but there was a full company of "Representative Men."

Again, Mr. Bryant writes in 1871 : —

"I can no more get up the necessary excitement for writing a poem at the present time than I can go back to the days of my youth. I have the Odyssey on hand, which takes up most of my leisure; then there is the 'Evening Post,' which I cannot neglect, and other matters, small in themselves, but numerous, the effect of which is to load me with so many petty tasks, and keep me fussing so, that I sometimes feel what used to be called, when people had no scruple about using a Latin word now and then, — *tedium vitæ.* So you see that you ask what is as impossible as if you were to wait a few years and ask it of my tombstone.

" I am, dear sir, very truly yours,

"W. C. BRYANT."

" NEW YORK, *April* 25, 1871.

" MY DEAR MR. FIELDS, — There was no need that you should exhort me to be diligent in putting the Odyssey into English blank verse. I have been as industrious as was reasonable. I understand very well that at my time of life such enterprises are apt to be brought to a conclusion before they are finished, and I have therefore wrought harder upon my task than some of my friends thought was well for me. I have already sent forward the manuscript for the first volume. You may remember that I finished my translation of the Iliad within the time that I undertook, and this would have been done without any urging. In the case of the Odyssey I have finished the first volume two months sooner than I promised.

" I do not think the Odyssey the better part of Homer except morally. The gods set a better example and take more care to see that wrong and injustice are discouraged among mankind. But there is not the same spirit and fire, nor the same vividness of description, and this the translator must feel as strongly as the reader. Let me correct what I have already said, by adding, that there is yet in the Odyssey one more advantage over the Iliad. It is better as a story. In the Iliad the plot is to me unsatisfactory — and there is besides a monotony of carnage — you get a surfeit of slaughter. . . ."

The following brief extracts from the diary giving a sketch of Mr. Bryant in his own beautiful home at Roslyn, may not be out of place : —

"*June*, 1871. Last night Mr. Bryant met us in the train for Roslyn. He is nearly eighty years old, hale and strong, his intellect clear as ever. He showed us Long Island with pride, as having a kind of ownership in the whole place apart from his actual possession. His influence has been incalculable in the proper planting and civilizing of the whole district. He pointed out the farm where Cobbett lived and wrote his book upon

American Agriculture; the plains where the Indians cut off the trees — where the railroad now runs; indicated the growth of towns, Jamaica especially, which was a very small place twenty-five years before when he came to Roslyn. . . . In the morning Mr. Bryant walked to the village for the mail, and we wandered about the place rejoicing in the beauty of the trees and flowers. Everything in the way of foliage contrasts strongly with our own rugged shores of Massachusetts. . . . Wandered into the library. The broad window where the poet's table stood overlooked the garden with its white lilies and the lake below. The Odyssey, opened at the fourteenth book, lay upon the table, where he had already been at work in the early morning. It was the library of a student and scholar."

In the spring of 1863 Mr. Fields found a comfortable farm-house on a hillside in Campton, N. H., about a mile from that village, where during several consecutive years he "met the spring" and rested in absolute retirement. There was no railroad nearer than the town of Plymouth, eight miles distant, over a sandy and difficult road, and no post-office nearer than the village of Campton, whither the mail was brought by an express wagon, which was a whole long day toiling between Plymouth and that place. But for one who loved the country as he did, to whom the green growing things were a constant joy, who reveled in them always as children do, — not like a botanist, or an astronomer, or story-writer, or thinker, and still less like a man of business, or an editor,— but going out to play, finding wild roses, or columbine, or pimpernel, whatever it might be, and bringing it home, forever guiltless of the Latin name, like a conqueror, as if it were just created; to one who loves nature in this way she is sufficient; she takes him to herself and gives him rest on many a green pillow.

He was never tired of going to New Hampshire. "They are my native hills, you know," he would say half in excuse, and although the climate of Campton itself did not suit him he continued to go thither for many years.

The following notes of the life there will give some idea of his love of country enjoyments.

"*June* 7th. Raining like a day in April; began our walks before breakfast. The ferns are only half awakened and the wayside is blue with violets. The hermit thrush and robins are busy enough. What the farmers call 'real growin' weather.' Mad River bridge is unsafe. They say here 'the buttonments' are weak. The ford too is impassable from the heavy rains. Read Niebuhr's letters aloud, also the memoirs of Lord Herbert of Cherbury. The only external excitement is when the country wagons pass up and down the road to and from Plymouth. . . . Heard the Peabody bird here for the first time. . . .

"*Sunday* — Went to the village church. The sermon

was not unsuited to the hearers, and the service was earnest and interesting. In the afternoon climbed to the very top of Willey's Hill. We saw the sun go down while still near the summit. What an evening! The streams are fuller than we have seen them before."

"*June* 11. Drove to Sanborn's Inn, and wandered about in the sunshine all the afternoon. Two boys were fishing for trout in a full blue pond near by, where logs were floating. We sat on one of the logs near to the brink, and watched their agility in springing from one to another, with utter fearlessness of slipping. 'No trout yet,' they said, in answer to our inquiries. Drove to Farmer A.'s. Met him just below his house. He walked by the side of the wagon, talking. Such a place! It was a Paradise. The mountains opened before us, the meadow and river lay below. What a magnificent residence this would be! Comparing favorably in natural features with the finest the world can show. . . . Think of it : a patriarchal domain at an expense of one hundred and eighty dollars a year !

"*June* 12. Went up to the W.'s farm on the hillside. There is no road leading there; only a grassy lane. Found the farmer hoeing his corn thoughtfully on the hillside. He believed there would be frost to-night. The northwest wind was blowing lustily over the young shoots, and it was quite cold. At the door of the cottage the mother greeted us joyfully. We went in to see her sick daughter. . . .

" The green hills stretch up behind the cottage, and slope down in front of it, and the solitude is undisturbed.

The lilacs were waving in the sunshine as we left the sick girl; the birds were hovering about the door, sunshine and health were everywhere without, — pain and fading were within. . . .

"In the afternoon walked to Farmer G.'s, and came home through 'June Avenue' (he christened all the walks and drives and climbs during these visits). Farmer G. said his taxes were very heavy, equal to fifty dollars a year, all told, but then ''t was wuth somethin' to live in the village of Campton!'

"Last night Don Santiago Duello arrived in Campton, 'the world-renowned contortionist.' The people said this morning he did all he said he would, and they had their 'money's worth.' Seeing him drive away, Mr. Fields said, 'A more decayed, miserable set than the "Don" in his buggy, . . . his wife and child and baby and rattletraps, which preceded him, could not easily be conceived.'

"*June* 15. Hills veiled, — rain, rain, rain. Later, — thick fog, and signs of clearing. Finished Massey's book on Shakespeare's sonnets; read Mozart's letters in the evening. Walked many miles; visited the school-house; was interested in the teacher, a lame girl, with a passion for study. She intends going next year to the Seminary at South Hadley; earns about three dollars and a half a week, besides her board, while teaching here. Has forty-two scholars. These people pick up much of the knowledge they possess from experience. Mr. Fields asked, 'how old is the school-house?' 'Well, I can't tell ye exackly, but I helped to take up the old fence the other day, and the oak-posts was rotten; naow it takes jest twelve years for oak-posts to begin to rot, so it must have been built twelve years at least.'

" The air is filled with a chorus of birds. We strain our ears to listen, and, as far as sound can travel, there are the birds' voices calling to each other in the silence. The sun warms us through; soft white clouds come upon the sky to break the fierceness of the sudden heat, ferns unroll, the trees are odorous, —

" ' All the world is gay.'

" Found the linnæa in bloom. Drove to K. Hill; asked the younger daughter of the house to accompany us, and climbed the height. The hill-top was like a baronial park of perfect maple trees. We found a mighty sugar-house there, with two hundred buckets and huge pans, suggesting plenty of sweet spoil. ' How dull it looks here now,' said the girl. ' In sugar time it is lovely ! The snow is on the ground, but the air at mid-day is not very cold at the season we generally choose. It is real pleasant going up to the sugar-house then.'

" We climbed to the very top, and, sitting on moss thick as a good sponge, looked off upon Moose Hillock, and down into the Franconia Notch, over the winding, glancing beauty of the Pemigewasset, with the fertile meadows. Upwards of a hundred sheep were nibbling on the near hills belonging to the K.'s; saw also oxen and cattle and a large orchard of apple and pear trees.

" These people are proud as the lords of old, but they need assistance in their labors, and, failing this, their whole farm life is, in one sense, a failure. They overwork, and neither attain their ends nor enjoy their lives.

"*June* 16. Walked over the hills before breakfast. Startled a cow, who gave quite a human jump of astonishment.

"PLYMOUTH, N. H. (en route for Campton), *June*, 1868. Sunday — Passed the morning on the piazza of a deserted house on the hill-top overlooking the town. The whole Franconia range in sight. Whittier was our companion (in pocket form this time). It was a heavenly season. Mr. Fields told me he dreamed last night that L. had returned to pass a few hours with him. They talked very fast, there was so much to be said, and yet when he asked about the honors conferred on the banks of the Cam, or the public demonstrations, L. would only laugh, with a characteristic gesture, and say nothing. He talked incessantly of the loveliness of England, of the lake district in particular, while he hummed from time to time the refrain of a poem. ' I know you have written something to show me,' said Mr. Fields. ' You would never have come without that.' Then L. took out a short poem ; but they soon fell again into talk ; this time about C. D.'s house where L. is now staying. ' It is perfect,' said L. ; ' you cannot hear the wheels go round.'

"CAMPTON, *July* 2. One of the farmers amuses us by talking of *sidlin'* land, meaning hilly.

"*July* 3. Very, very warm. The morning clear and of unspeakable beauty. We read ' Comus ' before breakfast. The thrushes sing plenteously and life is harmonious, silent, and apart. How far apart it seems, indeed, after such close contact with it as we have had !

"*July* 4. Hot, hot. The trees stand motionless. Mr.

Fields could do nothing yesterday afternoon but watch the cloud scenery, which was marvelous in its beauty.

"*June*, 1872. A splendid vision upon the mountains at sunset, and a rainbow in the east. We shall remember this sunset, with the scene at Interlachen.

" In the morning the atmosphere like crystal and deliciously melodious and fragrant. Read Spenser's ' Faëry Queen ' aloud in the evening.

"*June* 20. Roses in torrents. Climbed the hill towards night and saw a tree cut down, — a hemlock. He fell solemnly at last, and then only a short distance, being upheld by his fellows. Finally he was dragged down disgracefully by his hair. The squirrels ran for it ! "

One of the pleasures of this period of Mr. Fields's life was his acquaintance, nay friendship, with Mr. Agassiz, and any record would be incomplete which failed to recall the delightful hours passed in his society. " Did you have a pleasant Club to-day ? " " Yes, Agassiz was there ! " — was often the answer heard from his lips. The glimpses here of their association must be of the briefest, for every reason, but such memories are too precious to be omitted and allowed to perish altogether. Agassiz was so beloved by all who knew him, and all who knew Fields loved him so, different as they were, that I can but recall in this relation a passage from the writings of Lacordaire. He says, in speaking of Ozanam : —

" C'est un rare secret que celui de la popularité, j'entends la popularité veritable, celle qui ne s'achète point par de lâches concessions aux erreurs d'un siècle, mais qui entoure d'une auréole prématurée l'honnête homme vivant. . . . Toutes les conditions remplies, il n'est pas impossible qu'un homme échappe à la popularité, si quelque chose de bienveillant ne tempère en lui la force du caractère et n'abaisse la hauteur du génie. C'est la bonté qui rend Dieu populaire, et l'homme à qui elle manque n'obtiendra jamais l'amour."

In 1866 Mr. Fields one day accompanied a young English gentleman to Agassiz' Museum. They found the Professor hard at work, his hands in oil, fishes, and alcohol. " How sad for a naturalist to grow old," he said. " I see so much to be done which I can never complete." The stranger had brought with him specimens or drawings from Professor Huxley for Mr. Agassiz. He was at once cordially received and invited to lunch with him the following day.

Again, from the diary : —

" Mr. Fields received a call to-day from our consul at Mauritius, who has brought to Boston two skeletons of the Dodo, the extinct bird of that island. The consul is anxious to see Mr. Agassiz. It is said there are no other complete skeletons. He suspected the possibility of their existence in a certain tract of marshy ground, and sent the natives in nearly to their necks in mud and water to feel about. After a time they struck these bones, with which he returned at once to New England, being convinced of their value as belonging to the real Dodo. . . . Mr. Agassiz seems to have enjoyed the 'Dodo' bones. They are not perfect, but valuable notwithstanding, and the best we have in America. Mr. Fields asked him if the 'Dodo' was good to eat! 'Yes, indeed; what a pity we could not have the Dodo at our Club! A good dinner is humanity's greatest blessing. What a pity! But the Dutchmen carried a ship with rats to Mauritius who sucked the fine eggs, as large as a loaf, and everybody found the bird so good they did eat him, so he has become extinct. We know of but one other bird of recent date who has become extinct, — the Great Northern **Auk.** The Bishop of Newfoundland did send me his bones, — a treasure indeed.' "

New specimens overflowed from every side. His plans grew in proportion, and their only chance of fulfilment seemed to be in the continuous labor of those nearest him who could further the details of his great work.

Agassiz' friendship for and appreciation of Professor Pierce were always manifest when occasion offered. One day an album was produced in which Pierce had inscribed a half leaf about the stars and the far-reaching power of the mind of man transcending the limits of the spheres. The passage was most impressive in its eloquence. Agassiz was delighted, crying, " Do you hear! That is Ben! Who but Ben could do that! It is enough to say that."

In 1868 a private dinner was given to Mr. Longfellow upon his departure for Europe. Mr. Agassiz was present. Some one expressed a strong desire to see the Nile. "Ah!" said Agassiz, "I, too, long to see the Nile, but because I wish to study the fishes in it!" He sustained a hearty struggle with a Darwinite at the table, but was equally full of science and of fun. His gayety and tenderness were unusual even for him. It was on a subsequent occasion that he described the Brazilian woodland, where he had seen one hundred and twenty-seven different kinds of wood growing within the space of a half mile; also the splendor of the red passion-flower shut in by the dark green of the forest, green so dark that it is black.

A most interesting gathering of the Saturday Club came together to welcome him upon his return from Brazil. On that occasion he is remembered as seizing Dr. Holmes in his arms and taking him quite off his feet in the warmth of his embrace. He spoke there also of the greatness of Brazil, of her glorious woodlands; and described the Brazilian ants as swarming into the houses and remaining for three days at a time, forcing the family meanwhile to move away; said he had counted one hundred and forty-eight varieties of wood, whereas in New England we have only about fifty; and spoke of the vast room for enterprise in such a land where not a sawmill was then in existence. He enlarged also upon the distinguished intelligence of the Emperor, and mentioned his intended visit to this country. Agassiz accompanied Longfellow and Fields as far as Lynn after the dinner. As they looked from the windows of the car into the moon-lighted landscape, Fields asked if that scene were not as beautiful as anything Brazil could offer. "Ah!" was the reply, "I was just reflecting how sterile was the appearance of New England after the luxuriant beauty of Brazil." He was sadly troubled to find the "old hack politicians" whom he hoped the war had slain, coming out again in renewed force.

The diary continues: —

"Mr. Agassiz often seems to have left half his heart with his work when he is away from it, except when he is like a child running over with fun and frolic. . . . It was after Mr. Whipple's fine lecture on 'Bacon' that some one fell to discoursing about imagination. 'Let us stop here,' said Agassiz, 'we each define imagination differently. Imagination is to me the perfect conception of truth which some minds attain, of what cannot be proved through the senses. For instance, the planet Jupiter is so many miles from us, it has a certain determined size, and certain peculiarities. The mind that can comprehend and use this knowledge as clearly as if the senses had touched the planet, that mind has imagination.'"

Mr. Fields asked him at one of these gatherings if he thought man ever would draw nearer to the mystery of birth and death. "I am sure he will," was his reply, "the time will come when all these things will be made as clear as this table now spread before us."

Three Scotch professors were the guests at the Saturday Club of August, 1871, and it was proposed that Walter Scott should be remembered as if it were his birthday. Agassiz presided, and the matter in hand seemed likely to be forgotten. Fields recalled the subject for the day to the president. "Thank you," he said, "my dear Fields, I had entirely forgotten it. I have been busily discussing scientific subjects with my friend here. I ought also to confess to this company that I have read only one of the novels of Walter Scott, that is 'Ivanhoe'; but if God please, before my death I will read two more. My time is always much occupied in other directions, and it was not until I came to this country that I read even 'Ivanhoe.'"

This pleasant bit of autobiographical confession opened the hearts of all present and the talk which followed was of unusual interest.

I recall two memorable opportunities of the enjoyment of Agassiz' peculiar eloquence, an eloquence not to be outshone; one a social meeting

at his own house, when he described the **action of**
glaciers upon the surface of North America ; **the**
other a public discourse upon embryology.   They
are never to be forgotten, and were appreciated
by none more sincerely than by the " clear spirit "
of his publisher and friend.

In November, 1873, the diary continues : —

" Agassiz is very ill — probably dying.   What
a different world it will be **to us** without him.
Such a rich, expansive, loving nature.   The Saturday Club will feel this to be their severest
loss."

From his earliest years Mr. Fields had been a
lover of the histrionic art.   I have already referred to the opportunities afforded him for seeing
the best acting while he was still a youth, and it
was a taste fostered in his later years.   He was
not, in the common acceptation of the term, **a**
great theatre-goer.   The occasions were rare
when he did not prefer his own library to the
front box in any theatre, but when those occasions
offered, he made, as Charles Dickens used to say of
Madame Viardot, " an audience " in himself.   He
understood — as few persons outside the profession
have ever done, the difficulties to be surmounted
in order to obtain eminence, but eminence in any
direction once achieved he was among the first to
pay tribute to the artist.   **His** knowledge of the

literature of the stage was wide and accurate, and as Charles Lamb said of the fat woman sitting in the door-way, " it was a shrewd zephyr that could escape her," so it was a shrewd slip of the text, accent, rhythm, pronunciation, which could escape his keen observation and memory. The artists themselves were the first, of course, to recognize such an audience, and the almost universal tribute of their friendship was one of the pleasures of his life. Many members of the profession will recall happy hours passed under his roof, but of two or three of the most eminent who have gone from us, a brief record has been preserved. I have already spoken of Mrs. Mowatt and of Charlotte Cushman.

Among Mr. Fields's letters from one of the most famous of our living actors, I find the following sentence of pathetic significance : " Any notice of any actor now-a-days, which is assuredly both unsolicited and unpaid for, is a refreshing rarity, and deserves a place in the most important part of ' our shop,' among the curiosities."

We believe the day is happily past for neglect either of artistic painstaking or artistic success. In Mr. Fields's opinion, both painstaking and success upon the stage demanded the same recognition that these qualities demand in any other sphere of art. But his enjoyment of the society of actors was quite apart from any such reasoning Nature first, and afterward the business of the actor's life, has caused the entertainment of others to become his study. " Going to the play," means " a good time," and rest to the careworn. Any human being who has learned the science of entertaining, has indeed possessed himself of a beautiful gift. Many a dark mood may be cheated out of existence by this fine science. And it was a gift which always gave Mr. Fields an exquisite pleasure to see exercised. It would be a vain task to mention the names of living actors, men and women, who have turned to him continually as to a friend; but the satisfaction he himself took in these relations is no less a satisfaction to recall now.

His acquaintance with Charles Matthews must have begun with Matthews's first visit to America, for I remember an anecdote he used to relate of him long before the visit of 1871. Mr. Fields had enjoyed Matthews's playing sincerely; it seemed to him perfect of its kind. "Matthews," he exclaimed, when they met, " I enjoyed your performance beyond expression." " Ah, that is just it," said Matthews, " you don't express anything. How can your people expect to get the best out of an actor, if they don't speak or try to tell him so. They will never know what we can do. It is impossible to give one's best under such circumstances." It was an excellent suggestion to a thoughtful hearer, and left the door wide open for some kind of expression in the future. In June, 1871, Mr. Matthews returned to Boston. It was not a convenient time to go to the theatre, but returning to town just in season one evening, we took a cup of tea at a restaurant near by, and went to see " £1000 a Year," which was followed by a short comedietta of his own, called "Toddle-kins" (and something else). His acting had a last-century flavor in it; also it possessed the rapidity and perfection of the modern French stage, while it was altogether English. It was a very fine house, proving that the absolute perfection of his own style had at length brought him the recognition he deserved.

Later we saw him in "The Critic," Sheridan's play, but re-adapted by himself for our stage. The requisitions of the modern theatre were ingeniously engrafted upon the old play. Matthews had great talent, and inherited talent. He was at that time sixty-seven years old, without a sign of decadence.

Where could be found a more brilliant man, a more fascinating companion, than Sothern? As swift in wit as a French woman, as swift in action as a juggler, he combined with these gifts great tenderness and charm of nature. I am sorry to find no record of our intercourse with him except what is set down on the treacherous tablets of the memory, but I remember his coming was always a signal that the thermometer was rapidly rising and everything beginning to glow with a midsummer radiance of feeling and color.

I find in the diary : —

"*February*, 1870. Mr. Fechter came to lunch. Talked freely of his own conception of Hamlet. Finds his Boston audience wonderfully appreciative. . . . Told a touching story of Mademoiselle Mars during her last years. She came upon the stage one night to personate one of the parts she had made famous in her youth. When she appeared some heartless wretch threw her a wreath of immortelles — as it were for her grave. She was shocked: drops stood on her brow, the rouge fell from her cheeks, and she stood motionless before the audience, — a picture of age and misery. She could not continue her part.

"He spoke with intense enthusiasm of Frederick Lemaître. 'The second-class actors were always arguing with him (only second-class people argue) and saying, 'Why do you wish me to stand here, Frederick?' 'I don't know,' he would say, 'only see that you do it.' . . .

"It is odd that Fechter's eyes should be brown after all! They look so light in the play. . . . His description of Dickens, as Fechter often saw him from the lawn at work at his desk, or when he rose, to join him at lunch, ' with tears on his cheek and a smile on his mouth,' was close to life and delightful. . . .

" Saw Fechter in the ' Duke's Motto.' He was wonderfully fine. This is the play of which Dickens gave us
such a humorous description. Fechter wished *him* to
adapt it (John Brougham did it at last); and he went
through the plot in such a rapid way with a baby in his
arms, made up of a pillow which he snatched from the
couch in Dickens's study, that it was perfectly impossible
to understand a single word he said, English and French
getting entangled in an inextricable medley.

" *June* 14. Fechter has been here, plunged in deepest
grief for the loss of his friend Charles Dickens. He
was pathetic. . . . At the very hour we were talking together the body was brought into Westminster Abbey.

" *August.* Dined with Fechter at Nahant. He had
been in England, but had returned with many question-
able and perverted notions of people and things. He
was dramatic in his representations of persons, and made
himself entertaining."

" *December*, 1871. Just returned from seeing Fechter
in Ruy Blas. The public had heard the news that he
was to leave the Globe Theatre in four weeks. (He had
made an engagement there for the winter.) The result
was an enormous house. He played with great fire and
care. He had a wretched cold, and his pronunciation
was not only thick but very French, as it is apt to become when he is excited ; and we found it difficult sometimes to catch a word ; but his audience were determined
to be pleased, and they caught and applauded all his
good points." . . .

Dickens possessed a strong influence over Fechter, and while he lived seemed to keep him from

sinking. He said, however, when Fechter decided to come to America: "He will doubtless make a great impression, but whether anything can prevent him from overturning his own fortunes remains to be seen. I shall do the best I can for him."

The following passage from Mr. Fields's lecture on Cheerfulness will not be out of place here: —

"Whoever has the magic gift, like Warren and Sothern and Owens, and Raymond and Boucicault, and Gilbert and Clarke and Jefferson, and dear, sensible, funny, friendly Mrs. Vincent (whom heaven preserve, big bonnet and all, for many years to come), — whoever has that special endowment to raise a continued shout of honest laughter every evening in our various theatres, is a benefactor to be greeted everywhere. When I go to see and hear these genuine sons and daughters of Momus, who bring to us so many hours of unalloyed happiness, I can but rejoice at every peal of hilarious pleasure that rings to the roof from my over-brainworked countrymen and women ; for each outburst from the audience seems a direct expression of 'Down with the bridge of sighs and up with the bridge of joy !' Having been honored with the acquaintance (on and off the stage) of many of these ushers of mirth, these furrow dispensers from the brow of care, these helpers to good digestion, these half-fictitious, whole-hearted, most attractive people, I confess myself their insolvent debtor, who can never hope to pay even a dime on the dollar for all the delight they have given me."

I return to the diary : —

" *December*, 1867.   Ole Bull and his son came in. Ole was like a sunny apparition and stayed but a moment.   He proposes to return to-morrow, however, to breakfast.   He was eager to tell us of a young Norwegian poet, Björnson, thirty years old only, a man sure to be famous, who has written many beautiful things, among others a poem called 'The Merry Boy.'   Mr. Fields asked him which was his favorite audience.   The Norwegians of my native town, was his immediate reply.   His pantomime is extraordinary.   He half acted, half told how men, women, and children gathered about him there when he was to play, and how he drew his themes from subjects and objects familiar to him from childhood.   He was never more exquisitely expressive, nor his handsome little son more appreciative. . . .   One night, after playing in the Music Hall to an enormous audience, Ole Bull gave us the pleasure of his presence at supper.   He talked much of his scheme for a new piano, which was absorbing him.   'The idea was betrayed to you by your violin,' said L.   'Yes,' responded Ole, delightedly, with that long dwelling upon the short word of assent peculiar to him.   He described the various qualities of the 'Amati,' the 'Stradivarius' and other violins.   'How about strings,' one asked.   'Oh! there is a great difference even in strings,' said he, 'your muttons must not be too civilized.'

" In a letter to Mr. Fields describing his new piano, he says: 'Ericsson has been extremely kind in taking a lively interest in the instrument from the drawing only. He proposes to study the instrument after a hearing, and

9

thinks he can reduce the weight of it by more than half by compensation and change of material, and counteract the sudden changes of temperature, etc. . . . I do love you so much that I know you would be glad on my account that such a reward should be mine after so many disappointments and failures. But if this also should prove a disappointment, well, we must stand on the fulcrum and try to move the world. In coming to Boston I 'll try to induce Professor —— to come to the meeting surely, and illustrate my theories with some instruments from his laboratory. With my violin I shall explain the tone phases, the construction of musical instruments in general, beginning with the history of the violin, the essence and harmony of musical expressions. I do feel so grateful to you to have obtained for me the honor and delight in laying before the society my individual convictions in music. . . .

" Your ever devoted,   OLE BULL."

In 1871 I find another record of a visit from Ole Bull accompanied by his young wife. He was like a fine strain of poetry. In rather more charming English than usual, if possible, he described their beautiful home in Norway and his violin, " vo," he says, meaning who, "is seek."

This casual mention of Ole Bull, giving no hint of his beautiful poetic presence, would indeed be omitted as utterly unworthy if it were not that Mr. Fields himself wrote a few words in remembrance of his friend, which are to be printed in " Ole Bull's Life," now in preparation.

I wish it were possible in few words to convey the refinement and charm of Ole Bull's presence to those who have not known him. The childlikeness of his nature was admirable, and endured to the end. It was not necessary when he was to give his friends the favor of a visit to suggest that he should bring his violin. He never failed to remember that he could find his fullest expression through that medium, and when the proper moment arrived was always ready to contribute his large share to the pleasure of the time. There was a generosity about bestowing himself in private for others which was delightful. He was proud to give what he possessed. His friends cannot forget his manner of going and standing with his violin in one corner of the library with his little audience at sufficient distance, when drawing up his fine figure to its full height and throwing back his head he would stand silent until he was prompted to begin; it was a picture not to fade from the memory; or when exciting himself over his subject he would stop suddenly and explain in a torrent of words and with dramatic gestures what he wished to convey.

It was one of the valued privileges of Mr. Fields's life to know George Putnam, the Unitarian preacher, and to listen to his discourses. Frequently on Sunday, when the weather permitted, he would walk out of town to hear him. I find in the diary : —

"*Sunday*.   Walked to Roxbury to hear Dr. Putnam. The discourse was upon the love between brothers and sisters, and of Jesus as our elder brother.   Anything more tender or more simple can hardly be imagined."

Again, —

"Walked to Roxbury, and heard Dr. Putnam give one of his clear, strong pleas.   His style is simplicity itself."

"Heard Dr. Putnam yesterday on the advent of Christ, — the state of living expectantly which should possess the true followers.   A moving discourse." . . .

"Such a sermon from Dr. Putnam !   On worldly and unworldly gifts ; first, of the gifts our Lord has bestowed upon us by His teaching, and second, of the gifts that all the good and wise of the earth may give to men.   It was a most uplifting discourse.   The preacher, indeed, possesses the power given to the apostles of old ' to teach and to preach.' "

"In speaking of the presence of our Lord at the feast, Dr. Putnam said last Sunday, ' He rewarded the hospitality of his friends by his presence.' "

"*Sunday*.   Perfect day ; walked to Roxbury.   Dr. Putnam preached one of his noble discourses — touching, heroic, yet so reticent ! . . . The text was from St. Paul, ' Seeing we also are compassed about with so great a cloud of witnesses.'   The encompassing cloud of witnesses urging us to new struggles and farther heights had been seen by him in clear, spiritual vision. He could tell us of them; of the heroic and the lovely; of our own dear ones; how they were standing and calling to us, surrounding and inciting us.

"He rose to a height of eloquence of which he himself was totally unconscious. He had been listening to his beloved, who have gone before, and they had taught him what he should speak. He recalled the noble verse: —

> "'Lives of great men all remind us
> We can make our lives sublime,
> And, departing, leave behind us
> Footprints on the sands of time.'

He said our witnesses not alone regard but report our ways, and teach us distinctly the one lesson that we should live uprightly, dutifully, kindly, humbly; for our days are few; and what can any worldly good avail if we forget to listen to the loving ones who beckon us to come their way?"

It was often a part of Monday's relaxation for Dr. Putnam to go into the book-shop, and, when it was possible, to find the publisher in his corner and exchange a few words at least. One day, after the removal of Fields, Osgood & Co. to Tremont Street, he looked in, and, after a bit of personal talk, said: "Well, I suppose you anticipate a good many pleasant days to come in this place." "No," said Mr. Fields, "I don't, doctor. I don't look forward to anything." "That's right," was the reply. "Sufficient unto the day is the good thereof."

Many a pleasant talk have these two enjoyed among the books. Dr. Putnam was an appreciator of a first-rate novel, and I especially recall his enthusiasm over Mrs. Gaskell's beautiful tales of " Mary Barton " and " North and South."

They both seemed to " take comfort " in each other's friendship and society.

Of Mr. Fields's intimate friendship and correspondence with Bayard Taylor little or nothing can be reproduced in these pages. They exchanged many letters during the long period of their happy relation to each other, a relation which was never broken ; but in view of the record of Bayard Taylor's life, soon to be given to the public, and the late publication of Mr. Fields's own selection from Taylor's letters lately printed in the " Congregationalist," I will attempt to give nothing further here.

Nevertheless, the remembrance of many a pleasant social occasion recurs, especially during the season when his lectures upon German literature were given at the Lowell Institute. He had then finished his latest work, " Deukalion," and his mind and heart were filled with it.

His memory was not only a repository of literature, properly speaking, but of the freaks of literature, and it was as astonishing as it was amusing to hear the long passages he would repeat from Chivers and other eccentric authors.

His tender feelings for his friends, and his boyish ways with them, were peculiarly his own. His visits to Boston were a festival to him, and to them his coming was the signal for many a midnight talk and much wholesome festivity.

The brief record which remains in the diary of the years from 1861 to 1876 will be henceforth given almost without interruption.

" BOSTON, *Sunday, December* 8, 1861. At home all day, except a walk at noon over Cambridge bridge. The climate reminds us of Rome. It is almost too warm for fires until now as evening approaches. The morning rays came through a veil of soft gray mist which allowed the wings of the birds and the sails of the vessels (the latter like birds of larger growth) to gleam white as silver, and the whole bay looked for a few hours like a faded opal. At noon the sun poured out its warm, full rays, making it hard to guess if this were home or Italy. Some young and handsome boatmen darted under the bridge in their wherries as we returned. They were bound for a pull into the white waves of the harbor. Before the walk read aloud, 'One Word More with E. B. B.,' one of the most extraordinary poems in the language. We are reading 'Wordsworth's Life and Letters.' . . .

" Yesterday morning Artemus Ward breakfasted with us. We had a merry time. J. was in grand humor, representing people and incidents in the most incomparable manner. Artemus was complimented upon his success, and his power of amusing others. He said little but twinkled all over. Once, however, when asked how he was received by his very first audiences before they understood what he had to give them, he said: ' I was prepared for a good deal of gloom, but I had no idea they would be *so much* depressed!' . . .

" *December*, 1863. Mr. Hawthorne passed the night. He has already written the first chapter of a new romance, but he was so uncertain of what he had done as to find it impossible to continue until he asked Mr. Fields to read it and heard him express his sincere admiration for the work. This has given him better heart to go on with it. He talked of the 'Atlantic Monthly,' said he thought it the most ably edited magazine in the world, and was bound to be a success, 'with this exception,' he said, ' I fear its politics. Beware! What will you do in a year or two when the politics of the country change?' ' I will quietly wait for that time to come,' Mr. Fields answered, 'then I can tell you.' . . . Talked and laughed about Boswell, to whom Hawthorne accords a very high place, and Mr. Fields recalled Johnson's saying of a man who had committed some misdemeanor, and was on the verge of suicide in consequence, ' Why does n't the man go somewhere where he is not known, instead of to the devil, where he is known?' Speaking of the 'Atlantic Monthly,' Mr. Fields said the magazine profited by having the best living proof-reader. ' He is so interested in its success that I always say, No N——, no Fields.'

" *January*, 1864. J. T. F. passed yesterday in Concord. He went first to see Hawthorne, who was sitting alone gazing into the fire; his gray dressing-gown, which became him like a Roman toga, wrapped about his figure. He said he had done nothing for three weeks, but of course his romance is maturing in his mind. —— and —— had sent word they were coming to call, so Mrs. Hawthorne had gone out to walk ('thrown out on picket-duty,' —— said), leaving word at home that Mr. Hawthorne was ill, and could see no one." . . .

"*Sunday, October* 23, came news of Colonel Charles R. Lowell's death."

"*November*, 1865. Governor Parsons, of Alabama, lunched with us. He has sad stories to tell us of the suffering and destitution of the South, especially of his own State. He has seen cities laid waste and burned to the ground, with books and pictures, and every precious relic a home can contain. In Sherman's 'March,' the town of Selma, forty miles south of his residence, was burned in that way, and the suffering of the inhabitants was terrible to behold. We know nothing of the horrors of war in New England, he says; and when we look in his face, and hear his pathetic tales, I am persuaded that many of our people do escape a sense of this terrible calamity. He is a sad man. He comes here for the purpose of urging Massachusetts to forgiveness, and to send help to the sufferers. . . . He went last night to the Union Club, where Governor Andrew introduced him, and pleaded his cause. Charles Sumner spoke against it. . . . Governor Parsons has a negro slave whom he purchased for his body-servant thirty years ago. When there were no more slaves he paid him regular wages. Then other people came and offered him much higher wages than he was able to pay, but the old servant said: 'No, Massa Parsons lubs me, and I lub him, and we shan't separate now.'

" *November*, 1865.   There is talk of establishing another business house in New York, large enough to represent Ticknor and Fields.   It is an enormous ship already, and must be watched momently by the man at the helm, or she will drive upon the rocks.

" BOSTON, *July*, 1866.   Just returned from Berkshire. Glad to be at home again, where we can see the sunset over the bay, and feel the fresh morning breeze.   Almost every day something delightful occurs ; but the pleasantest of all occurrences is when the day rises and sets with nothing to break the stillness of midsummer. . . .

" *August*.   Left for the Isles of Shoals.   On our way we heard of the success of the Ocean cable.   What glorious reward to Cyrus Field after eight years of delay and disappointment.   ' Peace in Europe,' reported as the first message. . . .   The day was fair, the shores of the Piscataqua gleaming with white houses, waving trees, pleasure boats, and all the gay surroundings of human life in harmony with nature.   Reaching the islands we followed the troop of people over a plank walk to an over-crowded hotel, and bided our time.   After dinner, having seen our fellow-passengers safely reëmbarked for Portsmouth, we started to explore the island, walking over the bleached rocks, and threading our way through bayberry.   Dark clouds rolled up fold over fold from the north, summer's loveliness reigned in the south, and all around the rote of the never silent sea came up from the cliffs which hedged us in.   Everywhere, if grass were found, we set our feet on graves; if stones, they were white-bearded like Tithonus.   We peeped in clefts and crannies where the sea reached up awful fingers and shook them in the face of the intruder. There was no wind, only a brooding sadness overspread the scene. Something of the dread of the place came over us, a knowledge of the dreariness of winter and the loneliness of life when the busy crowd had been swept away by the breath of autumn. By and by, returning to the hotel, the cheerful look of the place was pleasant — young girls darting to and fro from the bath to their rooms, or walking on the piazza with their elders, or playing croquet, watched by gentlemen on the balcony. We walked to the cottage and lingered in the garden brilliant with marigolds, nasturtiums, coreopsis, and fragrant with mignonette; it was full of wild birds too, besides a parrot and two canaries, in cages, hanging in the porch. Sitting by the window was a large gray-haired woman wrapped in a white shawl. She was like the full pale summer moon, so calm, and fair, and sweet. There she sat lovingly watched over by her daughter, a constantly redeeming presence.

"Inside the little parlor was gay with pictures and flowers. Among the latter a crowd of glowing poppies. As we bent over them a pleasant voice sang the old song ' Poppies! Poppies! Poppies like these I own are rare!'

"There was a drift-wood fire that night and there were ghost stories, and voices were heard far into the night.

"Meantime, in the pauses, the sound of the sea came from every side and we knew its awful vast stretched between us and home.

"The morning was resplendent. We were soon in a

boat bound for Star Island. The place was very still in the sunshine of the day. The fishers were gone to sea, the women were at their household duties. We passed through their yards and over their walls seeing only a woman occasionally at door or window, whom our dear guide, C. T., would accost with 'Good-morning, Susan,' or, 'Are you well, Sarah?' as if they were members of her family. There are only about fifty families left of the old town of Gosport. It was comparatively a large place in the days when Spain carried her commerce hither for the dun fish, which was then beautifully cured by these people. At present they have nearly lost the art, for they have lost the art of taking pains. We crossed Star Island, picking our way among the graves, or stepping from fallen stone to stone, to the wild cliffs and chasms on the opposite side. How wild and desolate it was, even in the summer sunshine! Then we rowed to 'Smutty-Nose,' where our guide passed two years of her childhood before the building of the light-house. The story was not new to us, but the utter desolation of the place, in spite of the song-sparrow and the sunshine, the pimpernel, cinquefoil, morning-glory, and all the loveliness of summer, could not be forgotten. We heard the howling of the winter wind and saw the Spanish vessel on the rocks. . . . Rowed round White Island, but the sea was too high to land. . . .

" *October*, 1866. Mr. Fields received to-day the most extraordinary letter of all the many strange ones it has been his fortune to have addressed to him. It is from an English woman well born and well educated. She is now in this country, however, and called upon him last week. This letter is so long that although clearly written it required upwards of half an hour to read it aloud. She gave her personal history unblushingly, and if one half be true she has had as wide a run in the best society of Europe and puts as high a value upon it as any woman ever did. She estimates her own talents very highly, too. While reading our feelings oscillated between wonder and pity. . . .

" He has also received an autograph book from a man who left the volume himself with a polite request 'for Mr. Fields's autograph.' The book was very handsome, French, richly bound, and contained many good signatures and letters. In a few days the owner returned to get his book, left his thanks for the autograph, and said any time Mr. Fields wished his hair cut *he* was the man and would come to his house at any moment to do it! . . .

" Mr. Fields has found new papers, never collected, in Fraser's magazine, by Thackeray. He is making a book of them."

Mr. George William Curtis, with a kindness sure as his literary touch, wrote after this publication : " What a pleasant book you have made of Thackeray's dropped stitches ! It is really a new work by him. It is like finding a lost portfolio of a great painter's sketches. They have all his manner. If the fruit is small it is none the less a Seckel."

" Ah ! We saw Ristori last night, She was full of dignity and pathos. J. T. F. says she *was* Queen Mary and he will never be present at an execution again ! . . .

"*January*, 1867. A volume of Pope was sent to Mr. Fields to-day formerly owned by President Lincoln. The name, and a letter in the handwriting of our great president, are inscribed within.

" Bayard Taylor has sent us a picture in oils, by himself, of the Temple of Apollo Epicurius, also one of the ruins of Mantinea for T. B. A. So we had a grand opening last evening. Seeing these recalled what Bayard said of his little ——, now seven years old. She has a fondness for Greek history and was found the other day charging vigorously into the woodpile; when her mother asked what she was doing, she said she was an Athenian pursuing the Lacedemonians. So much for being born in Greece !

" Professor Felton's lectures on Greece are now in type. J. T. F. is delighted with them, and has already finished the first volume, though they only came from the printer last night ! . . .

" Very large meeting at the Union Club last night. The question whether the House should be kept open Sundays or no was proposed for discussion. Every room was open and filled. Governor Andrew made an excellent speech, full of his fine humanity, which is so sure to carry the majority over to his side. He proposed that the House should be open with restrictions, a few rooms, and no liquor.

" The question of sending aid to Crete was also brought up. . . .

" *Thursday.* Willis was buried at St. Paul's Church. A gracious circle of poets surrounded the body.

" *February, Wednesday.* Called on Miss Catherine

Sedgwick, who, although the shadow of many a year hangs over her, sits by her fireside talking wittily and wisely. Her presence and conversation are wonderfully attractive. She has the power of expressing tenderest sentiment, yet so relieved by a keen wit, that you are cheered and never offended by the quick contrast."

"PLYMOUTH, N. H., *June*, 1867. This place is now always associated with Hawthorne. Yesterday, sitting in the lustrous loveliness of summer, our thoughts were filled with his memory, when the mail arrived, bringing extracts from his diary. We read them together, with keen enjoyment; looking up to the hills, meanwhile, radiant in sun and shadow. Suddenly we heard the sound of martial music: it was a public funeral; the effect was very solemn and inspiring. One of the responsible persons connected with the house said he assisted Mr. Hawthorne to his room that night, — the one adjoining that of General Pierce, — and that Hawthorne passed from sleep in life to the sleep of death with so easy a transition that his posture was unchanged, and the flight of his spirit only discovered when his friend placed his hand upon him lovingly, in one of the wakeful pauses of the night, and found his body cold. The distress of General Pierce was indescribable, the narrator said, and 'indeed, sir, if one didn't know anything about his politics, it would be said of him that he was one of the best of men. There is nobody who comes to this house of more uniform and unfailing gentlemanliness than he.' "

"CAMPTON, *Monday*. Rose at half-past four, breakfasted at half-past five. Mr. Fields went to Boston. . . . The night shut down heavily."

" *Tuesday.* Still warm and raining. About three
o'clock in the morning is the time now to hear the birds,
They clamor wondrously then. Rain, rain, the livelong
day, with now and then a pause of perfect stillness, without bird or breath of wind, and then the rain again —
patter, patter, through the leaves. Watched for my
traveler at night from half-past seven until nine o'clock.
At length he arrived, wet and tired. The horse found
the roads heavy, and they came slowly. He met two
men in the cars who had been to see Booth in ' Hamlet.'
' I tell you,' said the youngest, ' you have to read that
play to see what he is talking about. You 'd better read
it the first chance you get. You 'll understand it a deal
better then.' ' Well,' rejoined the other, ' I like to see
him in " Hamlet." I always see him in that play. Why,
I 've seen it THREE times. I tried " Richard the Third "
once, but somehow it didn't seem natural, so I went back
to " Hamlet." ' They continued to recount stories of the
stage of more than doubtful authenticity. At last, one
asked the other if he had ever seen the elder Booth.
' No,' was the reply; ' but I 've heerd that he acted
" Richard Third " so true, that they would get up and
hiss, — not him, you see, but the wicked man he made
b'lieve to be.' "

. . . " Drove over what is called the New Discovery
Road, though it is years since the gap was discovered between the hills opening the way to Centre Harbor. We
are fifteen hundred feet above the sea, while passing a
portion of the road. The hills rise stern and bleak around.
Two lakes lie embowered in green at the foot of Mount
Prospect, and the whole effect is mountainous rather

than hilly. In our ascent we met several children, all perfectly untamed, as if they never had seen a stranger before. One witch-like little thing, a half-fledged Madge Wildfire, came careering over the top of the hill on her way from school, swinging her arms and kicking up her legs. Suddenly she caught sight of us proceeding slowly in our wagon, and, penetrated with fear, crept like a calf to the side of the road among the bushes. There she stood trembling, though somewhat reassured by our voices, but the moment we were sufficiently advanced to give her a chance, she went flying off down the road as if distracted. Afterward we saw a little girl about ten years old with two older boys. The valiant youths hid themselves behind their sister, who disdained to appear alarmed, though her eyes looked startled. The wildness of the scenery could not give us such a sense of savage solitude as these children did. . . . The day was so beautiful, that we lingered till the light faded and the stars appeared."

" PLYMOUTH, *June 21st.* We sit where we can drink in the beauty of the river and the hills, and J. has read aloud to me nearly the whole day. From our window we see the river winding through the wide interval until it becomes lost among the hills. We have seen few places in the world so beautiful. He astonished me in our walk this morning by going up to an old farm-house and declaring that was exactly what he wanted, and he meant to have it and live here six months in the year. . . ."

" BOSTON, *July.* Mr. Fields had a very busy day. Receiving perpetually, everybody, from —— to the drunkard, who insisted upon following him home. Indeed, he forgot his promise to dine out. I was obliged to go without him, trusting he would finally remember, which he did, three quarters of an hour after the time."

"Our beloved neighbors came to inquire after his hand, which is lame, — an affection of the nerves which prevents him from writing. . . .

"*August. Manchester-by-the-Sea*. Walked to the Dana Place; found Mr. Dana, Senior, sitting on the piazza as we approached — two or three fluttering dresses could be seen on the beach below and a child at play. Mr. Dana is anticipating his eightieth birthday. His white hair and slender figure are so combined with perfect vitality of expression as to prevent any thought of decadence in connection with his great age. It was a beautiful day, and the scene was one of loveliness and significance. The memory of Allston, the painter, who married a sister of Mr. Dana, is tenderly guarded in his household, and chairs from his studio, standing on the piazza, invited us to rest. Just at sunset, with the moonlight in the sky, we wandered through the woods. It was wild and dim. Returning we came out upon the lawn; the house-door stood open, the sunset streamed across, and young girls were moving about in gay dresses.

"Standing in the hall door the full view of the sea and its sad perpetual music from the sands below struck upon the eye and ear. Children were swinging in a hammock under the low pines on the edge of the cliff. Here we sat, while Mr. Dana told us how he and his daughter discovered this beautiful domain, and through what difficulties they had established their home in this

wonderful wilderness. But he chiefly loved to talk of
subjects such as poets choose : —

> "Dreams, books, are each a world ; and books, we know,
> Are a substantial world both pure and good;
> Round these with tendrils strong as flesh and blood,
> Our pastime and our happiness will grow.
> There do I find a never-failing store
> Of personal themes ; . . .
> Hence have I genial seasons; hence have I
> Smooth passions, smooth discourse, and joyous thought; —
> And thus from day to day my little boat
> Rocks in its harbor, lodging peaceably."

I venture to print here two notes from Mr.
Dana, as giving some idea not only of his own
tastes but of his relations to Mr. Fields : —

"DEAR MR. FIELDS, — While your proposal gratifies
me it also troubles me, for I feel that I must decline it,
and that looks somewhat ungracious. That you should
have thought of one who for a long while has been almost a stranger to literary circles, gives you a claim.
Above all, the fast friend of many years, who spoke so
many kind and bold words for me — when I most needed
them — what have I to say in not making him a trifling
return ? Nothing, but that I have been so long a mere
idle recipient of the good things of others, that I have
nothing of my own to give. I do not feel at the present
time as if I would do justice to B., or satisfy myself. It
is a special relief to my conscience that there are those
of your acquaintance who truly appreciate him, and
would do the thing thoroughly and well. You speak of
'Thanatopsis,' you remember 'The Past.' It just occurs

to me that years back I said to B., 'Could only one of your pieces be saved, short as it is, still, I should select ' The Past.' 'So would I,' he answered. ' Yet I have never seen it alluded to in notices of me.'   It has been spoken of since that time.

" Very sincerely yours,

" RICHARD H. DANA.

"43 CHESTNUT ST., *Nov.* 27, 1863."

" MY DEAR SIR, — Pardon my keeping Christopher so long. Was he not a man ? — Oh, large, brave heart, yet tender as a child ! *But no letter-writer !* What a pity that the bulk of the work should have been so increased by letters which are little else than so much dead weight, — scarce half a dozen of them worth the paper. Aside from these, there is a fresh air blowing upon us from out the spirit of the man, which seems to breathe over and through us something of his rejoicing health and strength.   With great regard,

" Truly yours,

"RICHARD II. DANA.

"43 CHESTNUT ST., *Nov.* 24.
"MR. J. T. FIELDS, Charles St."

" *August*, 1867.   Charles Dickens's agent arrived to make arrangements for his last visit to this country. The description of Mr. Fields given him by the ' Chief ' was so accurate that he was recognized immediately.

" *September*.   Mr. Fields gave me an account of his interview, to day, with Orestes Brownson, now a man of seventy years.   After studying theology he followed its suggestions in many different directions, espousing each form of doctrine in turn as the only true religion.   At

length, when by the independent action of his mind he
believed he had found the rest he sought in Romanism,
the stigma of frivolity was cast upon him. . . . He has
been chosen by Admiral Dahlgren and his wife to edit
the life of their son, the heroic Ulric Dahlgren. They
had prepared the book, but found they were in need of
a literary adviser. After some conversation upon the
subject, Mr. Brownson said the suffering of the Dahlgrens
was not exceptional : he had himself lost one son in the
war, and another was maimed for life. He said his mother
had only lately died, at ninety years of age. In the year
1861, her health being already enfeebled, she called her
son to her bedside and said, ' What is this I hear, Orestes ;
what is this trouble at the South ? ' ' They are trying to
destroy the Union, mother, and there must be a great
war.' ' Well, my son, what are you going to do about
it ? ' ' What can one man do, mother ? ' ' Do, why you
must go to the war, you and your sons ! '

" Eight of her grandsons were lost in the war : six
died, two deserted. She said the suffering caused her
by the last two was greater than that of the death of
the others. She was born on the day of Washington's
thanksgiving after the war of the Revolution. She
thought she should live to see the day of Lincoln's
thanksgiving, and so she did. She died the following
week.

" *Tuesday.* MANCHESTER-BY-THE-SEA. Mr. Fields
had a busy day in town. Mrs. Hawthorne brought him
fourteen closely written volumes of her husband's journal, — so fine as to be difficult to read, though written
quite plainly and entirely without corrections. Such ac-

curate notes of observation and such strange records of interesting people and places, have been rarely before made. There are also piles on piles of romances begun but never finished, — chapters here and there of exquisite beauty, but nothing completed. . . .

"Among other strange persons who called to-day is the poor man who was cast away in the steamer London, bound for Australia, and whose heart-rending description we read in the 'Cornhill Magazine.' He is young, and has a fine business in Australia; but says he can never go to sea again. He is anxious to have Mr. Fields print that portion of the history omitted by the 'Cornhill,' in which he explains why the accident took place and where the accusation should rest. Mr. Fields advised him to wait, because the young man was pecuniarily involved, until the case should come before the court, as it must do shortly. . . .

"Boston, *September*. Before breakfast he wrote letters from dictation on account of his lame hand. Among them letters of introduction for Mr. —— to American colleges. —— told us of Mrs. Carlyle's fondness for flowers. After her death Carlyle showed him plants, as they walked in the garden from Farringford and Eversley. He said, as Miss Cushman had said before him, 'she was cleverer than Carlyle.' 'Why she never wrote I cannot divine,' said ——.

"Mr. Fields told me to-day an anecdote he loves to recall of Willis (it may have appeared in print somewhere), of his watching a little ragged girl one day in London, who was peering through an area railing. A window of a comfortable eating-house gave upon this

area, and a man sat at the window taking a good dinner.
The child watched his every movement, saw him take a
beefsteak and get all things in readiness to begin, then
he stopped and looked round. 'Now a pertaty,' murmured the child. . . .

"Governor Andrew came in the evening. He said
the Rebel General Jeff. Thompson was coming to his
house and would we adjourn thither. Of course we said
'Yes,' and a strange evening we had. Thompson talked
without let or hindrance. A lank, bony man, with sin-
ews like steel, eye like a hawk, mouth thin and flat as a
fish's, high cheek-bones, feet out of shape, from his hard
marches probably, his legs twisted one over the other as
he talked. 'Waal, I'll jest tell ye how 't was. I was
the man that bought the rope to hang John Brown.'

"'We've been awfully whipped though, and our only
safety is in reconstruction.' His speech photographed
the various scenes he had been through. He swore continually, and ended by giving us an Indian dance. Jeff.
Thompson had been a guerilla chief, or as he himself
phrased it, 'had four thousand men under his command,
who reported to no man but himself.' One of his aids
was a wild Indian, who brought him a prisoner one day
who refused to surrender his sword. 'Surrender,' cried
Jeff. in a terrible rage, 'or my Indian shall scalp you.'
The man still demurring, Jeff. ordered the Indian to set
upon him. He began with a kind of wild howl, dancing
around his victim, and flourishing his tomahawk. In
another moment the man would have lost his scalp had
not fear caused him to succumb. The whole picture was
given with terrible vividness. We came home shudder-
ing."

"*November* 1st. Governor Andrew lies dead. Since the death of President Lincoln no man can be so great a loss to the country. To us, as neighbors and friends, the loss is doubled, for he failed in none of the hospitalities of daily life. He was benevolent and accessible always, and as charitable a man, in the largest sense of the word, as ever walked the earth. When Ole Bull's son was quite a child, he said to Mr. Fields one day in broken language, stopping short as they walked across the Common, ' Mr. Fields, you must thank God for your disposition.' Surely, we might say this also of Governor Andrew."

"*November* 2d. Funeral of this great good man! The sun shone through a veil of autumnal mist, as we walked across the Public Garden to the church, and the trees shook their last gold leaves pensively in the blue air. It was a lovely season, and tempered like the nature of the friend we had lost. Agassiz joined us, and we proceeded together to the church. Nothing could have been more fitting and inspiring than Mr. Clarke's service and tribute."

"*November* 4th. Great meeting of merchants to consolidate the fund as a memorial of Governor Andrew. Mr. Fields put down one thousand dollars for Ticknor and Fields. It was an eloquent and deeply enthusiastic occasion."

"*November* 19th. Dickens reached Boston yesterday. J. T. F. went down the harbor to meet him. He was in grand health and spirits. The night was glorious, and Dickens seemed impressed with its sublime clearness and beauty."

"*November* 27*th*. They have fallen into a daily habit of walking together, and J. comes home filled with C. D.'s inexhaustible and most interesting talk."

"*November* 29*th*. They dined alone together to-day, and sat four hours, amusing each other with endless characteristic representations. Mr. Fields gave his picture of the chimney-sweep, and Dickens in his turn gave the poet Rogers to the life, and Lady Blessington's receptions, 'to which I thought it was the thing to go when I was a young man,' also an excellent description of Mr. and Mrs. Lewes. The latter he finds most interesting 'with her shy manner of saying brilliant things.' . . . He talked of the mistake it was to fancy that childhood forgot anything; it is age that forgets.

"He spoke of Mr. Froude, saying, 'he is a brave man,' and with most cordial liking both for him and his works. . . . He repeated the story of his having burned all the letters of Sydney Smith when his daughter, Lady Holland, applied for permission to print them, and with these letters all his own private correspondence. 'For I thought if I should meet Sydney Smith in the Shades, and he should say, " what have you done with those letters "' —— a significant shrug expressed the rest, though he added immediately, 'Perhaps he would have said, " You should have brought them with you where they would crackle well." '

"*Monday night.* Charles Dickens's first reading. The audience seemed one vast ear and eye; the people sat fixed and speechless. Every one seemed drawn to that great sympathetic nature, and as if they longed in some peculiar way to give him their confidence! And how in the anteroom afterward he and his friend embraced and laughed, and then embraced again from the very excitement of the occasion !

" *Tuesday.* The reading was quite as wonderful but quieter in its character. We went, as usual, at his request, to speak with him after it was ended. He was in good spirits but very tired. 'You can't think,' he said, ' what resolution it requires to dress again after it is over !'

" *Monday, December* 9. First reading in New York. ' The Carol ' was far better given than in Boston, because the applause was more ready and stimulated the reader. Indeed the enthusiasm was rapturous. Dickens sent to request us to come to his room. He was much exhausted, but after taking food, his warmth and vigor returned.

" *Wednesday.* At four o'clock Dickens came to dine, later we went together to the theatre, and afterward back to the hotel, where we sat talking until one o'clock. Every moment was full of vivid interest. In speaking of that great railway accident described in ' All the Year Round,' he mentioned the curious fact of his chronometer watch, perfect up to that moment, becoming subject to eccentricities, yet this was rather as an illustration of the subtle effect the accident had upon *him* than remarkable in itself. The play that night was really very dull, and he sat talking, but with such care in managing voice and gesture that only a keen observer would have discovered he was inattentive to the stage. After our return he laughed till the tears ran down his cheeks at the memory of the laughter he had seen in the faces of his own audience the night before, representing the different phases of character and the different effect of laughter on each. Speaking of Fechter he said : 'If he were a writer how marvelous his powers of representation would be ! I who for so many years have been studying the best way of putting things have often felt utterly amazed and distanced by him.' At the ballet Dickens observed the honest faces of the women, and became much interested in one of them who seemed to have lost something, perhaps a trinket, and who wept as she danced. Poor child! Her tears only made her eyes shine the brighter to pit and gallery ! . . .

" Last night of the first course of readings in New York. Dickens was delighted with his audience: ' As good as Paris,' he said, when he invited us into his room afterward.

" BOSTON, *Christmas Eve.* Dickens came to dine and talked all the time as he will do when the moment comes that he sees it is expected. He is by no means a man who loves to talk. His dramatic touches are peculiarly his own, but are of course more difficult to recall even than his words. Describing a little incident which happened while in New York, and seeing some doubt of its verity on the faces of his friends, he said ruefully: ' I assure you it is so! And all I can say is, how astonishing it is that I should be perpetually having things happen to me with regard to people that nobody else in the world can be found to believe.' . . . Went to hear ' The Carol.' How beautiful it was! The whole house rose and cheered ! The people looked at him with gratitude as to one who held a candle in a dark way. Afterward he invited us to come to him, but he was so very tired we should have done better to stay away except that he sent for us.

"*Friday.* Quietly at home together. It was really a novelty.

"*Saturday night, January* 4. Mr. Dickens arrived punctually. He was in good spirits in spite of a catarrh, which only leaves him during the two hours at night when he is reading in public. He was full of amusing anecdotes. We were somewhat jealous because New York heard 'Marygold' first. 'Please God,' he said, 'I'll do it as well for you.'

"*Sunday morning,* bright and clear. His cold no better, but he is wonderfully gay; pleased and amused also with his new surroundings. . . . I hardly know anything more diverting than when he begs not 'to be set going' on one of his readings by a quotation or otherwise, and odd enough it is to hear him go on having been so touched off. He has been a great student of Shakespeare, which is continually discovered in his conversation. His love of the theatre is something which never pales, he says, and the people who go upon the stage, however poor their pay, or hard their lot, love it, he thinks, too well ever to adopt another vocation of their free will. . . .

"*February* 21. We accompany him to Providence to-night to hear 'Marygold.'

"*Saturday.* Have heard 'Marygold.' The audience was not responsive, but we were penetrated by it. Subtlest of all the readings, it requires more of the listener than any other. From beginning to end it is worthy of close study. Dickens was gentle, kind, affectionate.

We played a game of cards together, which was a pure effort of memory to try to wear away something of the excitement of the reading. It was not of much use.

"Boston, *Monday.* Dickens came to dinner. We sat four hours. He read a short extract from an English newspaper, the deposition of a child three years old against ' Mother Jaggers,' a secreter and killer of babies. The child called itself ' the baby-ganger,' whose duty it was to sit up in the middle of the bed with seven babies and give them the bottle when they cried. Deponent saw ' Mother Jaggers ' one day ' take a drop of gin,' when by some means ' the ganger ' falling into the fire, and no one being there who could extricate it, it has been disabled for life. He intends to look up this matter as soon as he returns to England. . . . Last night during the reading a telegram arrived bringing news of the impeachment of President Johnson. . . . The two friends walked about seven miles at noon, which is their average. . . .

" *Wednesday.* Dickens came to pass the evening. He was full of life and frolic, and kept winning the memory game with cards which he called ' Lady Nincumwitch ' in such a preternatural manner that at last we suspected him of some plan to aid remembrance which the rest of us had not the wit to discover. He explained after a while that he invented each time a little story by means of which the cards were strung together in his mind, but as the story seemed to us as difficult as the cards we acknowledged ourselves well beaten.

" *March* 6. Dickens dined with us. He made all manner of fun of his friend for trying to ' show him ' some new fruit-houses on their return from Cambridge, where he had already been shown so much that he began to think he should feel a bitter hatred to the man who should propose the next thing to be seen. . . .

" *March* 31. Dined with Dickens at the Parker House. Found him in the best of good spirits because his traveling is over, and he is within eleven readings of home. His catarrh still clings to him, yet he is better and will feel quite well if he can sleep, but with all his gifts he has no talent for sleeping. . . . Heard the 'Christmas Carol' yesterday for the last time in Boston.

" *April* 7. Dickens was very ill yesterday. Unremitting exertion has preyed upon his strength ; he does not recover his vitality after reading. We beseech him not to continue. Copperfield was never more tragic than last night, but it was no longer 'vif.' I should hardly have known it for the same reading and reader. . . . All agree in finding the readings very exhausting. It is not only the excitement and consequent loss of sleep, but the exercise of close prolonged attention combined with anxiety for the reader himself.

" *Friday, April* 10. Left home for New York with Dickens. . . .

" *April* 11. Mr. Dickens looks into my room to say that as C., who was to dine with him, most fortunately has the gout ! and can't come, we will all go, ' if I please,' to the circus to-night. . . . He looks in again shortly with a ' piece of dreadful news '; —— was to arrive shortly for a visit,— one of us alone ' could save him ! '

" The friends walked many miles together to-day. It was wet and uncomfortable at the last. They had been reading Governor Andrew's speech upon the Prohibition Act and found it very moving. 'I could not put it down till I had finished it. That man must always hold a high position in your country,' said Dickens.

" *Wednesday, April* 15. The anniversary of Abraham Lincoln's death, now three years ago. Monday night was Charles Dickens's first reading of his last course. The night was very stormy; the audience large but unresponsive. We returned directly to the hotel; in a moment heard a tap at our room door. It was dear C. D. who begged us to come over for a bit of supper with him. He was wretchedly tired; but after a few moments he seemed to recover and became the most exciting and amusing of hosts until after midnight.

" *Tuesday.* Audience large but less demonstrative than yesterday. The reader came home very, very tired.

" *Wednesday.* After dinner we went to the French theatre, walking both ways. The lights in the park and in Broadway, and the soft spring-like air, were delightful. The play was wretched, but Dickens's presence and conversation were far more agreeable than any play could have been to us.

" *Tuesday.* Last night came the final reading. The exertion is too great, and to-day he is utterly prostrated. He went through with it bravely in spite of the pain in his foot. His desk was covered with flowers. After all was over when Mr. Fields went to speak with him, he shut in his hand as he took it a velvet box containing his favorite studs, then worn by him for the last time. . . .

" *Wednesday, April* 22. My husband went to the

steamer with Dickens to say farewell. He returns to his own home, and the splendor of England's summer. He leaves us the memory of our joy, and the knowledge that we can see him no more as we have done. Never again the old familiar intercourse, the care for him, nor can he ever feel again perhaps quite the same singleness of regard for us.

"*May* 2. Our home life has lost nothing; indeed it has gained. Do we not see him here too, added to all other tender associations! How delightfully the rain shuts us in. J. read me at breakfast a grand new poem by Lowell, it is called 'June.' Last evening he took down Irving's works to try to find a description of a summer thunder-storm which Dickens said was one of the closest pictures he knew and the most vivid.

"Failing to find that he read me the story of the 'Stout Gentleman,' the scene of which was laid on as wet a day as I ever experienced! Reading this recalled to his mind an incident told him by Leslie the painter, years ago, which, if it be not already in print, deserves a place. He said, Leslie was walking one afternoon with Washington Irving in England, when as they crossed a little churchyard they saw a most extraordinary stout gentleman just in front of them, who presented such dorsal amplitudes and comical aspects that Irving was convulsed with laughter. Whereupon Leslie made a sketch of the same stout gentleman on the spot, and from this sketch, which served to keep his memory green, Irving afterwards worked up the little paper called by that name. . . .

"E—— has just returned from New York. He

looked in upon his publisher a moment saying, ' How is the guardian and maintainer of us all ? '

" *Sunday.* To-day the quiet of home once more. J. is busy among his books. . . . Some one asked him yesterday for an antidote against sea-sickness, saying he had heard that brown paper worn on the chest was considered good. ' Yes,' was the reply, ' a lady in whom I have no confidence assured me that was the fact. You had better try it ! '

In September, 1867, was published " The Guardian Angel," by Oliver Wendell Holmes, with the following dedication : —

" To James T. Fields, a token of kind regard, from one of many writers, who have found him a wise, faithful, and generous friend."

This tribute was one of the pleasant incidents which marked the closing months of the year.

In the autumn of the same year, also, John G. Whittier's poem, entitled, " The Tent on the Beach," was published. Mr. Fields is introduced into this poem among a group of friends, as one of the actors upon a scene " made of such stuff " as dreams, and memories, and thoughts of summer days long past. It is a genial and characteristic picture, and one many a reader will be interested to recall.

A publisher's experience is not altogether easy nor agreeable. Having to deal with the most sensitive portion of the human race, authors, and persons of artistic temperament, unwonted to business and often untrained in character, misunderstandings arise, and worst of all, unfaith.

"Unfaith in aught is want of faith in all."

Such tokens of confidence and sympathy, therefore, are a positive encouragement and assistance, inspiring courage for days to come.

"Plymouth, N. H., *June*, 1868. One of the loveliest villages in New England. There is a little black boy here full of impishness who was in high excitement yesterday at the arrival of a traveling band. He was set in motion immediately, showing a real talent for dancing just as soon as the harp and violin began. The barber joined with his flute, having invited the company into his room. Country people soon collect at the sound of music, and the place was quickly filled. The boy, who was as heavy as a feather, danced away with one eye on the keeper of the house (fearing his disapproval of such gayety), and one on Mr. Fields to see if he appreciated the performance, with lapses of perfect obliviousness, when the love of the dance filled his whole little being, and he became forgetful of everything except the pleasure of rhythmic motion. By and by an old farmer of eighty years joined the group. He stood and watched attentively for a short time. Suddenly he said, ' I can't stand this,' and stripping off his coat joined the dance — doing the double shuffle with the vigor inspired by his memory of the flying blood of twenty years. . . .

"*July,* 1868.   Drove to Newcastle, the island at the mouth of Portsmouth harbor, where there is a fort, old now and disused, also a new one begun and left unfinished.   A sea-mist and a gray sky prevented us from enjoying the colors of the ocean and the shore, so beautiful here on a clear summer afternoon, but the cool damp air was very grateful.   ' J.' had not visited this place since a child.   It seemed to him then the *Ultima Thule,* the distant fountain head of holiday delights. The same three bridges remained to be crossed to-day which he passed over then ; the little islets on either side were unchanged, and the looks of the people.   He knew the name of the old toll-keeper and inquired for him, but the young girl who ran out to take the money only remembered the name of such a person as having been toll-keeper there many years ago.

"There are few places in America so primitive as Newcastle is now, the small neat cottages with sea-chest and pictures within, reminding one incessantly of Dickens's immortal Yarmouth.   One old fat man was smoking his pipe in the decayed fort as we crossed the yard, but the sentry-box was empty, and the round tower or lookout was capped with green, recalling the famous old buildings of the same shape on the Appian Way without bringing disdain upon its own head.   Visitors were evidently an unaccustomed sight.   Even the minister, who was bidding ' good-day ' at a cottage-door as we came into view, ended his visit rather hurriedly as I alighted by the road-side, that he might plod leisurely onward, his books under his arm, and gain opportunity for an occasional furtive glance in our direction.   As I have said, Mr. Fields had not seen the place since his childhood, and there was a pleasing connection in his mind between boyhood's holiday and the quaint town delightful to see. The houses were hardly changed at all. If our horse had not proved himself more competent than ourselves to untie the clumsy fastening with which we bound him, we could easily have lost an hour around the old light-house.

" Returning to Portsmouth the length of our journey was beguiled by his quaint fancies as to what the boys 'Shindy Cotton,' or 'Gundy Gott,' would think of this new school-house, or that widened street. Passing an old bridge he remembered to have been fishing there one day when the 'boy's company' (there was always a boys' company in Portsmouth) drew up by the side of the bridge, and saluted him and his companions. It appears he had been the captain of the company himself previously, but graduated from that honor as he grew beyond a certain age. He christened it 'The Woodbury Whites.' Also he pointed out an old-fashioned house where three young ladies, the beauties of the town, then lived. As we drove through one of the pleasantest streets he would tell me without looking what the names were on the doors. Some of the large houses looked very comfortable and lovely with their grand trees and gardens sloping to the water side.

" As we drove home with the sea-mist in our faces, the road growing moist and cool as night approached, the place seemed as redolent of associations as it was of country odors. Passed the night at the Rockingham House, formerly the governor's mansion, and as yet very little changed. The rooms are still haunted by the stately figures which so few years ago walked up and down the halls.

" Went to Kittery Fore-Side, and to see the residence of Sir William Pepperell. It is much disfigured, though still retaining the old hall and a cupboard of real beauty. An old woman opened the door; ' I 've been a nappin,' she said, ' and I 'd no idee the door was locked.' When we involuntarily expressed pleasure at the fine old hall, she replied : ' Well! I don't think you 'd like it if yer lived here ; it 's a dusty old place, and stands just as it did when the old gentleman was alive.' It was not difficult to fancy vessels landing at the foot of the pleasant green slope, or to see gentlemen in small clothes, and ladies in hoops moving through the stately entrance. . . . On our way to the Pepperell mansion we passed another house of apparently equal antiquity. Nothing had been done for many years to preserve the place from decay, and even in the cheerful light of that exquisite afternoon it would be hard to find anything more dolorous than its aspect and suggestion. The windows were, many of them, broken, the roof of the barn had fallen in, one of the other out buildings had only one wooden wall still standing, which creaked in the breeze as it swayed towards its fall; the luxuriant shrubbery, with the freshness of the season upon it, was the only thing that chimed with the living. As we came upon this spectral habitation J. recalled the strange history of the family to whom the place belonged. It looked utterly deserted now ; even the fence and the gate were in ruins, and a panel had fallen from the front door. We pushed the gate, but the hinges were rusted and would not allow us to go in. Finding an aperture in the broken fence, we clambered through. As we went toward the house a window opened, and a woman as gray as the moss on the surrounding trees looked out and asked what we wanted. She was bleared and wandering, and wretched, but her voice was neither rough nor untaught. The sight of such lonely misery was terrible. It was like holding parley with a ghost. . . .

"How blue the water was, how beautiful the sails, how brilliantly the light-houses shone in the afternoon sun, — these things can never be told! Nor the solitude of that life!

" *October* 29, 1868. The firm of Ticknor and Fields no longer exists. Fields, Osgood & Co. is the new name; it sounds unfamiliar to the ear of the public, who for many years have seen the above imprint.

"I find that Mr. Fields has edited several books of late for which he has seen a place. In 1861, 'Favorite Authors,' containing a portrait of Hawthorne; in 1864, 'Household Friends,' with a portrait of Tennyson; in 1866, 'Good Company,' with an engraving of Whittier. Also, he has printed privately a small volume of poems called, 'A Few Verses for a Few Friends,' inscribed to E. P. W. In response to this little book he received the following poem from John G. Whittier : —

TO J. T. F.

ON A BLANK LEAF OF " POEMS PRINTED, NOT PUBLISHED."

WELL thought! who would not rather hear
The songs to Love and Friendship sung

Than those which move the stranger's tongue,
And feed his unselected ear?

Our social joys are more than fame;
Life withers in the public look.
Why mount the pillory of a book,
Or barter comfort for a name?

.   .   .   .   .   .

We are but men; no gods are we,
To sit in mid-heaven, cold and bleak,
Each separate, on his painful peak,
Thin-cloaked in self-complacency!

.   .   .   .   .   .

Let such as love the eagle's scream
Divide with him his home of ice;
For me shall gentler notes suffice, —
The valley-song of bird and stream;

The pastoral bleat, the drone of bees,
The flail-beat chiming far away,
The cattle-low, at shut of day,
The voice of God in leaf and breeze!

Then lend thy hand, my wiser friend,
And help me to the vales below
(In truth, I have not far to go),
Where sweet with flowers the fields extend.

The diary continues: —

"*November*, 1868. Mr. Fields met Charles Sumner at dinner, and advanced the subject of copyright, saying he hoped that question would still be foremost in his mind as he prepared to take his place in the new government. 'But do you know,' said Sumner, in his most serious way, 'what a pecuniary loss it will be to your house to have this measure carried?' 'Yes,' was the reply, 'but *fiat justitia, ruat* House of Fields, Osgood & Co.' Of course, a hearty laugh was the immediate response. . . .

A gentleman called, who gave Mr. Fields a pleasant anecdote of Halleck. He and his wife chanced to be coming to Boston in the same car with Halleck the year before his death. He intended to stop at Stamford, which was then his home, but being in a conversational mood, to their surprise he did not move when they arrived at that station. 'Are you not to stop at Stamford to-day?' the lady asked. He looked up in amazement, saying, as he took his friend's hand, 'The conversation of your wife has so interested and absorbed me that I have been, what never occurred before in the course of my long life, unconscious of the journey.' The good lady had scarcely opened her lips; but what genius for listening! . . .

"Dr. Brewer came to talk about birds. Always an interesting subject to Mr. Fields. First, he read a paper he had written for the 'Atlantic Monthly,' and between and after the reading gave us little glimpses of his experience. Once he was in the woods of Nova Scotia studying the Hermit Thrush. He had just begun to suspect there were two varieties, and was eager in his pursuit of the study. He came upon a nest of the rarest variety in the thick woods, and finding the old birds gone hastily took the nest and its contents, consisting of several eggs, away into the light of an open space not far off. Just as the eggs were blown, and the nest arranged for transportation, the old birds returned. Their cry of lamentation was so touching that 'I would have

put the eggs all back in a minute if I could,' he continued. The sound was quite unlike the birds' ordinary
cry.

"He spoke of the mocking-bird, and referred to Longfellow's beautiful lines upon him in 'Evangeline.' He
once owned a mocking-bird, one accounted of superior
value not because of his song, but from his tender fa-
miliarities. He lived chiefly out of the cage, which
made him a cause of household anxiety, and in spite of
all care finally drowned himself at the wash-stand in his
master's room. In fly season he would perch on the finger and be carried round the walls, darting at every fly
as he went and devouring them with astonishing celerity.
One day Dr. B.'s mother having made a fine batch of
pies for Thanksgiving, — mince, apple, and squash, —
and spread them out in 'the spare room' to cool, the bird
selected one made of the minced meat, pulled the crust
off, and began to enjoy himself. Being discovered at this
crisis, the old lady put all the pies on a large tray and
was about to shut them up, when, seeing her intention,
and her hands being fully occupied in holding the sides
of the tray, the bird flew down and pulled her cap off.

"Speaking of the robin, he told us his daughter
watched a pair on the piazza for twenty days, feeding
their young with the larvæ of insects every half hour
until they were strong enough to fly. In this way the
garden was preserved from innumerable enemies. His
paper was an indirect plea for the introduction of the
English house sparrow, of which so much has been said
lately.

"*January*, 1869. — William Lloyd Garrison came in.

He had been sitting with Charles Sprague "comparing notes." Mr. Sprague told Mr. Garrison he could never forget three sights he had seen from the windows of the old Globe Bank in Wilson's Lane, where he was em-ployed for many years. One was seeing a man with a bald head (meaning Garrison) maltreated by an angry mob and borne along the street; the second, the capture of Anthony Burns; the third, the marching of the first colored regiment, under Colonel Shaw, on their way Southward. In return, Garrison was able to tell him of the delight he had in setting up in type a certain Shake-speare Ode."

A letter from Mr. Garrison, written in 1866, may not be out of place here : —

"Roxbury, *March* 26, 1866.

"Dear Mr. Fields, — I fear it may have seemed to you either a singular forgetfulness, or something of in-difference, on my part, that you have not received any definite answer from me in regard to your proposition, made some time ago, that I would write a history of the Anti-Slavery movement for publication by your firm. Be assured, however, that while that proposition was very gratifying to me, and while I have had it constantly in mind ever since it was made, I have deemed it worthy of the gravest consideration before committing myself *pro* or *con*. But I will not delay any longer. Let me state, with brevity and frankness, some of the difficulties in my way.

"In the first place, I have been so closely connected with the movement, from its inception to its completion,

— not with any design or expectation of my own, *ab initio*, for I never thought of rising to public conspicuity, but only of inducing such as had already won distinction to lead in the great undertaking — that to virtually ignore that connection, by the most incidental reference to myself, might seem to savor of affectation; while on the other hand, it would be a delicate task to decide to what extent I might refer to my trials and labors without seeming egotism. Personally, I feel no interest in the matter, whether made visible or invisible in the pages of the contemplated history; for as I espoused the cause of the crushed and fettered millions at the South without dreaming of notoriety or fame, so, now that their emancipation is achieved, I have no wish to take any other than the humblest position of all who have labored to the same glorious end, and feel willing to be wholly dropped out of sight.

" My next difficulty (and it really looks very formidable) is the great condensing power, — equal to anything found in hydraulics or hydrostatics, — that will be requisite to embody, in a popular shape, the various phases and ramifications of the mightiest and most protracted struggle in behalf of the rights of human nature that the world has ever seen.

" How shall the ocean be put into a gallon measure? And if only a gallon is furnished, what idea of the ocean is given? To say nothing of preliminary chapters respecting the rise and progress of slavery and the slave-trade, particularly as relating to our colonial history and to the pro-slavery concessions made in the formation of the Constitution of the United States, —

there have been thirty-six years (from 1829 to 1865) of discussion and conflict, shaking Church and State to their foundations, and culminating in the dismemberment of the republic *pro tempore*, but happily ending in a restored Union, the Anti-Slavery amendment of the Constitution, and the total abolition of slavery. An almost incredible number of books, pamphlets, tracts, periodicals, speeches, essays, reviews, narratives, reports, etc., etc., all directly bearing upon the subject, have been published during that long period, the careful examination of which would prove a laborious task indeed. A faithful and reliable history, therefore, would require I know not how voluminous a work; but I feel sure that the materials furnished by each decade would amply suffice for a duodecimo volume of four hundred pages. What size or shape would make the work the most salable, and therefore best suit the market, you are far better able to judge than I am.

"Another serious difficulty is to know how to 'keep the pot boiling' while devoting so much time to the preparation of such a work, with no adequate pecuniary resources of my own, and with no way of augmenting them, except by engaging in something that will secure me immediate and regular remuneration. For if I once began, I should wish to be unremitting in my labors to complete the history in the shortest time practicable.

"In a day or two, I will see you, and learn what you may be able to suggest or propose concerning these difficulties.

"Very truly yours,
"WM. LLOYD GARRISON.
"JAMES T. FIELDS, ESQ."

" *March* 15. — Mr. Fields had an unusually turbulent and exciting day. A constant series of interviews with every variety of person. One of his most absorbing calls was from a young man who has lately abandoned the Shakers. For three years he has been trying to get away and has only just now succeeded. He is a man of marked intellect. At the age of sixteen (he is now a little over twenty) he was placed at the head of their school in Canterbury as chief instructor.

" He awakes at night, he says, in paroxysms of horror at the memory of the terrible life and terrible deeds he has seen performed among this people. He came to them when he was two years old, his father being a religious fanatic, and wishing his wife and two children to go with him. They did so, but are now all free. He left the Shakers with ten dollars in his pocket to face the world. His friends are all among them and he is perfectly ignorant of the ways of the world. In two or three cases he has known of young girls becoming unhappy and leaving the Shakers only to fall into wretchedness and misery. He says he has been slain intellectually and morally. When he remembers the confessional (for they have it also as in the Catholic churches), and the foolish things he has been led to recount as sins to the elders, he can hardly contain his indignation."

" LONDON, *Tuesday*, *May* 11, 1869. Dickens has been to see us four times to-day, beside a long walk with Mr. Fields along the new Thames embankment. . . .

" *Wednesday.* Dined with Dickens. Arranged to go to the little hospital at Stepney. 'A small star in the east.'

"*Friday*, he came at half-past ten A. M. to go to the hospital, bringing with him some small alleviations for colds, with recipes. Started promptly, and by aid of omnibus, cars, and a short walk, arrived before noon at our destination. Dickens was perfectly at home in this part of London. He was full of interest also in the young physician and his wife at the hospital, who looked upon him as one of their best friends. It was evidently always their gala day when he arrived. He could not say enough to express his admiration for the simple, reverent earnestness of their lives. 'How they bear it,' he said, 'I cannot imagine. I wish you could have seen,' he continued, 'the little child I wrote of, who died afterward, so exquisite in beauty and so patient, its rounded cheek so pale. Certainly there is nothing more touching than the suffering of a child, nothing more overwhelming.' The doctor carried us, before our return, into one of the poor-houses in the neighborhood. A mother, father, and seven children in one room! And yet, he said, this was not an extreme case. . . .

"ISLE OF WIGHT, *June*. Walked to Mrs. Cameron's quiet cottage near the sea. She was expecting us, having expressed a wish to photograph M—— and J. She drew the latter into a darkened room, rearranging his dress to suit her artistic ends, and began her work. It was not the labor of a moment, but the result was most satisfactory. She said, characteristically, of the persons whom she invited to sit, that she only 'took the young, the fair, and the famous.' Her eye was quick as an eagle's to detect the qualities she wished to convey into her pictures; and her vision was as individual as it was keen. Her appreciation of her friends, her enthusiasm for them, was unbounded. Writing to Mr. Fields after we left, she says: ' Mr. and Mrs. Tennyson have spoken with pleasure of your visit, and I can entirely understand the eternal delight it is to you to have dwelt with them in their dear home. . . . Only in this way can one fully estimate either his or her most beautiful and endearing qualities. His immortal powers, of course, are conveyed in his books, but very few come to a perfect and real appreciation of him who have not seen him in the intimacy of private life. . . . You will see how perfect and valuable these impressions are (of photographs which she presented with this note), and I delight in making a gift of them to those who I know to be so worthy of the gift as you are. . . .

" GAD'S HILL PLACE, *June.* Mr. Fields has himself recorded, in ' Yesterdays with Authors,' whatever he considered interesting to the reader connected with this visit.

" AMBLESIDE. Mr. Fields enjoyed a few hours with Harriet Martineau, who had just received a letter, full of good cheer about India, from Florence Nightingale. She was eager to talk of her ' Autobiography,' trying to arrange everything in view of her death, although she was constantly seeing friends pass before her into the Unseen. She was full of interest in public affairs, and talked unceasingly.

" Miss Martineau's letters, as the world knows, are replete with valuable suggestion and characterized by clear, individual expression. In view, however, of the careful selection already made by herself and her friends, it is thought wise to include nothing further here.

" After leaving Miss Martineau, we drove over Kirkstone Pass, and walking a short distance from the hotel, which is said to be built at the highest elevation of any house in England, looked down into the Vale of Patterdale. A more lonely spot could not be imagined than it looked that summer afternoon, from the height of Kirkstone.

" At Furness Abbey we found a dwarf of the smallest possible dimensions, hardly taller than the tall grass among the stones. In spite of the solitude in which we found him, he seemed to possess an equal love for ruins and conversation. His hair and cap appeared to be of exactly the same fibre and color, looking as if black grass had grown up tall through a barred helmet. When he pushed back the cap in his excitement to show us 'how he did it,' that is, how he went in among the lions and bears, and pretended to be eaten, it was a sight worth going far to behold. He wanted a dummy to play the part of a bear, and looked wistfully at J., but suddenly gave him up, in his own mind, as inappropriate.

" At Lowwood, where the perfect stillness allowed every sound to be heard across the water, Mr. Fields amused me by relating one of his escapades. He was standing on the edge of the lake in a curve of the road, with a portfolio of photographs under his arm, which he was bringing to show me, when an old gentleman with his two nieces approached. They had not the least idea they could be heard. 'I lay ye half a crown,' said the old gentleman, 'that he's not an artist.' 'I'll take you up, uncle,' said the prettiest of the girls. 'What makes you think so,' rejoined the uncle. 'Because of the stoop in his shoulders,' said the girl, 'and when I come up with him I 'll ask him.' 'I 'll lay ye ninepence ye wont do that,' said he. 'But I will,' said she, 'if you say I may.' True enough, when the party approached, the blushing young girl stepped up to him and said, 'Excuse me, sir, my uncle and I have made a little bet as to your profession, if you don't mind telling us. I shall be glad if you decide in my favor. Are you an artist?' 'I shall be most happy to decide in your favor,' he replied, and with a low bow, in perfect sobriety, departed, leaving the shrewd old man, who evidently hated to part with his sixpences, counting them out in the road to the satisfaction of his niece.

" He heard a bell tolling in the tower of the little church near by, and seeing two old men sitting on a gravestone, said to one of them, 'What is this bell tolling for ?' 'Please, sir, 't is one of our hold friends, sir, who be just gone to his long 'ome, sir, and we wos just awaitin' 'ere, sir, till his body do be brought along.' This form of speech is common here.

" The old gardener at Dunster said, speaking of Minehead church, which we could barely see on the distant hills, and the Luttrell possessions: 'They do hown, sir, about as far as you can see, sir, from Minehead church, sir, as far as *we*.' Again of the ivy: 'He 's a fine plant, sir, he 's a werry old plant, sir.'

" *July* 4. Stratford-on-Avon, with those loyal friends to America and Americans, Mr. and Mrs. Flower. . . . Thence to Malvern. Climbed the Malvern Hills on don-

12

keys. Found an old woman on one of the summits sell-
ing gingerbread and beer. It was blowing hard with a
thick fog. Mr. Fields inquired of her respecting the
weather : ' Well, sir,' she said, ' I've 'ad the plumbago
now for two days, sir, wich is as good as a halmanac, sir,
honly not so conwenient.'

" Came to Clevedon, sacred to the memory of Arthur
Hallam. High, overlooking the river Severn. We lingered there ; the place possesses a deep interest for all
lovers of Tennyson and the Hallams. Came to Devon-
shire. Found an old-fashioned garden behind the inn at
Tiverton quite at our service. . . . We begin to find
quaint names — Innocent Witherstone, Ezekiel Hear,
Elizabeth Bobby, Selina Skipwith — good for a novel.

" *Dunster.* Wonderful old place. Again we could
fancy traces of Tennyson's observation and description.
Hotel, formerly an abbey, with ancient garden behind.
Terrace overlooking the sea. At the castle an old gardener, proud of the family and his position, which he has
held for sixty years. A sleeping palace — beautiful in
decay. Came into the village at dusk ; saw remains of
all kinds of birds and animals, inimical to the farmers'
good, nailed up outside the door of an old stone barn ; a
singer in the streets, dancing as he sang, and shouting to
the children, ' get off the carpet, get off the forum ;' the
old church doors open, the choir preparing for Sunday
service ; fresh girlish voices.

" *Sunday*, at Lynton. A little garden outside our window bounded by a hedge, thence a steep descent to the
sea, with pines, chestnuts, and beeches covering the slope
to the shingly shore below; the sound of the water is

heard perpetually. In the distance the beach curves as at Baiæ, giving a perfect view of the strand and cliffs sloping in enormous waves of red and green declivity to the opal sea. Drove from Lynton over bits of moor, between high hedges, with the purple heather coming out in fringes along the way ; rounding headlands with the sea constantly in view. On to Ilfracombe, where the chief delight was to lie on rocks and fancy ourselves at home. . . .

"SWITZERLAND, *August.* Talking of the Grimsel in bad weather, Mr. Fields said : ' He hated to be dragged up where the Devil carried the best man that ever lived.' We did *not* go over the Grimsel ! . . .

"BOSTON, U. S. A., *November*, 1869. We light the first fire on our library hearth, and somehow feel a little solemnity about it, as if it were for a high festival. Our boxes have all arrived at length from England. The original portrait of Pope, painted by Richardson, master of Sir Joshua Reynolds, and purchased by Mr. Fields while in London from the gallery of the Marquis of Hastings, is hung up."

In the autumn of this year James Russell Lowell printed his poem, "The Cathedral," with the following dedication : —

"TO MR. JAMES T. FIELDS.

"MY DEAR FIELDS, — Dr. Johnson's sturdy self-respect led him to invent the Bookseller as a substitute for the Patron. My relations with you have enabled me to discover how pleasantly the Friend may replace the Bookseller. Let me record my sense of many thoughtful services by associating your name with a poem which owes its appearance in this shape to your partiality.

"Cordially yours,

"J. R. LOWELL.

"CAMBRIDGE, *November* 29, 1869."

In the winter of 1870 Mr. Fields's health began to give way. The voyages, the excitement of travel, and his return to business responsibilities, proved too much even for his excellent constitution. His sleep was broken and his spirits suffered. He who had been the life of every feast was often silent and fatigued. His strength seemed to fade away from him, and after any little exertion or excitement he would fall asleep from utter exhaustion. That winter was like a valley of shadows which led us in June to Dickens's grave.

The summer was a very warm one, and Mr. Fields continued to go to town from Manchester-by-the-Sea daily, with few exceptions. There was cause for anxiety about his health. He seemed tired, as Mrs. Hawthorne once said of herself, "far into the future." Nevertheless those days by the shore were restoring in their influence, and the autumn found him better and slow to leave.

"Who knows if we shall ever see that glorious sight again together! The waves were very high, a gorgeous sunset sent its late yellow shafts out over the gray sea, the foam broke on the distant rocks like a sudden burst of soft white blooms, it was all vast, glorious, indescribable. We sat on the sandhills, overlooking the beach and the wide scene for an hour. It never appeared to us more lovely. Coming back we scrambled over Thunderbolt Hill, and saw the sunset among the red sumach and ripening apples.

"TUESDAY, *November* 1, 1870. We begin this month with different feelings from any I could have anticipated. . . . The weight of this great business house is no longer to rest where it has done. It is a cloud behind us. Mr. Fields is like a different man already. . . .

"*January*, 1871. A visit from William Hunt. One of the most dramatic creatures who ever lived. He told a story of a student from the South who came to Harvard University with a colored servant. Returning to his rooms one night (or day) at four o'clock in the morning, he found a company of negroes leaning back in his chairs, smoking his cigars and drinking his sherry. With a grace Hunt could not sufficiently admire, the young man walked through the rooms as if he did not see its occupants, whereat they all crumbled away, nobody knew where, only his own man remained, who, as quick as thought, gathered the bottles under his coat, and when his master *did* look round was furiously dusting the room with a feather duster. Hunt's mimicry of the whole scene was inimitable.

"His delight, too, over the Cameron photographs! 'Go 'way,' he said, getting into a corner with one of them, as if it were a piece of cake, and he four years old. 'I don't want anybody to see it till I 've done with it.' I held a second one for his inspection. 'No, no,' he said, '*he* may have that, (pointing to T——), and I 'll keep this!' It was so absurdly like a child, and yet done with such real feeling that it was very comic.

"He loves to tell stories of animals, especially one of going to a place in Paris, where the man had only a monkey and an elephant to exhibit. He was determined, therefore, to make the most of the show. He arrayed the elephant, (who just fitted in to the apartment with no room at all left over,) with a napkin about him, as if he were dining; and the monkey, dressed as a garçon de café, came dancing in with the plates one after another He would enter with long strides, flinging down the tin plate before the elephant with perfect nonchalance, so long as it contained salads and the like; but when it came to the nuts and raisins, his dance was altogether vertical, he being occupied with gobbling up the contents on the way. Finally, on arriving at the elephant, he would fling the empty plate before him with a grand air. In Hunt's hands this became a little drama, in which he played all the parts with infinite amusement.

"He caught himself, as he said, the other night, daring to look at a little charcoal drawing of his own, hanging on the wall behind him in our room. 'That heather,' he said, 'with the starry blooms! the paper is left, there is no white laid on; there never could be any white put on to shine like that! I wonder who the fellar was who did it! It was done with a great piece of charcoal which just left the spots clear. Ha! I 'd like to see the man who could do that again! I could n't! By George! I tell you what, look at that little bit (drawing his finger round and round the heather-top), the fellar must have known he had done a good thing by the time that was finished.' . . .

Last night Hunt came. He 'played' he was a manikin, — figure of Napoleon at St. Helena, also Mrs. Smith; nothing could be more laughable. He sang, too, with much feeling, always protesting he had forgotten both words and tune.

" Tried to read aloud, which he said he never could do. He so bewitched the meaning that we were overwhelmed with laughter. As for E—, Mr. Fields said he laughed until ' his eyes left their wonted sockets, and went to laugh far back in his brain.'

" Putting down the book Hunt launched into a sea of talk upon his own life as a painter ; of his lonely position here without any one to look up to in his art ; his idea being misunderstood; of his determination not to paint cloth and cheeks, but the glory of age and the light of truth. He became almost too excited to find words ; but when he did grasp a phrase it was with a power that sent his meaning, barbed with feeling, home. ' If the books you wrote were left dusty and untouched upon the shelves, don't you think you 'd try to write so that people should want them ? I am sure you would.'

" BOSTON, *May* 12, 1871. Third meeting of officers of the Army of the Potomac. [Bret Harte was expected to read the poem. On the previous evening he wrote to say he could not come in person, but would send his verses. It was an important occasion. Generals Sheridan, Meade, Hooker, and many others, were present, who had won the right to be forever loved and remembered by the people. A committee waited upon Mr. Fields to ask him to read the verses. Bret Harte was then at the height of his popularity; public curiosity was alive to see him, and a feeling of disappointment must greet any one who should stand in his place; beside, the verses did not arrive. It was an unwelcome duty at the best, but accepting it as the least he could do for the men who had fought as these had done, Mr. Fields wrote a few verses himself which might introduce the others in case they arrived, or preface some apology, telegraphed to Harte, and one hour before the ceremonies opened at the Globe Theatre, received his manuscript from New York. In that short time it was studied, read and re-read, and prepared for public presentation.]

"CATSKILL, *June.* Our boy-driver had never read Irving's story, but had often heard of Rip Van Winkle. 'Who wrote the story, do you know?' asked Mr. Fields. 'Washington, did n't he?' was the reply. He said his father came 'from those parts,' and had told him the story over and over until he was curious to come and see the place. It was 'all flat' at the West, where he passed his boyhood, 'and the fust time I saw this, I tell you! I never thought there could be such a place. Well! I just come to see it, and I 've stayed here ever since, nigh on three year.' The place where Rip had his long sleep, and where a small wayside inn now stands, overlooks a wonderful valley through a natural gorge. The sunset light made everything radiant as we ascended. Coming to the summit with hands full of laurel blooms, we went out upon the magnificent plateau, and hardly left it again until we were obliged to come away altogether. In the

moonlight we heard the tree-toads calling, and everything else that lives and stirs in the woods in the deep-
ening hours. The sky was 'living sapphire' where the
sun had left it long before, the stars and planets were
appearing in the east, the trees stood as if cut upon the
steeps of heaven, and the whole scene was solemn with
night and loveliness. . . .

" Some one was speaking of the dishonest manage-
ment of the Erie Railroad. Mr. Fields said, ' The Bible
says : Buy the Truth and sell it not ; the Erie men say,
Buy the Truth and sell it out for a profit.'

" *November* 6, 1871. Mr. Fields 'lectured' in Boston.

" *December.* Continues to lecture ; making additions
and changes continually in his essays. . . . Went to hear
Horace Greeley 'On Wit.' It was a singular agglomera-
tion of matter. Old Miller jokes, combined with quotations from the dramatists. Strange enough in manner
also. His sole gesture being to paddle the fingers of one
hand as if he were thrumming a piano. He was dab-
bling his finger-tips in water he had spilled from the
tumbler upon the table in order to turn the leaves more
easily. It was a bad night, and the audience was small,
but Greeley was content with his one friendly listener.
' Good, ain't it ? ' he said, after it was over.

" *January,* 1872. Mr. Fields is continually lecturing
and overflowing with singular 'experiences.' He is writing a paper upon ' Tennyson ' (this was the first sketch
of the future lecture), to read before a small private
company next week.

" *January* 25. Lectured at L——. Crowded house ;
pretty town ; the moon was up, but it was very cold ;

walked out on the snow between moon-set and sunrise; returned to breakfast at home in Boston. Described the good man who kept the hotel in L——. 'Now,' said he, 'after the lecter to-night, I shall give ye,—oysters,— hot.' Returning, there was some delay about the oysters. Presently the landlord appeared, bringing them himself. 'Military ball here last night, — cook as mad as thunder, — but here are yer oysters!' putting them down triumphantly. When they were fairly on the table he turned to Mr. Fields : 'I was in to-night.' 'Yes,' said Mr. Fields, 'I saw you.' 'Did!' (with faint intonation of surprise). 'Well, Mr. Foster and I was a-talkin' of it comin' out, and sayin' we thought 't was abaout as good a lecter as we 'd ever hed here.' "

Mr. Fields was subject at this time to severe colds, which attacked the lungs, and occasionally prevented him from fulfilling his engagements; to be stopped coming out of a lecture room to hear " a good story," which somebody had been saving till that unfortunate moment, or to be detained on a windy corner, were sure to bring him more or less discomfort.

" *May.* Revolving plans for a course of free lectures for women upon English literature, to be given during the autumn ; something to bring the audience of women together who are longing for a better education ; to be able to look it over and understand the need."

As a result of Mr. Fields's labors in behalf of a larger opportunity for women desiring an education, the following article from his hand soon appeared in the newspapers of the day, shortly followed by the advertisement appended. These serve to show how generously his friends responded to his appeal for their assistance in his plans : —

"Good News for Women. — During the months of October, November, and December of this year, on Saturday afternoons, at three o'clock, in the large hall of the Technological Institute, there will be given a free course of twelve lectures to women on subjects connected with English literature. These lectures are not to be reported in the papers, or printed in book-form. The following eloquent lecturers are already engaged for each Saturday in the above months, beginning October 5: Ralph Waldo Emerson, Phillips Brooks, Oliver Wendell Holmes, Edwin P. Whipple, Wendell Phillips, George S. Hillard, James Freeman Clarke, William R. Alger, John Weiss, George William Curtis.

"It is the design, we presume, of this course of free lectures to introduce a scheme of instruction for women which shall give to them the advantages so long afforded to students in universities. It is the beginning of a plan which will be hailed with delight wherever the full and proper education of women has been discussed. This course will no doubt be followed by others in the sciences, etc., and Boston will have the credit of starting a plan which is sure to end in university education for women in various parts of the country.

"We understand there are to be no tickets of admission issued, but that all women (and only women are to be admitted to the hall, as there will be no room for others) who wish to avail themselves of such a course in English literature will go early enough to take their places. The hall will seat between eight and nine hundred only, and is to be opened at two o'clock and closed promptly at three, to avoid any interruption after the lecture of the day has commenced. School teachers especially are to be benefited by this course, and if the hall were double its size it would not be large enough to accommodate all the women who will wish to be present.

"The idea of this provision for the instruction of women is a noble one, and is another evidence that the world moves."

Later the following advertisement appeared : —

"A free course of twelve lectures to women on subjects connected with English literature, will be given in the large hall of the Technological Institute, during the months of October, November, and December, 1872.

"To commence on Saturday afternoon, October 5, at 3 o'clock, and to be continued every Saturday afternoon following, at the same hour, until the series is ended in December.

"The lecturers for October are Mrs. E. D. Cheney, Edwin P. Whipple, John Weiss, Oliver Wendell Holmes.

"The lecturers for November are George S. Hillard, Phillips Brooks, Wendell Phillips, Robert Collyer, William R. Alger.

"The lecturers for December are Ralph Waldo Emerson, James Freeman Clarke, George William Curtis.

" The hall will be opened at 2½ o'clock each Saturday, and closed precisely at 3. Seats are provided for nine hundred ladies, who will be admitted without tickets."

Perhaps there can be found no more suitable point in this " story of a life," than the one we have now reached, to incorporate a beautiful tribute to Mr. Fields received from Mrs. Mary A. Livermore, and written during a rapid tour in Europe in the summer of 1881. This journey, prescribed to Mrs. Livermore by her physician after a season of unusual fatigue, was to be a period of rest ; therefore surprise and gratitude were both aroused by the reception of this letter from her in the early summer. Mrs. Livermore writes : —

" LONDON, ENGLAND, *June* 15, 1881.

" I shall never forget the first time I met Mr. Fields. It was during the war, and when I was living in Chicago. The great need of funds to carry on the work of the Sanitary Commission had driven the women of the northwest to the last resort — a grand fair. It was the first of the series of great fairs which yielded immense sums of money to the Sanitary Commission, and, unlike those which followed it, it was projected and carried on almost entirely by women. All available women were harnessed into the various departments of the fair ; and the committee having in charge the publication of the daily fair paper, desiring that its brief life of three weeks should be a brilliant one, I was despatched to Boston for assistance.

" I was instructed to secure, if possible, the services of a lady, then 'a bright particular star' in the literary world. I only knew that Mr. Fields was the lady's publisher, and so, without letters of introduction, and unaccompanied, I sought him at his office, and introduced myself and my errand. Fully aware that my errand might seem quixotic or infinitesimal to the great publisher, I was prepared for a cool reception.

" I shall always remember the great courtesy and kindness with which Mr. Fields received me. I was at ease directly. He listened with interest to my story, kindled with enthusiasm as I told him of the preparations for the fair, all eminently western, of the patriotic audacity of the women of the northwest, who proposed to raise $100,000 for their sick and wounded 'boys in blue,' and immediately put himself at our service, and sought to make my errand successful.

" I failed of accomplishing what I sought, but it was not through any indifference or lack of effort on the part of Mr. Fields. Seemingly intent on aiding us, he discussed with me the details of the paper, was fertile in suggestions and hints by which we profited, and promised to solicit contributions from eminent people with whom he had relations, — a promise that he kept.

" As I rose to leave, he made inquiries concerning my experiences in hospitals, on transports, and among our sick and wounded soldiers. His face glowed, his eye moistened, as I spoke of the marvelous heroism, the indescribable patience, and the sublime resignation of men, young, with families that needed them, to whom life was full of promise, — and yet bravely suffering, and calmly dying that the nation might live.

"'This,' said he, 'is the side of the war that the people can never learn from the reports of officers, or the letters of war correspondents. When the war is over you must give us a book of your experiences, must show us *the heavenly side of the war*, and I will help you get before the world with it.'

"My interest in Mr. Fields dates from that day. I never afterwards heard his name spoken, or saw it mentioned in the papers, without recalling his courtesy and kindness, and thinking of him as a man to whom a woman might go for advice and assistance.

"Years after, when I had returned to New England to reside, I remember how all who believed in the enfranchisement of women were thrilled with his speech, made, I believe, in Portsmouth, N. H. In strong and grand words he expressed his sympathy with the struggling reform, not as hopeful in its promise as now, pronouncing it founded on eternal justice, and predicting its ultimate success at no very remote day. Glad and grateful, I hastened to write him a note of thanks, and to tell him of the good cheer his words had given us. His reply was even stronger and more earnest than his public address; and the brief note soon found its way into one of the autograph albums, arranged and sold in aid of a public charity.

"Once more Mr. Fields increased woman's indebtedness to him by organizing and successfully carrying out a free course of twelve lectures for women on English literature. So excellent were they, and so highly prized, that hardly was the large hall sufficient for the accommodation of those who sought to attend them. We had all come to recognize in Mr. Fields a friend of woman, who desired for her equal educational and legal advantages with man.

"If he arranged for women a course of literary lectures, his programme included women lecturers as well as men. If, at his charming summer retreat by the sea, he provided a series of Sunday discourses for his townspeople, he invited women to the pulpit, which he temporarily controlled, and gave them the same hearty welcome he accorded to clergymen.

"Was a woman in doubt concerning the worth of her untried lecture or undelivered essay? he placed his time, talent, and experience at her service, criticising so kindly as to win her gratitude, even when the criticism was severe. Ay, and when sometimes an unasked loan of money was needed, because of the poverty of the would-be debutante, it was voluntarily tendered; — and I have heard Mr. Fields declare that rarely were such debts unpaid.

"In conservative and cultivated circles, where his interest in woman's advancement was not known, in the far West, where his advocacy of woman suffrage had never been advertised, he was as generous in his recognition, and as just in his demands for woman, as in the society where this had come to be expected of him.

"He never passed me on the street so hurriedly that he had not time for a word of cheer or encouragement, or an inquiry into the progress of a reform, in which he believed as strongly as myself. It is not yet possible for me to realize that all this is over, that these kindnesses are ended, that his work is finished. For he was so full of life and heartiness, that it is impossible to think of him as having passed into the land of silence.

" During my brief stay in England I am continually reminded of Mr. Fields. For he brought us into such acquaintanceship with the English ' Authors of Yesterday,' that, as I come upon reminders of Dickens, Thackeray, Wordsworth, De Quincey, and other masters of literature, — sometimes in galleries of pictures, sometimes in abbeys, cathedrals, and churchyards, — their historian and interpreter immediately rises to my memory, who has now, like them, solved the eternal secret, and divined the great mystery of death.

"I cannot think of him as dead, — nor will I. For as he passed through the low gateway that opens outward, and never inward, who can doubt that he entered ' another chamber of the King's, larger than this, and lovelier ? '   Yours very sincerely,

"MARY A. LIVERMORE."

Again I return to the everyday incidents of the diary : —

" A young gentleman at dinner yesterday gave me the following anecdote of Dickens. He went one day to hear him read, and was invited afterward by a friend to be presented to Dickens. C. D. (this was most characteristic) unnecessarily asked him what he, the young listener, thought of his reading ! 'Since you ask me,' he replied, ' I think the only criticism I could make upon

13

anything which has given me so much pleasure would be to say, quite frankly, that I think it somewhat too dramatic!!' Whereat Mr. Dickens bowed, thanked him for his opinion, and the scene terminated. Years after, this gentleman was himself reading from Tennyson's poems to an audience at the Isle of Wight. After it was over, Mr. Dickens came to speak to him from among the audience. Mr. —— expressed himself greatly honored, and said he was glad to have been unconscious of his distinguished auditor. 'But what, sir, do you say of my reading?' 'Since you ask me,' said Dickens, bowing, with a laugh running all over his face. 'I must tell you that I do not find it quite dramatic enough!'

"MANCHESTER-BY-THE-SEA. *August,* 1872. The fog-bell tolls all day and all night. It is very silent here, yet nature is melodious, the airs are soft, the odors exquisite.

"Last night Mr. Fields read aloud a manuscript poem called 'The Children of Lebanon,' with great pride and feeling, as a surprise to our little circle.

"The fog-bell continues tolling. 'Are we not to have some rain,' he said, to an old farmer here. 'I guess we be,' was the reply. 'I see them 'ere thunder-pillars leanin' up agin' the Northwest!' The sea still groans. Mr. Fields fell into talk yesterday about his boyhood. The best of Scott's novels were not in his boy's library! Whatever there was he learned to know thoroughly. 'Thaddeus of Warsaw,' of course, was a prime favorite. There was a poem called 'King Alfred,' which obtained a horrible reality in his eyes. He heard his two old uncles talking it over one day, when he was a child of

six or eight years old. 'How they bent the old man,'
he heard them say.

"CHICAGO, *October*, 1872. Most hospitably received
and entertained. Beautiful autumnal weather; leaves
aglow in the park (chiefly oaks); the great lake Michigan quiet and blue. Went early to see the burnt district. Long rows of new stone fronts rise loftily where
one year ago all was dust and ashes; but the trees standing with naked arms stretching to the sky, give pathetic evidence of what has been. The fine stone and
iron walls, too, cracked and ruined, show where grand
residences, surrounded by gardens, once stood. Everybody thinks everybody else 'much changed.' The people begin to meet socially now, almost for the first time
since the public calamity. —— tells me she has never
been to see the ruins of her home, although living in
close proximity. It is hard to find people. Our first
desire was to discover Robert Collyer; but although
Unity Church was rising from its ashes, there was no
clue by which we could immediately find its pastor.

"Lecture in the evening. 'Masters of the Situation.'
Large audience, and very enthusiastic. . . . Went to
Davenport to lecture. Rode nine hours in the cars, and
spoke that same evening; took the train again after the
lecture and returned to Chicago before the world was
fairly astir. Noble audience at Davenport; first glimpse
of Mississippi River. . . . Surprised to find many
Greeley men hereabout. The farmers believe in Greeley; they like his sympathy with them, and his endeav-
ors for settling the new country.

"BOSTON, *November*. Mr. Fields is at work on his

'Tennyson' lecture, which he gives again to-morrow night. . . .

" *November* 9.   The most fearful fire New England has ever known is raging in Boston.

" *November* 21.   Mr. Fields gave ' The Masters of the Situation,' before the Young Men's Union.   The subject seems doubled in significance since our disaster, hundreds of young men and women being thrown out of employment for the winter.   Everybody's time is more or less devoted to trying to bridge over this ugly chasm. . . . Our home never looked so beautiful, nor seemed so refreshing ! . . . I look with great satisfaction at the long row of good books Mr. Fields brought into the American world while he was still a member of the publishing house. . . . Our great treat this week has been reading the second volume of Forster's ' Life of Dickens,' which was forwarded in sheets.   We hardly breathed till we had read every word. . . . Such unending power of work, such universal care for others, such intense absorption in whatever was before him, has never been portrayed before. . . .   The fun and pathos of the book brings his dear presence back to us again with intense vividness. Mr. Fields wrote at once to Forster. . . .

" Hunt's studio having burned, — utterly burned to nothing, — he has bravely taken a new one, and is at work, though his whole youth, he says, seems to have gone up in the flames.

" *April*, 1873.   Mr. Fields at home writing away upon his Charles Lamb lecture with great assiduity.   He is enjoying his work, but writes only too steadily.   I must contrive some kind of diversion.

" HANOVER, N. H., *June*.   Most hospitable reception. Pleasant old-fashioned house under green elm trees.   The lecture was given in the church where Webster, Choate, and others have addressed the College for many years. Every kind of festivity proper to the occasion ; even a serenade !

" MANCHESTER, *Sunday, August*.   Walked to church. Mr. Fields found himself lame ; returning stopped at the doctor's, who pronounced serious trouble at the knee, and gave iodine wash.

" *Monday*.   Mr. Fields went to town, saw a surgeon, and came back bringing splint, etc., etc., also two guests. . . .

" *September*.   Knee is no better.   Neighbors and friends all kind and attentive.   The hours do not seem to be long to the patient.   He is cheerful.   Reading Channing's ' Life of Thoreau ' with great satisfaction.

" CHARLES STREET, *October*.   Mr. Fields still lame, but has had a comfortable week.   Charles Sumner dined with us.   He seemed less well than of late.   He said it was frequently his habit to spend fourteen consecutive hours at his desk or in reading.   The active exercise of composition was, of course, agreeable to him in certain moods, but the passive exercise of reading was a never-ending delight.   He spoke of Lord Brougham, Mrs. Norton and her two beautiful sisters. . . . There was much wit and humor that day at table.   The ladies lingered long after coffee and cigars were brought, that they might not lose the conversation.   Heard a good story of a deaf man lately married, who was asked at the Club about his bride : ' Is she pretty ? '   ' No,' replied the deaf gentleman.   ' No, she is not, but she will be when her father dies ! '

" *November*. Mr. Fields's course of lectures at the Lowell Institute began while he was still wearing a splint. Amusing anecdotes connected with his lectures are continually recurring. He met a man a day or two ago who said he liked his lectures, 'for there did n't seem to be any of that shycanery in 'em so many people now-a-days put in.' Another said, 'his wife was amazed to see how interested she got in hearin' about these folks she 'd never known nothin' about before; but she 'd like to ask who that ' North ' was anyhow ! (This was said after the lecture on ' Christopher North, John Wilson.')

" His own relation of an evening in a certain town of Massachusetts, where a long train of people came up to be introduced in succession with a ready-made speech, was very dramatic and comic. Last in the line came a grandmother holding her grandchild by the hand. Having made the regulation speech herself, the child also addressed him with the same words and in a piping voice, which proved almost too much for the gravity of the lecturer. A certain definition of eloquence by one of his hearers was also given that same night. 'That 's what I call ellerquence,' he said ; ' I tell my wife I allus know what seems to me ellerquence by kind o' shivers which runs up and down my back. Well! In one of your pieces I felt them shivers all over ; — that 's what I call real ellerquence.'

" *August* 31, 1874. Ground broken for our sea-side house. The stone-cutters turned in with a will.

" BOSTON, *September*. Very hot. Glad to think that ' Thunder Bolt Hill ' is ours.

" PLYMOUTH, N. H. Mr. Fields continues at work on

his Wordsworth lecture. He has just read, first with
amusement, and then wonderingly, that characteristic passage where Wordsworth says of his own poetry : no one
who has come at length to an admiration of his (Wordsworth's) poems has ever been known to survive their
satisfaction."

" *Monday Evening, September* 14. A soft haze has
overspread the hills to-day, indicating heat, but the cool
breezes blow so delightfully about this place that we have
not felt it. Took a long drive to Squam Lake and Hol-
derness over a steep hill. It was very like some of the
passes, perhaps Kirkstone, in the English lake country,
and no less beautiful ; but the solitude here is more vast
and unbroken. We passed a square brick house with a
roof of shingles, belted around by a forest, several miles
from any settlement, and a mile at least, I should say,
from a neighbor. The side-door was wide open, and I
caught a glimpse of a woman reading there as we drove
by. We found the blue gentian and wild apples by the
roadside.

" Mr. Fields has gone this evening to give his lecture
on Tennyson to the Normal School, the only school of
this character in the State. It has struggled hard for
existence, and is barely on a firm foundation now. He
likes the principal of the school, and finds him interested
in his work.

" Walked across the broad meadows in the sunset,
and paused under the drooping elms to watch the long
shadows and yellow light play over the grass, and finally
left the whole in dusky shade, with a glory shining on
the hills around.

" HANOVER, *Thursday Evening, September* 17. In the house of our kind friend, Professor S. We came from Plymouth to Hanover through the Pemigewasset Valley, and went thence to the Connecticut. The mist which has lain over the hills for the last few days, prognosticating the much needed rain, was thick enough to conceal some of the high peaks, but the soft gray light made the landscape only more beautiful with its gay maple boughs and brilliant green.

" We soon came to the little town of Haverhill, beautifully situated in the valley of the Connecticut. The hills rise all around it. Nature in New England can hardly be seen to better advantage. Young girls were strolling, and perhaps studying, on the hill-sides, — flowers are cultivated; there is a seminary; altogether the people seemed in a fair way to use and understand their resources. There had been a three weeks' drought, and the roads were ankle deep with dust, but the clouds were gathering, and a tender gray sky overspread the beautiful scene as we drove across the river and through the village of Newbury to the hotel. We found a neat and comfortable harbor. A room high up, but the view across the meadows to the neighboring hills was entrancingly beautiful. We stationed ourselves at separate windows, and could not take our eyes from the scene. Presently we sallied out for a walk to a hill called Montebello, which overhangs the lovely vale. The day was calm. with an occasional sunbeam straying through clouds and walking across the soft green carpet, perhaps two hundred feet below. The sheep and cows wandered slowly and luxuriously over the cool vast feeding ground, and large elms and maples cast shadows hardly less beautiful than the trees themselves. The birds were chattering around us, and their voices alone broke the silence. The calmness of eternity seemed to reign there. I felt sorry for those of our countrymen who, in ignorance of these blissful retreats, fly to Europe as if all beauty had been left behind by the stern Pilgrims. There is nothing in the world more beautiful than the valley of the Connecticut and the Vermont hill-country. It is yet to be appreciated fully.

We drove away the next day, although a soft misty atmosphere let down a little rain from time to time. Went on to Fairlee and Orford, — the river always in sight, and the scenery rich and various. Rain came fast by the time we reached the hotel at Orford, and it was dark early. A queer hotel, full of drovers and countrymen with no clean hands, who sat at the same table with us, and devoured endless varieties of excellent food as if it were all their right. The poor, pale little landlady, with a crying baby on her arm, told me, — in exchange for my remark that I should like another jug of water in our bedroom, — that she buried her eldest child, a beautiful boy, in the spring. She seemed to have left her heart chiefly in the child's grave, and the house went on as best it might. When I thought of that little woman attempting to provide pies and cakes, and the various niceties with which the table was covered, for those exasperating drovers, who ate as if they were enlarged locusts sent to create a famine, I grew quite indignant. We walked about the beautiful village in the dusk, but the rain began to fall heavily, and we were driven indoors and thence to bed, for lack of good lights and a place to sit.

"Drove to Fairlee in the rain, and ordered crab-apple trees of a good old man, who has made this whole region of the country beautiful from his orchard, sending the trees up and down the river wherever people are wise enough to want them. Saw another country interior. A gray-haired woman, the mother of several children, all dead save one, the youngest, who was playing about. She was at work making the everlasting pies. She said 'the country was beautiful about there for those as had time to look at it. For her part, there was so much work to do in their house she never had time to go out much!' She was rapidly moving between her huge cooking-stove and the ironing-table as she talked. Called to decide on the apple trees, and returning to the sitting-room a young girl was ironing at the table. From her rather trim costume, cut in city fashion, I ventured to ask if she lived there. 'Oh no!' she said, 'her home was in Chicago. She had come to make her relatives a short visit, but as there was only one laundress in the village, and she was busy, she concluded to do up her own dress.' All of which was very commendable, but she did not seem to find pleasure in her novel experience. I said, 'How you must delight in this beautiful place after Chicago.' 'Well,' she said, lowering her voice so that her kind hostess should not hear, 'this is all very well for a few days, but it 's terribly lonely.'

"We were glad to get away from the atmosphere of those women. In a paradise of natural beauty, with kind neighbors and some interesting people, too, within the

radius of a mile, they allowed themselves to be utterly
ignorant of the glory of nature as well as the human companionship they might have had.   Drove a mile farther,
into a solitude indeed, upon the hills, to the cottage of
————.   We had no time to get out, neither could we
do so, because the grass grew all round the door and was
very wet.   We sent in word who was there, and Mrs.
————, slipping on overshoes and taking shawl and
umbrella, ran out to speak to us.   Here was a difference !
‘ I never go out of that little brown hut,’ she said, ‘ from
the time of the first snow-fall until spring returns, and
sometimes when I get discouraged with the dull routine
of things I go into my own room where I keep all the
books you have sent me, and I take down Emerson or
Carlyle, or some other friend, and I have all the society
I need, and go back by and by refreshed to my work.’
Tears sprang to our eyes as she talked.   It was good to
see her, and we shall not meet again as strangers.”

“ *October* 9.   The busy season of the year is again
opening.   Mr. Fields has lectured three times this week
in different places.   At one town a little girl of nine
years came up to him after the lecture, put her arms
around his neck and kissed him !   The child clung to
him until he left, although she had never seen him before.   He brought home superb flowers.

“ In the train he met a man, a total stranger, who introduced himself, and then proceeded, little by little, to
give him the full story of his life.   A strange and moving history it was, and the way in which he clung to his
hearer was something extraordinary.   He was a student,
and a man of digested learning also, who had already

made his mark in literature, but 'the sorrows of that line' were unfolded with the directness of childhood."

"NEW YORK, *February* 7, 1875. Dickens's birthday. A cold, raw, clouded day, contrasting with the wonderful floods of yellow sunshine which we have enjoyed ever since we left Boston.

"Came to Saratoga, where Mr. Fields spoke the same evening. On the way in the yellow of the cold sunset the monument to young Ellsworth was pointed out to us on the summit of a hill. The marble eagle on the top shone in the bright air.

"Pleasant reception and warm fire at Saratoga. The night very cold, clear and starry, the ground covered with snow. A 'lovely audience' assembled to greet the lecturer, who came home warmed by the exertion of speaking. We had a comfortable little supper, chiefly on baked potatoes, by the side of our bedroom fire, and went most comfortably to sleep, in spite of the inquiring glance one must always cast at a strange bed in a hotel of mediocre achievements with respect to cooking. The next morning took a brisk ramble on the crisp snow. The change was delightful. We had left Boston almost impassable — the snow of the streets had been churned into a kind of gray meal, which clogged both wheel carriages and runners, and the sidewalks were like rivulets with slippery bottoms. Here everything was so clean! Cold, certainly, but fresh, and bright, and healthy.

"That day to Poughkeepsie, where Mr. Fields lectured again. Here on the banks of the Hudson, though still cold, there was little snow to be seen. He came home rather tired from his lecture. They had given him no lamp for the desk, only foot-lights!! and general lofty illumination. The result was, he cut his lecture very short. Again, supper in our room, but 'the man' had kept him talking some time below stairs, and he was a little more tired. However, we rose soon after six the next morning, and went to Vassar College, where at nine o'clock he made an address to the students. There were three hundred and seventy-five young girls in the building, and nearly that number must have attended the morning lecture. It was an audience of the best kind. He was as much pleased as they were. Afterward, we went over the building and the observatory, whither we went for the purpose of seeing Professor Maria Mitchell, whom the students love dearly. A bust of Mrs. Somerville was in her room, presented her by Frances Power Cobbe. We saw the telescope and instruments, also an arrangement or adjustment of lines for measurement which may be ranked among the 'discoveries.' It is Miss Mitchell's own. Instrument and room answer their purpose admirably, but twenty thousand dollars are required to perpetuate the work here begun. One pair of hands may hold it for a time, but without a foundation there is danger of loss in the future. . . . At night we reached New York. Mr. Fields was completely exhausted.

"*June*, 1875. First overtures from the Southern States to a real reconciliation. To-day three Southern regiments have arrived in Boston to help Massachusetts keep the centennial celebration of the battle of Bunker's Hill. One comes from Maryland, one from Baltimore, and one company from Charleston, South Carolina. The latter contains only forty-eight men, but it is the fact of their coming at all rather than the numbers which is impressive. Bayard Taylor came from New York to report the event for the 'Tribune.' After dinner went to hear Dr. Holmes and Dr. Ellis, at the opening of the exhibition of relics. There was hardly a dry eye when Holmes finished reading.

"William Hunt at tea. Took out a letter from Duveneck thanking him for the word of artistic recognition he so greatly needed. 'Ah! he's got the right spirit,' said Hunt, 'he loves art better than his native city. He loves the place where he was born and bred; we all do so, and we can't help hankering after it; but he loves art more, and he will go wherever he can find the most room for that. But how impossible it is to drum art into people if they can't see it. . . . They talk about Millet's not taking pains! Why, he worked several weeks in my studio in Paris one winter, and was three weeks constantly upon one hand. The truth is, painters should n't talk. They should have their mouths sewed up tight, and DO the thing, not talk about it.' . . .

"*July* 5, 1875. Writing in our own cottage at Manchester.

"This year an idea which was never absent from his mind, of teaching young people how and what to read, began to take shape in his thought. I find the printed title-page of a book before me, which was then projected. It was to be called, 'Talks with Young Scholars by an Old Scholar.' And the motto runs —

"'What at your book so hard? . . .
I'll talk with this good fellow.' — SHAKESPEARE.

" Several pages of the ' First Talk,' were also printed; but it is probable that the continual use he was able to make of all his material in his never-ending lectures caused him to postpone any such publication.[1] Lecturing (out of Boston) usually signified something more than the simple delivery of the evening discourse ; there was always a high school or seminary in waiting, asking for a few words on the following morning, or the previous afternoon. His tact with young people, and his power of interesting them in his subjects, was one of his peculiar gifts; perhaps I ought to add also one of his peculiar enjoyments, therefore he yielded the more readily to the continual solicitation of teachers for his assistance.

[1] The following sketch of topics for various chapters, with suggestions for titles, were found among his papers : —

(Half-Hour) TALKS

WITH YOUNG SCHOLARS,

BY

An Old Scholar.

Topics.

Habits of Study.	Self-Control.
Public Speaking.	Composition.
Reverence.	Patriotism.
Punctuality.	Enthusiasm.
Reading.	
Conversation.	
Exercise.	
Handwriting.	
Cold Water.	
Courtesy.	
Good Temper.	
Debt.	

Half Hour Morning Talks. Ten Minute Talks. Evening Talks. Talks with

"In the autumn of this year Mr. Fields again left home for Chicago, and a western lecturing tour.   Again, we enjoyed a hospitable reception, and saw much that was interesting under our friend Robert Collyer's guidance.   Among other friendships begun, not ended, there was one with William Clarke who, in what might seem unsympathetic surroundings, had preserved his youthful love and enthusiasm untarnished.   His treasures were not among seen and temporal things.

" Came to Beloit, Wisconsin.   A pleasant town full of comfortable homes; but the youth who had taken the responsibility of sending for the lecturer in a moment of enthusiasm, neither understood the business he had undertaken, nor had counted the cost.   It was too early in the season at best, and the town was a small one.   There was no audience.   The poor young man had no money to meet expenses, and was distressed beyond measure. Mr. Fields saw through the situation from the first moment, and fully appreciated the ludicrous side of it.   After all was over, he withdrew the frightened youth into a private room, saw that expenses were paid, and sent the poor fellow off rejoicing, and promising never to do so any more.

" Left Beloit before dawn, rising at four A. M. for the purpose, and going breakfastless to the station in the dark.

" MILWAUKEE, *Sunday.*   First Sunday afternoon lecture ever given in this city.   It was a great success; at the Academy of Music.   Beautiful city, but ' cold as Christmas.'

" RACINE.   Lectured.   Hotel overlooking the waters of

Lake Michigan in the moonlight. Starting early the next day, we hardly arrived at Evanston (for the evening lecture) in time to dress. Up early again next day, and on through Chicago to Rockford. Walked through the town in the afternoon. We crossed Fox River, made famous by Abraham Lincoln's story. Mr. Fields is a little more tired and homesick than usual, but this is the first really home-sick place we have seen.

" Madison, the capital of Wisconsin, one of the clearest, cleanest, and most beautiful of western cities. The College has four hundred students, an equal number of women and men. The State House is like a small Greek temple, surrounded with trees. We were most hospitably entertained in the beautiful home of Ole Bull. Left Madison at midnight for Chicago, where we found ourselves at half-past seven in the morning, and no carriages at the station. Gathering our wraps we walked across the still half-sleeping city to the hotel. The morning air and exercise revived us, but in a few hours we were in the cars again, hot and airless, and on arrival at a place called Sterling found a broiling fire in our stived-up bedroom. The lecture was on ' Cheerfulness ! '

" The hall was crowded, though it is a place of only five thousand inhabitants. People pressed about him eagerly ; one woman came eighteen miles to talk of her brother, Ralph Keeler, whom Mr. Fields had known, and to hear the lecture. As he walked out in the morning, a rough man driving a country wagon came up to him, jumped from his seat, pulled off his buckskin glove, and asked to be allowed to pay his humble tribute of grati-

14

tude for the lecture, which he said had done him a world of good. 'Long after you have forgotten this place we shall remember you,' one of his listeners said.

" OMAHA, NEBRASKA, *October* 17. Pretty tired after a long night and half day from Sterling to this place. The whole distance was like some noble garden, exquisite in sunset, moonlight, and morning. Here a fierce wind is blowing. It is dusty, and we begin to see the life Bret Harte describes in the faces, manners, and bearing of the people. We see fine horses and stalwart men. Everybody is kind and attentive to us. ' Opera House ' crowded. Men came in from the prairie in high boots to hear the lecture, leaving their horses outside.

" *October* 19. Arose at four o'clock, jumped into an omnibus which rattled rudely along over the soft earthy avenues, and into occasional holes, especially near the street crossings, which are of plank, sometimes rising a foot above the level of the road. The vehicle was full, two women with young babies, not to speak of children of all ages taken from their beds, — a company of the unwashed. We had time, however, for everything except breakfast! There was no express train. All day long we rattled on in cars heated by iron stoves, without dinner (they stopped somewhere and called it by that name, but we could not find courage to go in), until half-past six o'clock, when we reached Iowa city, where ' Cheerfulness ' was again given to a fine audience.

" *October* 20. Went to prayers at the University of Iowa, which stands in a park opposite the hotel. Saw six hundred boys and girls together. A fine sight. Later in the day we walked across the bridge which spans the Iowa River. The day was exquisite, warm as summer, with a soft haze. We sat on the hillside enjoying it, greatly amused in watching a family trying to get a drove of pigs to market. . . .

" BLOOMINGTON, ILLINOIS. Arriving at half-past ten at night, we found a reunion of the Thirty-third Illinois Regiment — with other soldiers, officers, and their wives, amounting to three hundred persons, — had taken possession of the hotel. It was a most interesting sight, however, as such reunions must always be. When they discovered Mr. Fields was in the hall, they would not rest until he had responded for Massachusetts. His speech, though short, was to the point, and the applause was simply terrific. There was no liquor on the tables, and the presence of women gave a cheerful aspect, which kept the memorial day from becoming too painful. One man who had lost a leg tottered as he rose to speak, whereat another one-legged comrade rose up and supported him.

" Were driven to see the State Normal School and Orphans' Home. Both noble establishments, of which Iowa may well be proud. Our guide wore a toothpick in his mouth, which he revolved restlessly with his tongue until you were perplexed as to the possibility of that member's evading any longer the sharp point inside. He wished to show us the museum, ' the first in America, sir!' also parks, kitchens, laundries, cupolas, and every imaginable corner. I took the lecturer's part steadfastly, declaring that, with a lecture before him that evening, he could go up and down no more stairs. Except for this excuse I know not what would have become of us." [1] . . .

" Arrived at ———. The place was full of kindliness, stove-heat, and enthusiasm for Mr. Fields! . . . School-house, — all house and very little school; teachers salaries worse than very little. . . .

" Reached Boston October 31st. November 3d Mr.

---

[1] We cut the inclosed out of one of the local newspapers : —

OATS AND BARLEY.

Fifty thousand bushels wanted at our oat-meal mill in Coralville, for which we will pay the highest market price.

TURNER & Co.

THE IOWA CORN CROP.

Iowa is a growing State — scarce thirty years old. Among other products she will this year add to the sum total, 140,000,000 bushels of corn. Now let us see what this means when put in a comprehensive form. It will require an army of 150,000 grangers twenty days to pluck and crib the ears. If shipped it would require 4,666 ships of 1,000 tons each to carry the crop. If transported upon cars, it will require 470,000 cars, and would make a train 2,750 miles in length, or space nearly across the continent. If loaded upon wagons, with carrying capacity of thirty bushels each, the train would form a line 27,000 miles long, or 2,000 miles more than the circuit of the globe. If emptied down upon the city of New York, it would overwhelm that city as were Herculaneum and Pompeii. If made into whiskey, it would float the United States navy, or make every man, woman, and child upon the face of the earth drunk. It means fat horses, fat beef, fat hogs, fat poultry, and fat pocket-books. It means that it will open bank vaults and start the wheels of commerce. Here in young Iowa are mines richer than California, or Ophir, or Peru. Fifty thousand square miles of surface diggin's and all " play dirt." Then why not come to Iowa? — *Council Bluffs Nonpareil.*

Fields left again for Williams College, where he lectured three successive nights. . . .

"BOSTON, *February.* Went to see Sothern in David Garrick. A beautiful piece of dramatic art. He said afterward at supper, in speaking of the vagaries of the mind, that he was always tempted when he came to the love-making of that play to astonish the audience by turning a somersault or two before them on the stage. He reminded us of Dickens again, as he always does. The flashing glance, the clear-cut speech, the love of effects, the keen, almost unobservable study of his companions, the very sound of his laugh, — but of course the measureless tenderness, the unselfish regard of which Dickens was capable, and which made him the master he was, can only be known once.

"Sothern amused us immensely telling us of his hatreds, 'musical boxes and photographs.' They are his red rags. He illustrated his own love of practical jokes : —

"He had invited a friend, who was going up to London to some entertainment, to sleep in his chambers, he himself having planned, just at that time, to be away. He changed his plans, however, for some good reason, and forgetting all about his invitation, went to his chambers to sleep on that particular night when his friend was to take possession. He had gone quietly in at a late hour, as was his wont, and had just thrown off his coat and collar, when he heard a snoring in the inner room. For a moment he was startled, but soon the ludicrousness of the whole thing burst upon him. Putting on his coat once more, he took a huge music-box, which some misguided friend had given him, wound it up, and put it under the bed. It was one of the kind that has hammers and bells and every sort of noisy accompaniment. Soon the thing 'went off.' His dramatic representation of the horror of the inhabitant of the bed, and his own enjoyment of the joke from behind the door, was very diverting. . . .

"Passed the evening in Hunt's studio. When we arrived he said they were just 'fixin'' for the company! He was moving about in his liveliest and most restless way. Every now and then he would hear a noise from a small nephew behind a screen. 'He 's arrangin' the cake,' said Hunt. Presently, when the cake was arranged! it was brought in a huge tin dish and placed on the top of a high stool near his easel during the evening. Then he began to show his work — the portrait of Agassiz, one of a lady, and many drawings in pastel and charcoal. Also a fine woman's figure holding a mandolin, with beautiful green drapery and yellow hair. Some one said, ''t is like Paul Veronese,' 'but softer,' said Hunt, ''t is softer now, is n't it,' in a kind of boyish and appealing way. We had delightful music. When it was time to go Hunt said, hugging himself and dancing about, 'if you *will* go, I 'm glad I have n't shown you everything. I 've lots more!!'

" WELLESLEY, *June*, 1876. The sun was streaming across the lawn and the great trees flinging down their shadows as we approached the college, a very fine building filled with three hundred young women. Six girls rowed us across the lake. It was a lovely sight, especially as we approached the garden shore. Returning,

Mr. Fields gave his lecture on De Quincey, and afterward enjoyed the evening with his host and hostess in the fine library of the college."

This is the first record of a series of visits to Wellesley, which ended only with Mr. Fields's death. His associations with the place and its founders were something more than agreeable, — they were those of friendship. These ties strengthened with the years, and as he always loved his friends in a way to help them, so his interest in Wellesley was deeply appreciated by its projectors.

" *October* 27, 1876. Lectured in Springfield *en route* to Buffalo and Niagara. The scene at the Falls was never more impressive. Walked about the place the livelong day except an hour for dinner.

" OBERLIN. Lecture most successful. The young men hung about his steps till the last moment. Rose at half-past five, and left before the sun appeared. The air was delicious, the horses strong, and we watched the perfect beauty of the dawn as we drove over the solitary road, heavy with black soft soil. How endless and forlorn some of these roads looked, branching out, no one knows whither, and reaching over utter solitudes. We were driven by a young student, who replied civilly to our questions about growing things, birds, even milk-cans, and all kinds of matters, such as beset the wandering eyes of the traveler. The milk-cans were indeed prodigious in that district. They were explained when we understood that we had entered the town of Wellington, one of the largest cheese depots in the world. Some quick eye, seeing the name on our trunk as we drove through the town, a deputation waited on Mr. Fields at the station to pray him to stay over one day and lecture.

"It was very warm as we rode on across the vast State of Ohio, with its gathered corn, its springing winter wheat, its vast cultivated plains and rather slow rivers. Mr. Fields was deeply interested in the sight, especially as we drew near to Dayton, where is the Soldiers' Home, dear to us because of the fine library that belonged to one of our young Massachusetts soldiers who fell at Ball's Bluff. It was presented to this Home by his mother.

"CINCINNATI, *November* 3. Dark November weather.

"*November* 4. Lecture last night on Wordsworth drew a crowded house. Everybody is more than kind. This morning a fog deep as that of London covers everything.

"Lectures continued daily — all very successful.

"CHICAGO, *November* 9, 1876. Intensely anxious as to the result of the election. Eager crowds at every station on the way to snatch the newspapers.

"The next evening Mr. Fields lectured at a place called Princeton, traveling all night after speaking, and returning to Chicago at seven o'clock, A. M. . . . Left Chicago for a week of lectures throughout Wisconsin. . . . Returning Friday, lectured Friday evening at Beloit, and again traveling all night, reached Chicago at day-break. He is not well; after resting we walked down town, and dined alone together, which seemed to do him good.

"*Sunday*. McCormick's vast hall crowded to hear

the 'Plea for Cheerfulness.' Everybody enthusiastic and aglow.

"Buffalo. Walking out in the afternoon to see the lecture-room for the evening, Mr. Fields stumbled over the steps in a dark entry, and sprained his ankle. With the aid of cold wet compresses and a physician's care, he gave his lecture, sitting, but otherwise as if nothing were the matter. Thanksgiving day dined at East Buffalo railway station. Much amused by a party, apparently the Fezziwig family, also dining. It was a wonderfully clean little place with the best of home-cooked dinners. We were waited upon by a young woman in the cleanest of clean gowns. She said, in answer to our inquiries about the jolly party, 'Oh, it's the family, and they ain't all here neither!' So 'the family' was making merry in its own restaurant!—and who should have a better right.

"New York, *December*, 1876. Mr. Fields lectures in New York, Swarthmore, and West Chester, alternately, every week."

With this month the diary ends. It never was resumed. Engagements and occupations absorbed the time and strength of both, and personal interests gave way to other claims. I cannot, however, allow Mr. Fields's lectures, which will never be printed, to pass into oblivion, without striving to rescue some memory of their peculiar qualities and influence. For this purpose, in order that no mistake may be made by substituting private opinion for genuine public recognition, I turn to the tributes paid him through the newspapers and periodicals. In one of the Philadelphia newspapers I find : —

" We do not attempt to criticise Mr. Fields. No one can, without loving him, listen to his soft, gentle voice, in the quiet, conversational tone with which he puts his audiences in warm personal relations with him."

A writer in Worcester, Mass., where he always found a delightful audience, says : —

" The lecturer spoke of the good done the world by pleasant people, meaning by pleasant people those who are to the manor born, seeing everything and everybody at the best and under a certain illumination, not those who are pleasant now and then or at times when they are pleased. Somewhere in a new England cemetery, on a gravestone, said the speaker, is to be found, with the name and age, the line, 'She was so pleasant.' 'Think,' said he, 'what a delightful character she must have been to have an epitaph like that. It makes one think that a choir of nightingales is perched upon her grave and singing melodious chants to her memory.' "

Also, from Worcester, came the following private note, one among many from other quarters of the same nature ; the source of which remains undiscovered : —

"WORCESTER, MASS., *January* 11, 1879.

" MR. JAMES T. FIELDS : — I must ever count among my chief blessings the privilege of hearing the course of lectures upon English literature you are now giving in our city. It cannot be a matter of indifference to you that you have greatly blessed and helped one in sore need.

"I thank you from my heart for showing me that a great noble learned man can yet be modest and simple, as our Saviour's type of his own pure kingdom, a little child. Whereas I was once, to a great extent, blind, I believe I have now both eyes open, and please God I will never shut them again.

"May you have many, many happy useful years,

"A GRATEFUL HEARER."

Again in a paper from Pawtucket, Massachusetts, I find : —

"The lecture, from beginning to end, was an absorbing literary treat. He spoke of the importance of novels and the influence they exerted upon the mind and society, commended the good and warmly denounced the bad; in the latter case amply illustrating the debasing effect the pernicious trash, from the dime novel to the so-called periodicals for boys and girls, which take up the larger portion of our newsdealers' counters, has had and is liable to have upon the readers of the abominable stuff; and his words upon this portion of his subject ought to be printed in circular form and spread broadcast over the entire country."

And from Exeter, New Hampshire : —

"Mr. Fields has done more than any other American to familiarize us with the men of letters of the old world and their works; and the nation owes him a debt of gratitude which will become greater as the ranks of our scholars increase. His opportunities have been peculiarly advantageous, his memory is prodigious, and he has gathered in a store of fact and narrative that renders him the most charming lecturer of the day. . . . He is able to surround his subjects with an interest, a freshness, and a wealth of reminiscence of which no other lecturer is capable."

From the New York "Tribune" : —

" The effect of such a course of lectures on the great public cannot easily be estimated. At every discourse there must be at least a small number to whose minds a new world is suddenly opened. The mind which has been favored with the advantages of education in its more practical sense, may find a never-ending interest and pleasure in the labors of science, the studies of political economy, the pages of history, the puzzling problems of higher mathematics, or the wondrous progress of mechanical invention; yet unless the lights of modern English literature have beamed upon their libraries they must pass through earth-life in a shadow."

Finally a writer in the " New York Post," having heard one of his lectures in Boston, remarks : —

" Mr. Fields was clearly of the mind that Bostonians had the opportunities for too much education, and it was a timely suggestion, that if the public libraries could not be weeded of some of their sensational trash, well qualified indicators should be appointed who should gauge the requirements of applicants, and tell them what books they ought to read."

This paragraph revives the memory of an idea which was a growth from his experience, and which he always believed to be perfectly feasible. Public libraries, he considered, could effect but a small part of the good for which they were intended until persons of judgment and sympathy could be found and appointed as indicators to assist readers in the selection of proper books.

The kind of affectionate personal interest which grew up in the minds of his hearers toward him was exceptionally noticeable. During the lecture season his house was seldom without flowers, offerings from his grateful listeners. He did not often return empty handed from his evening reading. This was but one expression of the influence he exerted.

In vain, during these pages, have I hoped to recall in words something of the vitalizing, encouraging, sympathizing, and above all simple and human presence which Mr. Fields was to all who knew him. I fear it may not be! But there is, at least, one striking characteristic of him not yet expressed,— he could bring the most adverse natures together, and, if war were not previously declared between them, they would separate liking each other better than they had ever believed possible. He was born to harmonize, and the amount of such business he was called upon to do was very unusual.

Meanwhile he was continuously occupied at his desk, as the subjoined list of twenty-seven lectures, which he had ready at this period, will show.[1]

He found it difficult to shake off his old occupation altogether. "Once a publisher always a publisher," he would say. Sometimes, however, the applications were too much even for his patience, and I find the following paragraph, cut from one of the daily papers : —

"Mr. J. T. Fields is compelled again to request publicly that no more manuscripts may be sent to him for examination, as he has not been connected with any magazine or publishing-house for several years, and cannot undertake to find publishers for either prose or po-

---

[1] Importance of the Study and Reading of English Literature. Literary and Artistic Life in London, Thirty Years ago. Fiction, Old and New, and its Eminent Authors. A Plea for Cheerfulness. Masters of the Situation. John Milton (two lectures). Alexander Pope. Oliver Goldsmith. Samuel Taylor Coleridge. Robert Burns. Mr. and Mrs. Browning. Walter Scott. Lord Byron. William Cowper. William Wordsworth. Charles Lamb. Alfred Tennyson. Thomas Campbell. Sydney Smith. "Christopher North" (John Wilson). Thomas Hood. Keats and Shelley. Thomas De Quincey (the "English Opium Eater"). William Cullen Bryant. Nathanie. Hawthorne. Henry W. Longfellow. Rufus Choate.

etry. He regrets that he has no leisure to read or give
opinions on unprinted matter, as 'he would gladly do if
differently situated,' and respectfully begs to refer all
applicants to Messrs. J. R. Osgood and Company, or to
Mr. Howells, the editor of 'The Atlantic Monthly.'
During the last two months forty bulky manuscripts
have been sent to Mr. Fields, from various parts of the
country, with no provision inclosed for return postage or
express charges."

In April, 1875, Mr. Fields visited Jesse Pomeroy
in his cell. It was altogether out of his usual plan
to do anything of the kind, believing it to be a
mistake to gaze upon misery or wrong which you
can do nothing to alleviate. In this case, however, it will be seen he had a definite end in view.
He had long held the opinion, that if the influence
of good literature was beneficent, the opposite was
also true, — the effect of bad literature must be
deteriorating. In an unpublished paper upon this
subject he says : —

" I have for a long time been of the opinion that the
increase of crime is largely owing to the reading of im-
moral and exciting cheap books. . . . Traveling about
the country I see young people everywhere absorbed in
reading, to say the least, a doubtful class of literature.
On the railroads I see school-boys secluding themselves
from observation busily occupied in reading 'Dime Novels,' as they are called. If I go into the engine or bag-
gage apartment, I always find one or two workmen off

duty, earnestly devouring the 'Police Gazette,' or other illustrated journals devoted to crime. On steamboats, the corners of settees, and boxes on the freight deck, are frequently occupied with readers all intent on the garbage thrown out to them by infamous scribblers who pander to all the worst passions of human or inhuman nature. . . . I found the advertisements of low theatres in all our cities holding out cheap inducements to crowd the pit and gallery when Helen Western played Jack Sheppard, and made robbery heroic to that extent, that the high sheriff of Suffolk told me, when this woman played that character at the Howard, young thieves multiplied perceptibly in Boston during her engagement. The popular play that crowds the Howard Athenæum this very week every night with boys from ten to nineteen, is called, 'Escaped from Sing-Sing,' and is based, I am told, on the easy immunity from the punishment of crime. . . . Having been so long interested in hunting out, if possible, proofs that demoralizing cheap literature was working bad results, I resolved to visit the Pomeroy boy in his cell, and question him as to the books he had been reading from childhood. . . . I began my conversation by frankly telling him why I wished for an interview.

"'I see, sir, that you come from no morbid curiosity,' was his prompt reply. I then asked him if he was fond of reading. He said, 'Very, I read everything I can get.' 'When did you first begin to be fond of reading?' I asked him. 'I guess about nine years of age.' 'What kind of books did you first begin to read? 'Oh, blood and thunder stories!'

"'Were the books small ones?'

"'Yes, most Beadle's dime novels.'

"'How many of Beadle's dime novels do you think you read from nine years old upward?'

"'Well, I can't remember exactly, but I should think sixty.'

"'Do you remember the titles of most of them?'

"'No, sir, but " Buffalo Bill " was one of the best.'

"'What were the books about?'

"'Killing and scalping injuns and so forth, and running away with women; a good many of the scenes were out on the plains."

"'Were there any pictures in the books?'

"'Yes, sir, plenty of them, blood and thunder pictures, tomahawking, and scalping.'

"'Did your parents know you were reading those books all through those years?'

"'No, I kept it away from them.'

"'Do you think you read more of those books than any of the boys who lived near you?'

"'Yes, sir, a great many more, I had a kind of passion for 'em.'

"'Do you think these books were an injury to you, and excited you to commit the acts you have done?'

"'Yes, sir, I have thought it all over, and it seems to me now they did. I can't say certainly, of course, and perhaps if I should think it over again, I should say it was something else.'

"'What else?'

"'Well, sir, I really can't say.'

" ' Would you earnestly advise the other boys **not to** read these books you have read ? '

" ' Indeed, sir, I should.' "

This visit left a deep and painful impression. Pomeroy confessed a sense of irresponsibility, not knowing what " I might do half an hour from now, though I feel so quiet, sitting and talking with you," which increased the mystery and the difficulty of the case; but I think it will be felt that Mr. Fields's visit was not without fruit, in the discovery that he had a mania for literary poison above any of his fellows, had secretly indulged his taste, and had lived to hope that other boys might be saved from a like indulgence.

In the spring of 1874, Mr. Fields lectured again at Dartmouth College. Afterwards he wrote from his favorite Plymouth : —

. . . " Had a crammed church-full last evening at the Hanoverian Court ; shook hands with untold students before retiring. ——'s all charming and most attentive. Rose at five this A. M. Took cars to Wells River. Glorious ride through forty miles of apple blossoms, and a background of mountains. . . . Drove to Willeys. Porch, excellent and popular. [One we had ourselves suggested and, in an amateur fashion, designed.] An exquisite vista opened in front of the house according to your direction. They can't make anything creep up the porch. Will you send some Virginia creeper."

In the autumn of the same year he gave courses of lectures during the month of November in Philadelphia, Baltimore, and Washington.

He was cordially greeted everywhere, but such incessant labor was altogether incompatible with social enjoyments, and in one of his letters he writes : —

" Painfully harassed with invitations of these good people to dine, sup, sleep, lunch, drive, and make speeches in their houses."

While in Philadelphia he says : —

" Went yesterday to the Great Normal School and had to 'say something,' contrary to my wishes. They seemed to expect it, so I got up, and they were happy although I was not. My audience last night at the Academy (Lamb), was simply delightful. Never saw such attentive and so many wet faces over poor Charles and Mary at the closing passages. . . . I am all right, with the exception of great heat and plenty of mosquitoes. They are lovely people here in this house, from the baby to the father and mother. . . .

" What a season it is! Here the warmth is oppressive. . . . You make me hear the sparrows chirping outside our windows. . . . I never read such notices of the lectures as appear in these newspapers. They could say no more if Dickens or Thackeray were lecturing. It is really too preposterous an outbreak of praise even for a man to send his wife! No, I won't.

" I cannot bear to think of you as alone. Pray send

for —— and go to all the concerts you can, and to Toole also. God bless you, and bring us safe together in a few weeks. . . . Think of my journeys to and fro! On the 9th in Westchester; next day over the road to Baltimore; next day back to Philadelphia; to-day at twelve Baltimore again; next day to Washington; next day back to Philadelphia; the day after to Washington again; then back to Philadelphia; next day to Germantown; next day on the road back to Washington; next day back to Philadelphia; then back to Washington, and thank God! that is all!

"PHILADELPHIA, *Monday*. I rose very early yesterday (Sunday), and went from eight to ten to hear Moody and Sankey, who spoke and sang to 10,000 people. Very impressive from its true earnestness. . . .

" This lecturing *is* fatiguing work, and my throat gets so full of dust on the railroads that I feel sometimes at my journey's end like a scraped carrot. But it will be over soon now, thank God, and I shall set my face sternly against lecture halls for awhile. They want me at Baltimore to begin at once at the Mercantile Library Rooms, four lectures as a course, but I can't and I won't. . . . We are to have your health proposed at dinner in a royal bumper. [It was our wedding day.] . . . I could not resist making an offer in Baltimore for that Stuart (original) head. . . . If it arrives pray tell me if it is not beautiful? . . . My legs ache so this morning that I could not run away even from ——'s mother!"

" The Fifth Avenue Hotel mistook me, as usual, for somebody else, and gave me a beautiful room on the first floor, although my **fellow** travelers were sent up **four** flights! How will all this end, when they find out that I am not Cyrus, or Dudley, or John! . . . I found —— at the hotel and lonely last night, so I took him to see Raymond in Mark Twain's new play, which is simply delicious. We bought fifty cent tickets for the gallery, but Raymond sent up and had us brought down into the stage-box. His success is tremendous in this piece. The house was crowded, and he has already played the piece fifty nights. It is to run one hundred more, probably. I don't know when I have laughed more than over Raymond's fun in the play. I fairly disturbed the audience twice. . . . I don't expect much of an audience myself to-night. The election has dissipated all interest in anything else, I apprehend. The Massachusetts news of yesterday is black! black!

"*Thursday morning.* Good audience. All pleased; some enthusiastic. To-day I must rest, as I feel somewhat leg-weary. I will *not* go out to dine six times a day, or to supper after lecture. . . . It is just five o'clock A. M., and although I did not go to bed until one this morning, four hours ago, I am up and at work. The truth is, I could not sleep. My audience at the Academy last night was a most exciting one, and slumber was banished from my eyelids. My subject was 'Literary and Artistic Life in London,' and I had touched it up in the afternoon with new things, and I suppose it was more than usually exciting. Harry Brown said afterwards it was the great hit of the course, and my hearers behaved as if it were. . . . I have answered and declined seven invitations for dinner on Friday of this week."

Henry Armitt Brown, whose opinion is quoted in the previous letter, died in the flower of manhood. Apart from all private grief, his loss to the city of Philadelphia has left a gap which will long remain unfilled. He possessed distinguished ability as well as attractiveness, and his local reputation as an orator was fast breaking local bounds, when he was snatched away from this world's ambition and labors. I find several affectionate letters of his to Mr. Fields, from which a few extracts may be in place here, showing readiness and grace with the pen, as well as glimpses of those higher qualities which justly distinguished him : —

"113 South Twenty-first, Philadelphia, *June* 16, 1875.

"James T. Fields, Esq.,

" *My dear Friend:* Had you been able to have seen my delight when I opened the package from Boston, yesterday afternoon, you would have felt, I am sure, that the reward of a good action is *peace.* Selah! I was sitting in my den, — a bundle of most wretched law papers lying in front of me, threatening the utter destruction of my happiness for the remainder of the day, — and feeling, as I am apt to do under such circumstances, miserably dull. There is, to one of my temperament, no doll quite so full of sawdust of the driest kind as the purely *legal* doll. To me, then, sitting alone and waiting for courage enough to attack my juiceless bundle, entered a maid-servant, armed with a suspicious looking package. 'By express,' quoth she, and laid it by my side and vanished. The purple ink and the peculiar twist of certain letters struck me at once: I heaved a sigh — up from the deepest depths — and murmured to myself but half aloud, 'Fields!' Breaking the string, and opening the wrapper, I soon extricated the venerable book, and beheld with reverential delight the book-plate of the great D. W. I guessed the rest, and needed not the words you had written on the fly-leaf to understand the whole. I am a thousand times your debtor. Not for its own sake merely — nor for old Walker's, venerable soul, — nor yet for mighty Daniel's, now alas so long ago gone to judgment, — shall that sturdy old volume be dear to me, but for yours, O my friend, and the associations which shall make it ever 'a sweet remembrancer' of you. Thine ever,

"HENRY ARMITT BROWN."

"PHILADELPHIA, May 4, 1876.

"MY DEAR FRIEND: As pants the hart for streams and things, I wait thy coming. The humble cot is ready, the tea-urn sings beside the crackling log, and the latch-string hangs far out, inviting your longed-for touch. The town is full, the streets crammed with gaping strangers, the cars go to and fro heavily laden, there is a buzz and bustle everywhere, and, yonder in the Park, the great Leviathan stands up overwhelmingly big and awful. The huge portals are still shut, but the din of hammers comes resounding from within, and the murmur of many voices in as many tongues. Philadelphia is dressing for the *fête*, and there is a sense of expectation in the very air we breathe.   Come and stand with us on the threshold.

> "Always sincerely,
>> "HENRY ARMITT BROWN."

"Certain fishers of men are in an ecstasy of happiness.   None of your occasional catches for them to-day! Imagine some of our 'leading citizens,' with drag nets out, and the waters fairly swarming with distinguished strangers! Prophets and kings may have yearned to see such things, but died ignobly without the chance."

"*June* 5, 1876.

"MY DEAR FRIEND: Praise from Sir Hubert, you know, and recommendations from you, are valuable indeed.   I don't know exactly how to get up the subject you suggest.   I might prepare a lecture on the social business of a hundred years ago, and ditto on the political.   Could the subject be expanded into three or four, think you? and, if so, can you give me any suggestion? A hint always helps me amazingly, and I should rejoice to have one or many from you apropos of these discourses. Thanks for the thoughts of me, again."

A few days later Mr. Fields writes again from Philadelphia : —

"On arriving here yesterday, P. M., dead beat with fatigue from Washington, I found your letters. . . . My Washington audience is a delight.   I go again on Friday. . . . To-day I find myself with a tormenting cold. . . . This cursed traveling, a hundred miles a day on an average, is not the best thing for throat and lungs." . . .

It was the old story; traveling and speaking proving too much for human endurance. The excitement of audiences, the pleasure of responding to the social kindnesses extended on every hand, the ceaseless efforts of mind and body, cannot be borne without serious results.

From Baltimore, at the same period, he wrote : —

"Had a fine audience here last night, and the old Plea ' made them roar.' It never took better anywhere. At West Chester the night before I gave them ' Longfellow,' and the success beggars my descriptive powers. One man made me go home with him to have a glass of champagne, for he said he was an old fellow, and might never hear me again. Mr. H., at whose house I slept, had a large dinner party the P. M. I arrived, and we had a jolly time with the clergymen and the doctors and lawyers, — a bad preparation for the lecture at eight o'clock ; but the party was all made up for me days ago without my knowledge. Your dear letter of Friday met me on the way, through Philadelphia to Baltimore yesterday, by the kindness of H. F., who is incontestably the finest host I ever knew. I will tell you all about it on my return. Here comes the omnibus."

Again from Baltimore : —

"Only a word to say, ' All right,' and that Baltimore is the prince of cities to lecture in. . . . It seems that the Catholic people here are my staunch friends. To-night I am tired, and have got my books and a soft coal fire, and here I shall sit until twelve or one o'clock to get the kind faces out of my brain. . . . The heat in the cars to-day roasted me, and when a woman opened a window on my back I resolved to give up lecturing."

"WASHINGTON, SATURDAY, *November* 21, 1874.

" Great and glorious time last night at Lincoln Hall. I never saw an audience more bent on hearing. They waited for me as I came out and seized my hand, and wrung it as if I had saved a nation. I was glad to get into the carriage."

In January, 1874, he wrote from New York : —

" Last night I went to the Intercollegiate dinner, as most earnestly requested by the chancellor and faculty of the New York University. I never saw a more interesting occasion. The young prize student sat on the right of the chancellor, and I was placed on the left. . . .

" During the chancellor's toast, proposing the health of the prize student, in most fitting words, it was delightful to read the feeling and modesty in the young man's face. When he rose to reply, it was done so admirably I declare I never was more touched. What he said was perfect ; the point being, that if he had succeeded it was all owing to his instructors who had presided over the college during his four years' study. It was most lovely to see how real and unaffected the little fellow was. It was a study of grace and earnestness. His father sat near me, and never was parent more delighted. The whole scene was touching to the last degree. . . . I was the only man beside Whitelaw Reid who was present from the committees."

This dinner was a result of the first year's work of the Intercollegiate Literary Association, in the establishment of which Mr. Fields had taken a lively interest. Much against his will, in face of his other engagements, he was chosen one of the judges, and during the previous months had been obliged to examine and pronounce upon a large number of essays in company with his co-workers, Thomas Wentworth Higginson and Richard Grant White. The judges of oratory that same year were, William Cullen Bryant, Whitelaw Reid, and George William Curtis.

In January, 1875, he again went as far west as Buffalo, returning to Philadelphia and the vicinity, always meeting the same untiring kindness and hospitality.

From Buffalo he wrote : —

"I have just come back from St. James Hall (where Dickens read), and am to send off a few words before I go to roost on my strange perch. And first, it seemed as if old 'Cheerfulness' never did hit the mark so straight before. It took like vaccination. They wanted me to promise to come again before I left the hall, but darn 'em, it's too far away from you and home. We don't know what cold weather is in Boston. Yesterday, when we got to Batavia, the glass stood at ten below ! The pipes in the cars had to be thawed out by red hot irons constantly run into them. I thought we should never get here, and I wished Buffalo had been further, and I never had heard of it. I started from Boston at half-past eight A. M., and arrived here at four on Tuesday morning, nineteen long hours. How I hated my vocation! But a good fire was burning in my room here, and I warmed my feet and went to bed, to be up early this morning and off to the Falls, tired as I was all over when I opened my eyes. But I thought I would go, and am glad I did. Fine as the sight was, in its way, I am glad you did not come, for the weather was awful. The wind was terrible. It blew on the Suspension Bridge to such an extent that I thought the sleigh would go over. The horses seemed bewildered by it, and stood motionless several times. What I saw was a sight not to be forgotten, but it is not Niagara as I like to remember it. It is too awful, and I much prefer the glory of summer flung over it. Winter is to me ghastly and out of place over such a spectacle, and I hurried away from it unreluctant and gladly.

"To-morrow I start from this cold country, clad in storm, for Pittsburgh and smoke. I shall be at least twelve hours on the road, and perhaps twenty, as the trains are all obstructed by ice, they say. Everybody is furred and freezing in this region. The wind from the lake cuts like a scythe. My eyes all day feel like peeled substitutes, and I long to exchange them for the old ones in Boston.

"Two young men rode forty miles to hear the lecture to-night, and came up on the platform to ask me to speak in their town next week. One of them had a face of exquisite beauty, and quite touched me by his enthusiasm. I should like to meet him again, but I cannot go to his place among the Alleghanies. This life of travel in cold and solitude is dreadful. It is only for what it brings and is necessary, that I would do it any longer. The experience on this trip was most dreadful, and I am thankful, much as I miss your dear companionship, that you were not suffering with me the dreary way. To cross the icy platforms from one train to another, and the changes are constant, would have exposed you to chills you never felt before. The air was full of needles, and they filled my lungs till I could feel the blood trickling after them. It was infernal. A man told me to-day that Boston air in winter was hot compared to the Buffalo atmosphere.

" And now, God bless you, my love, and keep you safe from all harm. Don't be without some one near you, to whom you can speak in the night if you wish to. I shall try hard to get back for a day between Canonsburgh and Rondout, but cannot say now, for I don't know the routes. I hope to find a letter at Pittsburgh to-morrow."

From Pittsburgh : —

" Here I am in this city of smoke, and feeling like a lump of soft and smutty coke. I am thankful you did not start with me. The journey across here from Buffalo was beyond cursing, and I rejoice you were not here to suffer the discomfort all the way. There were no drawing-room cars, and the heat and cold were awful even for old salts like myself. Twice I became dizzy with the suffocating horrors of the stove, and once half chilled to death by a transfer. I got here at midnight, and found a room heated to ninety awaiting me, and so I scuttled off into a cold one, after warming my feet and hands. . . . You can have no notion of the dirt of this city. It beats all the English atmospheres I have ever seen. London is bright compared to it. To-night I speak here ; to-morrow in Canonsburg, and next day I start for Philadelphia and New York. Whether I can go on home or no before I go to Rondout, I cannot now say, as I don't know the times and seasons yet. But I thank Providence you did not attempt this journey. You never could have endured the fatigue and no comforts. Nothing to eat between Buffalo and here but the steak of wild-cats and tigers. I never saw such meat offered to man before. The expense of railroad travel is simply monstrous, and the hotel bills are preposterous."

Again he writes from a small town on the Hudson River : —

" I can't help laughing at myself for being here! Of all the god-forsaken places yet, this beats the world. I have just been out into the streets to look at my probable audience, and I wish I had anything bad enough to offer them this evening. The men all look like pirates on low wages, who, having killed off decent people, have the town to themselves, and are now out of employment. Hardly a decent woman is to be seen, and the children are awful in their ugliness. The views, per contra, are glorious. I mounted a hill just now and looked up and down the river of ice which sparkled with wonderful beauty. I had to cross from ——— in an ice sledge drawn by two horses and filled with market people. Coming out of the hot cars after a three hours' ride, and getting into the open sledge, was simply suicide to my throat, which, with swelling of the glands, punishes me for being such a fool as to go round the country in this wise."

Again, after amusing descriptions of people and things, he writes from Philadelphia and Baltimore : —

"So much time in the cars destroys me, and I feel giddy half the day. I feel as tired and dull as if my name were ——, and I lived in B—— Street. But I must tell you of a young man who called to-night and kept me hating him for an hour. He said he belonged to one of the oldest families and wanted my advice as to his education. He wanted to attach himself to me, he said, and be with me constantly. He wished ' to be carried up as high as the mind of man could go, to the extent of human knowledge.' He brought a pocket full of poems he had translated from the German, and he troubled and detained me to that extent I could have roasted him and then declined to eat him. A letter has just been handed in from another young man who wishes an interview to-morrow. Another from a youth who wishes to give a young lady friend some books to improve her mind, and I am to select them ! Also notes inviting me to dinners, and cards from people with strange names ! The lectures are slipping off the string and soon all will be over. . . .

"I have just written to Redpath to cancel all engagements in the West from the 10th of February to the 5th of March. I cannot stand it. Traveling takes all vitality out of me, and I do not speak so well and vigorously as audiences demand in my case. I can't come up to expectation after a railroad headache of two or three hundred miles daily. . . . This constant call to read manuscripts must be crushed out. Yesterday a man sent up his card, and from the name I imagined he might be some lecture committee, so I said, 'Let him come up.' I sat writing letters, a batch of which comes every day, when entered, smiling, a tall, well-dressed chap, who asks 'if he can engage me for half an hour.' 'For what purpose?' To read me a poem he had written and get my opinion of it!! I sent him off, telling him I was hard-of-hearing-poems-read. . . .

"Last night, here in Philadelphia, the rain poured and the streets were washed as with a flood, but my audience was a beautiful one, both in numbers and quality. The night before, in Baltimore, the largest audience ever assembled in the Peabody Hall to hear a lecture crowded the building. Being Thanksgiving night I supposed very few would come, but the aisles were full and overflowing."

Again he writes from a college town : —

"I can't say when I shall return. I find the Faculty wish me to give another lecture, and if I don't do it I am afraid the course will be incomplete. Last night the President gave a levee in the lecturer's honor, a most pleasant company. But the plague of the whole thing is that everybody wishes you to do everything : to drive, to dine, to sup, to visit halls, to become a member of societies, to hear classes recite, and hop about generally. This, as you know, I HATE! I have just returned from a drive behind two fast trotters, an act for which I deserve to be roasted. I had not the wit to decline the invitation, and so I went and nearly froze in my boots. It began to snow on the mountain we were to cross, and for eight miles I had sleet in my eyes, my nose, my mouth, my neck, and everywhere else. How I inwardly cursed my fate, albeit the gentleman who drove me was most kind and interesting."

To conclude the extracts from his letters I will print here a few of later date, and thus close the subject of the lectures out of Boston : —

"WILLIAMSTOWN, MASS., *Thursday*, 1879.

"All goes well ; grand reception ; great enthusiasm ; and crowded chapel. This country is glorious ; I never saw anywhere such superb hills, although they are now covered with snow. The valley is quite as fine as Westmoreland vale. The moon came up to-night over Graylock grandly."

"BAGG'S HOTEL, UTICA, five degrees below zero,
"*Tuesday morning, January* 21, 1879.

"DEAREST A.: Fine audience ; great enthusiasm ; papers all jubilant ; can't reach Potsdam this time I think. Mrs. P. of the Seminary is a very exceptional lady ; has a grand building full of pupils, and does things expensively. She only cares to have her pupils in the lecture room. Autograph books flowing in abundantly.

16

Invitations ditto. To-night, after the lecture, must attend, they say, the fashionable club of Utica, at somebody's house. Carriages here do not close with doors, but only with leather curtains. Would not have come if I had known this, darn 'em. But such rivers of kindness ! Such delightful expressive folk !

" To-night at the Seminary again ; to-morrow night at the Opera House here, on ' Cheerfulness ; ' next night in Brooklyn ; then back here for Clinton, and then toward home on Saturday.

" P. S. This hotel is comfortable, but full of mediæval smells. Sometimes I seem to detect older whiffs, as if Pharaoh and his host had been dipped up out of the Red Sea, and put in pickle, all over these premises. Opening a drawer just now I nosed a mummy, or something to that effect."

" UTICA, NEW YORK, 25*th.*

" Clinton insists upon hearing me on Saturday evening. So I cannot be home until Sunday P. M., about three.

" Perfectly well, and discontented.

" Ever yours."

In the year 1860 Mr. Fields received a cordial letter from Charles Cowden Clarke, in reply to a wish expressed by him that Mr. Clarke would write out his Recollections of John Keats for the " Atlantic Monthly." This letter was the beginning of a delightful correspondence with Mr. and Mrs. Clarke, which has never ceased.

In 1861 Mr. Clarke wrote : —

" As Mr. Montague Tigg would say, 'There must be a screw of enormous magnitude loose somewhere,' or I should surely, ere this, have heard something substantial and satisfactory of the four-and-twenty numbers of the ' Atlantic Monthly.' It is my opinion that you all, on the other side of the great water, are in such a ferment with your never-ending, still beginning politics; and with your secession and non-secession; your union and separation; and with your foolish tariff (the *free trade* of France and Belgium, and soon with the kingdom of Italy, will make your selfish legislators wise — perhaps — in time), all these circumstances have loosened this ' enormous screw' of my monthly Atlantic parcel; and my belief is that THE one of your ' helps,' whose business it is to pack and send out London packages, has been attending some Republican meeting, and that the twenty-four numbers are now in the packing-room of Messrs. Ticknor & Fields!

" I hope you have received long ere this the manuscript of ' The Cornice in Rain.' . . .

" My brother has purchased an estate at Genoa, and I dare say my next letter will date from there. My address will be ' Villa Novello, in Corignano, Genoa.' When we are settled and at peace (for we are now in the turmoil of moving), we will try to think of some things we remember in dearly beloved Charles Lamb.

" With *our* kind regards,

" Yours, my dear Mr. Fields,

" Very faithfully,

" C. COWDEN CLARKE."

This was the first intimation we received of the new life of Charles and Mary Cowden Clarke in Genoa, at the beautiful Villa Novello, whence letters full of English literature and Italian landscape scenery, during more than twenty years have been gratefully received.

Early in 1877 came the sad news of Mr. Clarke's death. In May of that year Mrs. Clarke generously wrote : —

" I despatch by book-post to-day a memorial that I — knowing your genial nature and your appreciation of that of my beloved husband — feel sure you will like to have. It is the original copy of my Charles's first lecture on Shakespeare's characters ; one which he most frequently delivered of all the series. . . .

" Your tender hearts will take joy to know that mine had the comfort of seeing vouchsafed a peaceful close to an exceptionally peaceful, happy life ; it was soft and gentle, a painless and gradual ceasing to breathe, while the spring afternoon sunshine streamed in upon *us both.* Thank God, my health never broke down while he was ill, so that I was able to be with him hourly, night and day, to the very last moment. Patient, contented, placid was he throughout, and true to his beautiful, trustful nature. His own most characteristic lines, the ' Hic jacet,' from the ' Carmina Minima,' have been inscribed on one side of the gravestone, and on the other his chosen crest and motto, with simply his beloved name and the date of his birth and of his quitting earth. Violets and daisies grew amid the turf near about the spot, that March morning when I first looked upon it; birds and bees come there; the green hills slope up around on every side, and all seems to embody the very 'cheerful quiet' he himself desired for his resting-place. So many years of joy, so many granted mercies, ought to tranquillize me, and fill me *only* with gratitude; but you, dear friends, will understand the anguish that is mine, even when I am most grateful."

With the date of 1859 I find the first of a series of letters also, from Mrs. Lydia Maria Child, which lasted to the end of her life. They are full of wisdom, wit, and character. She has apparently a very slight acquaintance with Mr. Fields at the first writing, because she says, after requesting him to do her some slight favor in forwarding a book to London: —

"I venture to take this liberty with you in preference to any of my relatives or personal friends; first, because I wish to do the thing privately without exciting any conversation about it; and secondly, because your countenance gives me the impression that it is a pleasure to you to oblige others. Trusting to this assurance, I believe you will excuse the freedom I take.

"And I am very respectfully yours,

"L. MARIA CHILD."

In 1863 she writes: —

"I have a project very much at heart, in which I greatly desire your coöperation. In the course of my reading, for several years, I have been collecting articles to form a Christmas gift-book for the *old*. I have a collection of gems from various sources, English, American, French, German, Grecian, Roman, etc., poetry, stories, essays, extracts from remarkable sermons, etc. When I say *gems*, I do not, in every instance, mean it in a *literary* point of view, for some of the articles I have selected are extremely simple in their character, but they are all gems in the way of producing a *cheerful*, *elevating* influence on the minds of the old. They are all calculated to make them 'feel chipper,' as the old phrase is. I have also written eight or ten articles, which have the same character. While tending upon my aged father, I greatly felt the want of books serious enough to suit him, and yet *cheerful*. The great fault with all that is written or preached to the old is that it is too *solemn*. It is 'carrying coals to Newcastle,' for the old are too prone to take a solemn view of things.

"I have endeavored to carry out the idea first suggested to me by my father's wants, and it is a cherished wish with me to make this benefaction to the old before I die. A great deal depends on the manner of publishing, and above *all* publishers in the country *you* would be my choice."

Again in the same year Mrs. Child says : —

"I agree with you, that it would not be well to get out the book in a hurry, but I cannot deny that I am grievously disappointed. This year has been peculiarly full of sadness and disappointments. The sudden breaking down of my brother's vigorous health, ending speedily in death; my painful sympathy with the parents of Colonel Shaw, the earliest, the latest, the most reliable, the best friends of my life; the destruction of half our house by fire, with the consequent desolation, toil, and confusion, continuing up to the present moment, has made the year a very dreary one to me; and the *only* ray of happiness I had was the prospect of sending my book round to old acquaintances and friends, with the feeling that it may cheer and console their pathway to the sunset.

" But ' what cannot be cured must be endured,' and I have become an experimental and practical philosopher in that way.

" I would suggest the propriety of having more than one copy in existence. The manuscript is in the printer's hands, and if it should be consumed by fire, it would be a tedious and difficult process for me to restore it. In view of the uncertainty of human life, I would also suggest the propriety of having some contract signed. The book is so nearly printed, would it not be best to finish setting it up, and let it all stand in type? Then the manuscript might be preserved in another place.

" When I come to Boston, I will try to see you for a few minutes. We have so many workmen here, with piles of bricks and boards, and no pair of hands but my own to provide for them, that I cannot at present appoint a time, with any certainty of keeping my promise.　　　　Yours very cordially,

　　　　　　　　" L. Maria Child."

The next year she writes : —

" I *used* to begin with Dear sir, now Dear Mr. Fields

has slipped from my pen; perhaps the next thing will be Dear Friend. The length of our acquaintance hardly warrants it, but it would be only the spontaneous expression of my feelings; so, if it should so happen, you will not perhaps consider me obtrusive. . . .

"There is good taste in the suggestion about the title-page. My favorite red letters would need a florid, medieval vignette. They would pale Darley's vignette too much. They would be like a trumpet accompaniment to 'John Anderson, my Jo.' I am sorry to give them up, but I see that it is fitting.

"I take infinite satisfaction in looking at my photograph of Thorwaldsen's Winter. Thank you a thousand times for it. I have very little opportunity to see works of art, and my passion for them no amount of years or discouragements can chill.

"With kindest remembrance to Mrs. Fields, I am most cordially yours,   L. MARIA CHILD."

In one of her notes she says: —

"My sympathies tend as inevitably toward the masses as Willis's do toward the 'upper ten.' I have not the slightest talent for respectability. . . . I send a copy of 'The New Flowers for Children,' which you can transfer to some little friend, when you have read it. I send it, because I want you to read 'The Royal Rose-Bud,' founded on exceedingly slight hints in history. All who write *con amore*, as I *must* do if I write at all, are extremely pleased, I suppose, with everything they write at the *moment* of writing. At least that is the case with me. But very few pieces *continue* to be favorites. I grow indifferent to most things I have written, and have a decided distaste for some, but ' The Royal Rose-Bud ' is a permanent favorite with me, therefore I want you to read it. Cordially yours,

"L. MARIA CHILD."

In 1866 she continues : —

" I should have more heart for work, if that tipsy tailor were not so misguiding the ship of State. To have for captain, in a storm, a man not fit for a cabin boy !

" I feel very anxious and despondent about the prospects of my poor *protegés*, the freedmen.   There was such a capital chance to place the Republic on a safe and honorable foundation, and we have lost it, by the narrow prejudices and blind self-will of that ' poor white ! '

" Well, we *need* more suffering for our sins, and if it were not that the poor blacks have the *most* of the suffering, I could bow my head in patient resignation.

" I am very cordially your friend,

"L. MARIA CHILD."

In 1867 she says : —

" After you have read my manuscript I should like to have you write a few lines, to inform me whether you think the old woman's imagination needs ' the prayers of the congregation, being in a very weak and low condition.' "

" WAYLAND, *February* 27, 1873.

" DEAR MR. FIELDS: What bird of the air sung to you that I alighted on this planet the 11th of February ? If any one whom I like *knows* it, I am particularly grati-

fied to have them *remember* it. But I never imagined
that *you* knew the date of my advent. To be remembered by one's friends at Christmas and New Years' time
is pleasant enough, but *everybody* is remembered then;
but to send tokens of remembrance on a *birthday*, that is
something delightfully complimentary and exclusive. It
is, in fact, my pet weakness. I have never, you know,
outgrown my first childhood, and it will probably remain till I enter upon my *second*. I exult and crow over
a birthday present from any friend, or congenial acquaintance, as a two-year-old does over a new pair of red
shoes."

This series of extracts from Mrs. Child's letters
may fitly close with a tiny note written after Mr.
Fields ceased to be a publisher of books: —

"Dear Mr. Fields: Thanks for your note, giving
fresh indication of your kind interest in my little book.
I feel the more grateful to you, because I have no husband or son, brother or nephew, to care for my success,
and I have lived so much apart from the world, that no
circle or sect is in communion with me. This is a state
of things uncomfortably lonely, though highly favorable
to independence of thought.

"I have written with a conscientious wish to help on
the progress of the world, but whether any considerable
number of people *want* such help, remains to be proved.
It is a mere lottery. If the publishers do not lose by it,
I shall be satisfied.

"Gratefully and cordially yours,
"L. Maria Child."

In narrating the occupations and sequence of the years I have omitted any list of Mr. Fields's published books. I have mentioned that in the autumn of 1870 he was relieved from the cares of business, and it was in the following autumn that his first book, " Yesterdays with Authors," made its appearance. The cordial welcome this first venture received was a great pleasure; indeed, the book gave him a double happiness, first, in the doing, because the nature of its pages was like a renewal of old companionships rather than a labor, and second, in its hearty reception. In 1881 the book had passed through twenty editions.

To the completion of " Yesterdays with Authors," succeeded the work of writing and delivering the twenty-seven lectures, to which we have already referred elsewhere.

In the year 1877 he printed a collection of his brief papers in prose, under the title of " Underbrush." Of this little volume a new and enlarged edition was printed in 1881. In the autumn of 1878 appeared " The Family Library of British Poetry," the joint labor of Mr. Whipple and Mr. Fields, a book which has no rival of its size, numberless as are the collections of poetry. Finally, in 1881, under similar title, was published a thin volume, entitled " Ballads and other Verses," which did not fail to attract a large company of readers.

Grave and gay, old and young, wished to possess themselves of its contents, and " its excuse for being " was derived through public as well as private avenues.

Meanwhile the old habit of writing, more or less, for public journals, and private clubs and companies, was never altogether relinquished. He was one of the contributors to the " Youth's Companion," where he printed a long list of papers especially prepared to interest children in literature. Among the subjects treated in this manner I find Audubon, Tennyson, Washington Irving, Charles Dickens, Charles Lamb, Wordsworth, Tom Hood, Walter Scott, Mrs. Browning, Adelaide Procter, Thomas Campbell, Nathaniel Hawthorne, Macaulay, W. H. Prescott, Leigh Hunt, Miss Mitford, and " A Group of Famous American Authors." The editors of this paper continually proved the value they set upon his work, by their eager acceptance of whatever he would choose to send them. In this little paper also were printed many of his verses which he chose not to include in his last volume. I venture to preserve two stanzas, which should not be lost : —

" When the wind is blowing fair,
    Any ship to port may steer;
Prows that head-seas bravely dare,
    Master fate and conquer fear.

" Souls that, freed from prison bars,
    Struck the blows themselves that won, —
Grappling with their evil stars,
    Stand, like Uriel, in the sun ! "

It would be useless to try to trace his scattered literary productions. Mention has been made of the most important. It is interesting, however, to recall, with all his industry and achievement, how impossible it was to make him feel as if he were interrupted when he was at work. He was ready for others if he were wanted, and it was always somebody else who said he was busy; he seldom made the excuse for himself. This record has, however, failed of its purpose if it has not been able to convey, otherwise than by mere words, the generosity, kindness, justice, and self-poise which characterized him. Many tributes to his generosity and kindness lie around me, but to make evident that these qualities were the every-day atmosphere of his life, is far more important than to be able to recall a generous deed or a kind word which might be set down here. Of the joyousness and elasticity of his nature, tempered by his other qualities, we are reminded by a verse from William Blake : —

" He who bends to his life a joy,
    Does the wingèd life destroy;
But he who kisses the joy as it flies,
    Lives in eternity's sunrise."

Of his helpfulness the world has often spoken, but it may not be out of place to say, that if money were to be taken in charge for aunts or cousins, James was the person called upon. If New York editors wished a new man for some important post, they would send for Mr. Fields's advice and suggestion. Public readers would come to rehearse their parts, and learn what to read as well as how to read; young lecturers with their lectures; graduates, girls and boys, to know what to do next in life; and of authors and their manuscripts, as I have before said, he was never free. His judgment and good sense were as sure and as swift as his sympathy.

Mr. Fields had not the time, or perhaps lacked the inclination, to make extracts from books for his own use. His memory was so faithful a servant that he generally knew where to find any passage which had once impressed itself upon his mind; but, long before Mr. Bartlett's excellent book of " Familiar Quotations " was published, Mr. Fields had printed a sheet of four pages for the convenience of replying to the many persons who were constantly sending to him to find the origin of certain much quoted passages.

There is a large volume, however, which was a kind of common repository for such things as we feared might slip away from us, on the fly-leaf of which he inscribed the following motto : —

This is the coin that ne'er grows light in use,
The gold that oftenest handled brighter glows.

OLD PLAY.

Between the two covers lies a kind of epitome of the books we enjoyed, more or less together, during the last fifteen years of his life. Here, beside the sifted gold of literature, I find occasional quotations from conversation. In one place,

" Agassiz says that the world, in dealing with a new truth, passes through three stages. First, saying that it is not true ; second, that it is contrary to religion ; third, that it was known before."

" Kingsley said one night, if he could have but one book for the rest of his life, he should choose the ' Faërie Queene ' above all and without hesitation ; nothing so rested him and took him out of himself."

"BROOKLYN, N. Y., 1874.

" Every attention is paid here to Mr. Fields. The people appear truly delighted with his lectures. One old lady, seeing the pleasure he felt in receiving some flowers, said : ' There ! I might have brought you my hyacinth. I have one growing out of a sponge, which I planted in the autumn ; 't is just in perfection now. I wish I had brought it ! ' "

One night while Dickens was in America, after a reading, as we sat at supper together, J., in his own laughing way, and partly to excite Dickens to repeat a certain passage in the evening's performance, began by giving a portion of it himself. "That's it," said Dickens thoughtfully, yet half laughing, "my dear boy, you'll be doing it yourself some day."

"NEW YORK, *Sunday, March* 8.

"Mr. Bryant said this afternoon, that no one could impress upon the people of this country so well as Mr. Fields the value and importance of the study of English literature. Also, that no one can know more than one language thoroughly well."

Sydney Smith's "Lectures on Moral Philosophy," was a favorite book of Mr. Fields, and I find several passages quoted from it, especially a fine one on the use of history, concluding with these words: "For the object of common men is only to live. The object of such men as I have spoken of was to live grandly, and in favor with their own difficult spirits; to live, if in war, gloriously; if in peace, usefully, justly, and freely." Among contemporary writers he read everything of Mr. Froude's with the deepest interest, and I find many traces of his books among these quotations.

A quatrain, quoted by Dr. Johnson, and said by him to have been written by an obscure poet, a clergyman by the name of Gifford, was a favorite of Mr. Fields. The poem to which this quatrain was said to belong has never been discovered : —

> " Verse sweetens toil, however rude the sound ;
> All at her work the village maiden sings ;
> Nor while she turns the giddy wheel around,
> Revolves the sad vicissitude of things."

I also find the following : —

" Quillinan writes to H. Crabbe Robinson (and Mr. Fields possesses something of the same feeling), ' I will not reveal to you, for you could not comprehend, my idolatry of Pope from my boyhood,' etc." [1]

" Finished ' Life of Lord Jeffrey.' How often lately we have said what I find set down here, ' The best use of going abroad is to make one fond of home.' "

Again : —

" Nothing shows Boythorn in more brilliant or enchanting colors than his declaration, with tremendous emphasis, that he had never in his life regretted anything so much as his having failed to carry out his intention of purchasing that house, 35 St. James Square, Bath, where the first idea of ' Little Nell ' came to Dickens in one of his birthday visits to London with Forster, ' and then and there to have burned it to the ground, to the end that no meaner association should ever desecrate the birthplace of " Little Nell." ' "

The following parody was also preserved by me in these pages : —

---

[1] See page 222, vol. iii.

17

LINES ON FINDING A WATCHMAN SOUND ASLEEP AT MIDNIGHT ON MY DOORSTEPS.

J. T. F.

How sleep the brave, who sink to rest,
By all the city-rascals blest !
When Night, with snowy fingers cold,
Returns to freeze the watery mould,
She there shall meet a sounder sod,
Than Fancy's feet have ever trod.

By fire-y hands our knell is rung,
By forms unseen our locks are sprung ;
There burglars come, — black, white, and gray, —
To bless the steps that wrap their clay :
While watchmen do awhile repair,
And dwell, like sleeping hermits, there.

See COLLINS'S ODE.

Again, the following quotation to recall an excursion to the hills : —

" PLYMOUTH, N. H., *June,* 1872.

" Arrivéd there the little house they fill,
Ne look for entertainment where none was;
Rest is their feast, and all things at their will;
The noblest mind the best contentment has.

SPENSER'S FAERIE QUEENE, CANTO I."

One of the pleasures of Mr. Fields's life thus far unmentioned was in listening to music. Few persons, themselves unskilled in the art, ever found so keen enjoyment in or comprehended better the best work of the best artists. That unusual pleasure, in the library of a man of letters, of hearing fine music, was often enjoyed in his. No one could take greater pride and satisfaction in the success of any new performance or special musical event than he. He lost many public occasions for listening to music from fatigue or preoccupation; but his delight in the neighborhood and friendship of one of Germany's most distinguished musicians, and his enjoyment while hearing him play in private, must be a compensation to recall among the many dissatisfactions attending any musical career.

"I would rather be a fine tenor singer," he used to say, "than anything else in the world."

He possessed the power of attuning the musicians themselves, which is so seldom seen. A moment appointed for music seems sometimes alien to the mood, unapt things are said or done, and everything drifts away from the musical atmosphere; but he could always bring the circle round with a natural ease both reassuring and stimulating.

His musical friends who must miss henceforth his "fine ear," will recognize the truth of these words, and will remember his gratitude for the pleasure they generously gave him.

Among the published tributes to Mr. Fields, I would place first the following extract from a discourse by his friend Dr. C. A. Bartol: —

"Having known him well for forty years, and lived with him summer after summer in the same house, I must swear I have not known a better tempered man, . . . but whoever suspected he would lack nerve made a great mistake."

From the tender and discerning words of Miss Elizabeth Stuart Phelps, printed in the "New York Independent," I quote as follows : —

"Of all men whom I have known, he was one of the most heartily and humanly helpful. Whether this was instinct, or acquisition, or both, I cannot say (in no respect do natures differ more than in the *naturalness* with which they lend a hand) ; but it was, at least, habitual and thorough. Those who think of him chiefly in the glitter of life, in the foam of things, doing what it was pleasant to do, receiving what was more blessed than giving, and giving what was better than receiving, know not of whom they speak. The scholar, the wit, the author, the host who rested his guest, the guest whom everybody wanted, the friend of distinguished men and women, the patron of struggling talent, the recipient and the bestower of select inspirations — all this he was. He had life's fine wine ; but he was and had because he earned and held. He was not one of the rose-wrapped, predestined sybarites. He got his good things, as Lady Holland once said, with her haughty smile, of the Order of the Garter, 'by deserving' them. . . .

"It was a phase of his essential fidelity of nature which gave him so marked a usefulness among the men who have had the graver interests of *women* very near at heart. His real chivalry surpassed that of almost any man I ever knew. He could not, even after his illness, ask a servant to help him on with his coat without a beautiful accent, like a deferent regret. She was a woman; he would have spared her. . . .

"I have wished that men who regard irritability of temper as a man's, and especially a literary man's prerogative, could have sat at his feet and learned how manly it is to be agreeable at home. All the genial, loyal, unselfish qualities in Mr. Fields *struck through.* They had the penetrative character of what are called the 'honest colors' in a dye."

Mr. S. C. Hall sent the following touching tribute from England : —

"I learn with deep sorrow the departure from earth life of a most excellent and estimable man, when it would seem to us his long career of usefulness might have been largely extended — even to an age such as mine — just eighty-one years! He had done his work well, and has his reward among 'good and faithful servants.'

"But the loss is a loss to all human kind; to his own great country first, but as certainly to ours. I can do little or nothing but honor his memory, and grieve that I have lost a valuable and valued friend. But it cannot be a far time hence when I shall see him again.

"I receive this day a letter written by him dated April 17.

"I do not postpone the sad but solemn duty of writing to whoever may be his representatives, praying God to console and comfort those who remain after him, to continue a weary pilgrimage on earth.

" For myself, I am waiting but yearning for the call that shall be a summons to join my beloved wife; to be with her as I know she is with me.

" May God in his goodness and mercy give to those I address the light He has given to me.

"S. C. HALL.

"To the Family of James T. Fields."

Dr. Oliver Wendell Holmes wrote privately of Mr. Fields (and I trust he and other friends, whose letters may be quoted, will forgive this public recognition of the value set upon their affectionate words) : —

" The regrets of multitudes of friends, more than you can hear or know of, have followed the departing spirit of him who has left us, and their deep silent sympathy abides with you. How many writers know, as I have known, his value as a literary counsellor and friend! His mind was as hospitable as his roof, which has accepted famous visitors and quiet friends alike as if it had been their own. From a very early period in my own life of authorship, I have looked to Mr. Fields as one who would be sure to take an interest in whatever I wrote, to let me know all that he could learn about my writings which would please and encourage me, and keep me in heart for new efforts. And what I can say for myself many and many another can say with equal truth. Very rarely, if ever, has a publisher enjoyed the confidence and friendship of so wide and various a circle of authors. And so when he came to give the time to authorship, which had always for many years been devoted to literature, he found a listening and reading public waiting for him and welcoming him."

Mr. Richard H. Dana wrote from Rome, May, 1881 : —

" It is chiefly with my father, after all, that I connect my memories of Mr. Fields. To him he was always faithful, kind, considerate, and attentive.

" Manchester-by-the-Sea became a new place after he made it his summer home. The sight of him walking over by the beach or the pasture, or driving up the avenue in his basket phaeton, was an assurance of enjoyment, an enjoyment with this characteristic, — that it demanded nothing of my father. It all came from the full, the overflowing resources of the guest, so cordial, so affectionate, so encouraging to a man of my father's temperament and habits. . . .

" Who has left so many friends to mourn him ? Who has given so much pleasure to his friends while he was with them ? He was greatly blessed in nature and temper, and he faithfully made the utmost of his gifts for the advantage of all others."

The Governor of our Commonwealth, John D. Long, wrote to express his sense of public as well as private loss; also, the President of Boston University ; and the President of Cornell University, then our minister at Berlin, Andrew D. White. Mr. White says: —

" My memories of Mr. Fields are among my cherished possessions. During my early professorial days he was exceedingly kind to me, giving himself trouble to smooth my path at home and abroad, and just at the time when such kindness was most valuable to me. Without exaggeration, most of the greatest social enjoyments I have had are certainly those to which he gave me access in Boston, Nahant, London, and elsewhere.

"I also owe him deep gratitude for daring, in the old days of subserviency to the slave power, to publish articles which other editors dared not touch. . . . Winning and devoted as Fields was, it was not that which bound me to him most. I always found in him a real nobleness of heart, a deep wish to help on whatever of good or true he found militant in the world. Let any appeal to his deeper feelings come, and all that wonderful playfulness upon the surface disappeared in a moment."

The Boston booksellers and publishers gave a united and heartfelt tribute to his memory, and Mr. James R. Osgood wrote privately : —

"In view of my long and invariably pleasant association with Mr. Fields, I cannot forbear telling you how grateful a sense I have of my many obligations to him, and how tender a place he will always hold in my memory."

Mr. Alden, editor of "Harper's Monthly Magazine," wrote : —

"The Messrs. Harper desire me to express their sense of the great loss sustained by American literature in the departure of one who, as author and publisher, contributed so much to its excellence, and to its good repute at home and abroad."

Also, in expressing his own feeling of personal loss, Mr. Alden writes : —

" Into the darkest hour of my life he came giving light and hope. I can never forget it. Turning to him first because I found help in him — how much else I found! Only those who knew him nearly knew his goodness and his greatness."

Robert Collyer wrote : —

" He was the dearest friend I had on earth outside my home. . . . I have been thinking of the great host of men and women to whom he was as sunshine and as all that is most welcome in our human life. . . . We are all rich through the treasure he gave us out of his heart, the great, gentle, sunny heart which was so true. The work he has done in this world is quite unique and all good. We cannot say better of it than time will say. Just such a man was needed, and needed just where he was and when he came. God's blessing be forever on him for his work's sake."

George Macdonald said, writing from Casa Coraggio, Italy : —

" He was so good to me and mine that from afar I can understand something of his loss. . . . I know, I will not say *knew*, and love, I will not say *loved* him."

Mrs. H. P. Spofford wrote : —

" His nature was like heaven's sunbeams, — a satisfaction and a delight. I loved him with a grateful heart, for he was a part of happy youth to me, a bright immortal shape in my memory of those days of his exceeding kindness, whose going never seemed possible."

Mr. Howells wrote : —

" Perhaps I have never told you, and may fitly tell you here now, how affectionately and with what unalloyed gratitude I have constantly remembered my connection with him. A look or word of depreciation from him would have made me very unhappy, in the place I held under him ; but in all the years I was with him, I had nothing but delicate kindness from him — forbearance where I failed, and generous praise where he thought I succeeded in my work. . . . I shall cherish the recollection of the little half hour he spent with me in the reception room, that night, before he felt able to go up-stairs. . . . He would not let me feel heavy or sad about him. He was still as he always has been, — the genius of cheerful hospitality. There is no one left like him ! "

Mr. Thomas Wentworth Higginson says : —

" I shall always feel that I was under great obligations to him at a most important time in my life. He was the best and most sympathetic literary counselor I ever had ; and I had much opportunity to observe his constant kindnesses to others."

Rev. M. D. Conway wrote from London : —

" But a few evenings ago Julian Hawthorne was here, and in speaking of Mr. Fields said, ' whom my father so much loved.' I had just received, also, a note from Mrs. Procter, in which she spoke of your husband among her

American friends. I, too, have been proud to call myself his friend, and of what literary contemporary of his was he not the best and faithfullest friend."

Mr. Whipple wrote privately : —

"I love him very deeply now, as I loved him when I was a lad of nineteen."

Joaquin Miller wrote : —

"While many stood nearer to you and yours, few, if any, admired or looked up to Mr. Fields more earnestly than I. . . . How much better he left this world than he found it! How many a heart was made lighter, happier, each year of his manhood all men know. This vast West world is a great deal better and wiser because he has been. Think how few can have this said of us when all is over, work with all endeavor as we may! To me Mr. Fields's life seemed the most rounded and perfect of all men's I ever met. Very beautiful he seemed to me in soul and body, and people loved him truly. How I shall always remember that evening in Philadelphia; the President, the Emperor, the strength, and the beauty of this new world!"

Mr. Edward Lear, writing from San Remo, Italy, said : —

"I used to think, years ago, if anything could prevail on me to cross to America, it would be that I should there see James T. Fields."

Mrs. A. D. T. Whitney writes : —

"I must, for myself, always remember the early welcome your husband gave me when I had just come to his knowledge as a new worker in letters."

And Mrs. Procter, writing from London, said : —

"I think you both knew how great a regard my husband had for yours, — what merry days they had together. . . . I was this morning reading his paper, 'Leigh Hunt in Elysium,' where he speaks of my dear Adelaide — so kindly — as he always did of all."

It will be seen that only those brief passages have been selected from these letters which bear testimony to the character we have been considering.

Another volume would be required to contain the words of sympathy and consolation, expressed in every beautiful form the human heart can suggest, which his friends poured out. The following sonnet, of unusual beauty and significance, from Parke Godwin, must not, however, be omitted : —

> "I cannot wish thee comfort in this hour
>   Of life's supremest sorrow; for I know,
> By aching memories, how little power
>   The best words have to mitigate a woe,
> With which, in its own bitterness alone,
>   The heart, amid the silences, must deal.
> But here, where ocean makes eternal moan
>   Along its melancholy shores, I feel
> How mightier than nature's loudest voice
>   Is that soft word, which to the ruler said,
> Amidst his desolated home, 'Rejoice!
>   Thy dear one sleepeth: think not he is dead:'
> All death is birth, from out a turbid night,
> Into the glories of transcendent light."

In the month of May, 1879, after a winter of many lectures, Mr. Fields went to Wellesley College one evening to fulfill an engagement. He was to reach home at eleven P. M., and a cheerful supper was awaiting his arrival. The hour for his return came and went, when a telegram was brought summoning me to his side. About midnight I reached the college. He had received every possible attention, but I saw that a violent hemorrhage from the head had startled everybody. He was very weak, a little incoherent, and indisposed to sleep. The next morning, a beautiful Sunday morning, with the consent of the physicians, who did not fear relapse from such an effort, we drove home to Boston, and in a few days, as soon as he was strong enough, removed to our cottage at Manchester. The night of our arrival, soon after midnight, he was wakened by a return of the hemorrhage. All ordinary methods of stopping the blood were ineffectual, and great loss and weakness were the result. Day after day the hemorrhage returned, after the slightest exertion, until the physicians prescribed entire quiet and forbade him to be moved. During the month or six weeks of his confinement no one entered his room, except the physician and very rarely a servant.

I look back with peculiar pleasure to those

days! He was seldom tired of being read to, and during the long hours of June, from morning until dusk, which did not fall early on that beautiful hilltop, I read to him things old and new, poetry, essays, and occasionally a story of Thackeray or George Eliot. I can recall one morning when the pulse of life was very low, how the music and significance of Milton's Allegro and Penseroso seemed to take "a sober coloring," and to swing with slow and solemn roar through the chambers of the brain as it never had done before. It chimed and rang with an immortal melody through a mist of tears. And so the days wore on, and called him back to me with a sense of divine and eternal nearness we never had before.

Of this period I feel as Maurice de Guérin has said : —

"Après le bonheur de mourir avant ceux que l'on aime je ne connais rien qui marque plus la faveur du ciel que d'être admis au chevet d'un ami mourant, de le suivre jusqu' où l'on peut aller avec lui dans l'ombre de la mort, de s'initier à moitié au mystère profond dans lequel il disparaît, de lever sur son visage des empreintes fidèles et incorruptibles, de se former enfin un trésor de douleurs et de pensées secrètes, qui puisse fournir à l'étendre de la plus longue vie."

The autumn found Mr. Fields restored, but in a delicate condition, which no one outside of his

home could understand. He looked in perfect
health, but his nerves could no longer bear any
strain ; therefore it was not a surprise when, in
the midst of his Boston lectures in 1880, he was
again attacked with the old trouble. This time it
was less alarming ; partly because no painful measures were taken to stop the bleeding, and partly
because we were assured that more dangerous
trouble was thus averted. Again, in the spring,
he returned to his beloved home at Manchester.
" I like to think," he said, " that I have paid for
everything about this place by my lectures." He
here passed his longest, and I believe one of the
happiest summers of his life, though he suffered
from attacks of pain in the chest if he took any
exercise more severe than walking on level ground.
For five or six years he had found himself subject
to this pain at times after climbing or walking in
the wind, and used to complain occasionally of
feeling as if his voice were " cut off " when he
was lecturing.

In the autumn and winter of 1880–1881, Mr.
Fields continued to speak in Boston and vicinity
as usual. His lectures in town were more crowded
than ever, and as they drew near the close an
appeal was made to him to repeat them. The
temptation was great, it was an agreeable occupation for him, and required less strength than many

other things, but he was easily dissuaded from it, and the wisdom of the advice appeared, alas, only too soon! One night of January, after a cold day and some little exertion, he was awakened by the terrible pain well known to physicians as Angina Pectoris, or the Breast Pang, and at intervals until the final attack, nearly four months later, he was subject to this suffering.

Again great quiet was prescribed, and during all these months he saw very few persons. The moment he could get any respite from suffering he liked to have me read to him. It could not be said of him, —

> He had " no minutes breathing space allowed,
> To nurse his dwindling faculty of joy,"

for this power grew day by day to the very end. Old favorites were the books he chiefly desired. Charles Lamb was re-read with undiminished delight, and " Southey's Life of Nelson," and in his restless uncomfortable moments, or when I was called away, he would amuse himself with " Mark Twain in Switzerland and Germany." Montaigne was one of his prime favorites, and we re-read nearly the whole of it. Indeed, to recount that reading, would be to enumerate a small library, for he slept very little, seldom or never fairly lying down again upon his bed, and the long hours were conjured out of something of their suffering by these beloved companions. "Carlyle's Reminiscences" was one of the latest books we read together, and Forster's "Life of Dickens" was the last book he laid down. "It does not require any effort, and I love to recall him," he said to me.

Sunday evening, April 24, 1881, a little excitement in the street caused another severe attack of pain, from which he recovered only to fall into the eternal sleep. His face wore unchanged the calm expression native to it in those later days.

His body lies at Mount Auburn, "the sepulchre, oh, not of him, but of our joy!"

Yet as a traveler on some forsaken road sees the light of the city whither he is bound glimmer before him on the distant hillside, so the light of vanished eyes "beacons from the abode where the eternal are."

It is written in the Holy Word:

"At evening time there shall be light."

18

AUF WIEDERSEHEN.

HENRY W. LONGFELLOW IN MEMORY OF JAMES T. FIELDS.

UNTIL we meet again ! That is the meaning
Of the familiar words, that men repeat
    At parting in the street.
Ah yes, till then ! but when death intervening
Rends us asunder, with what ceaseless pain
    We wait for thee again !

The friends who leave us do not feel the sorrow
Of parting, as we feel it, who must stay
    Lamenting day by day,
And knowing, when we wake upon the morrow,
We shall not find in its accustomed place
    The one beloved face.

It were a double grief, if the departed,
Being released from earth, should still retain
    A sense of earthly pain ;
It were a double grief, if the true-hearted,
Who loved us here, should on the farther shore
    Remember us no more.

Believing, in the midst of our afflictions,
That death is a beginning, not an end,
    We cry to them, and send
Farewells, that better might be called predictions,
Being foreshadowings of the future, thrown
    Into the vast Unknown.

Faith overleaps the confines of our reason,
And if by faith, as in old times was said,
Women received their dead
Raised up to life, then only for a season
Our partings are, nor shall we wait in vain
Until we meet again !